"Thor's Hammer!"

The large predator yowled again, and Halvar stared at the creature. It was a cat, to be sure, but larger than any he'd ever seen. He'd seen a lion's skin from Afrika; this animal seemed to be of a similar size. So, this must be the mountain cat he'd been warned about.

The animal bounded away as Avaram drove up beside Halvar with his cart, just visible by the light of the lantern hung on a pole jammed behind the driver's seat.

"Capitán! Are you all right?"

"Well enough...I think. Was that the mountain cat?"

"I didn't see it," Avaram confessed. "But you're bleeding. And your jacket's torn at the shoulder."

Halvar pressed a hand to his shoulder. It came away red.

"Thor's Hammer!" he swore again. "I've been shot!"

Also By Roberta Rogow

Murders In Manatas
Mischief In Manatas
Mayhem In Manatas
Menace In Manatas

MALICE
in
MANATAS

The Saga Of Halvar
The Hireling
Book 5

Roberta Rogow

ZUMAYA OTHERWORLDS   AUSTIN TX
2017

MALICE IN MANATAS

© 2017 by Roberta Rogow

ISBN 978-1-61271-345-8

Cover art and design © William Neagle

"Zumaya Otherworlds" and the griffon colophon are trademarks of Zumaya Publications LLC, Austin TX, http://www.zumayapublications.com

Library Of Congress Cataloging-In-Publication Data

Names: Rogow, Roberta, 1942- author.
Title: Malice in Manatas / Roberta Rogow.
Description: Austin TX : Zumaya Otherworlds, 2017.
| Series: The Saga of
    Halvar the Hireling ; book 5 |
Identifiers: LCCN 2017012604 (print) | LCCN 2017022035 (ebook) | ISBN
        9781612713458 (Electronic/Kindle) | ISBN 9781612713465 (Electronic/EPUB) |
    ISBN 9781612713441 (softcover : acid-free paper)
Subjects: | GSAFD: Alternative histories (Fiction) | Mystery fiction.
Classification: LCC PS3568.O492 (ebook) | LCC PS3568.O492 M34 2017 (print) |
    DDC 813/.54—dc23
LC record available at https://lccn.loc.gov/2017012604

To My Grandfathers

Harry Heller

and

Irving Weinstein

who introduced me to Sherlock Holmes stories and Rudyard Kipling's poems, both of which still influence my writing.

Acknowledging...

Lynn Holdom and Rachel Kadushin were present when I first invented the world of Manatas.

Liz Burton has stuck by me and encouraged me to continue to write the Saga of Halvar the Hireling.

Thanks to Debby Buchanan, who read the manuscript and made suggestions for improving the story.

And thanks to the many people who gave me nuggets of information that found their way into this story.

Manatas Town
And Environs

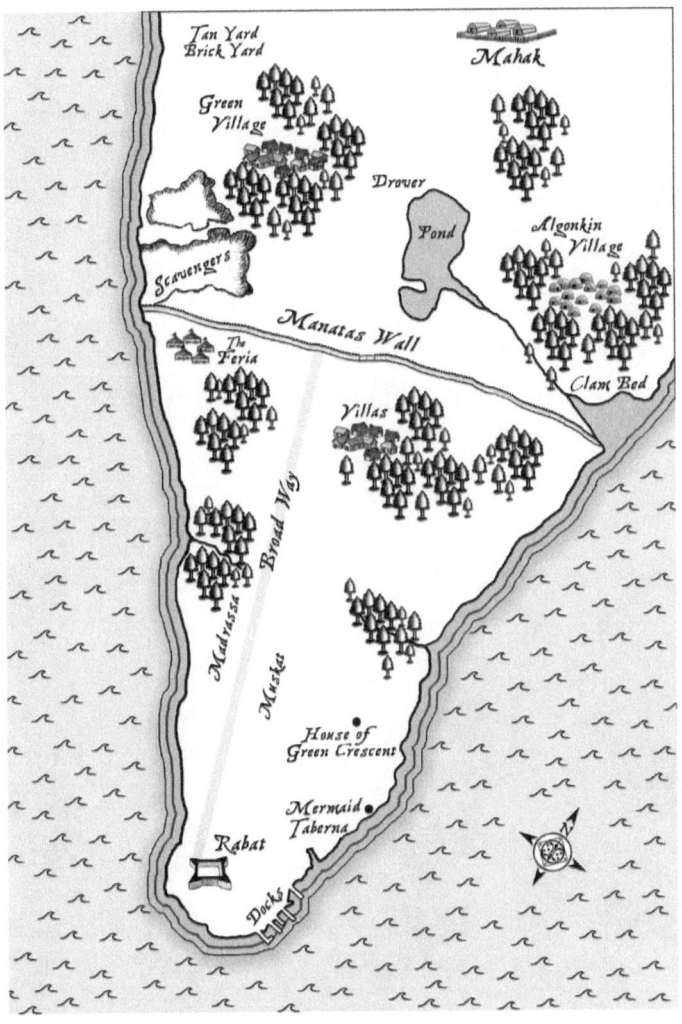

Part 1

The Murdered Messenger

Chapter 1

HALVAR TRIED NOT TO KILL ANYONE AT THE PARty. He sincerely hoped none of the other guests would kill each other, either.

It was supposed to be a friendly gathering of intellectual equals, a meeting of minds, held by the students of the Manatas Madrassa to honor their masters during the turning of the year when, as sometimes happened, the calendars of the three major religions of Manatas happened to coincide. The date of the Redeemer's Nativity had been fixed ages ago; and the Festival of Lights, when the Yehudit celebrated their deliverance from an ancient tyrant, was usually held at some time near the Longest Night. The End-of-Fast, however, when Islim marked the end of Fasting Month, tended to wander through the seasons.

This year, they had all come on the same day, and this party was supposed to be a unique opportunity for teachers and students to mingle on terms of relative equality.

1

At least, that was what Halvar had been told by his host, Benyamin ben Mendel, a stout young Yehudit whose assistance had led to the solution of several murder investigations. Benyamin had been most insistent that Halvar attend this social occasion, held in the Assembly Room of the largest of the many buildings that formed the Manatas Madrassa. That center of learning drew scholars from all over Nova Mundum to this island in the middle of the Great River between the Afrikan territories to the south and the Bretain and Franchen colonies in the north.

"It will serve to introduce you to the Madrassa elite," Benyamin had assured him. "They do not care to mingle with the rest of Manatas folk, but they can be very influential with the sultan and the Afrikan merchants who send their sons north for their education. Even the Bretains of West Caster send their sons to the Manatas Madrassa. Although," he added, "I hear there is some kind of collegium being formed at Bos-Town that instructs the Kristos in their version of our scientia." He sniffed derisively at the idea of any seat of learning that was not totally Andalusian in its orientation.

Once he had done his duty by presenting himself to the assorted masters of literature, alchemy, history, and natural philosophy, Halvar was free to mingle with the crowd.

They did not wish to mingle with him.

So, he stood beside a table loaded with foods he barely recognized and regarded the company sourly. He towered over most of those present, a tall Dane in the green coat of the Manatas Town Guard, which had been adapted with gussets in the shoulders to accommodate his muscular frame. His fur hat, worn over a leather-lined Danic cap, also distinguished him from the rest of the Manatas Town guardsmen.

Given the choice, he would have preferred to remain as the chief bodyguard of Calif Don Felipe, ruler of Al-Andalus-in-Exile; but Don Felipe had other plans for his Hireling. Halvar now faced the impossible task of organizing a militia and policing force in this northernmost outpost of what had become Hispania in Nova Mundum.

It was a position he had neither wanted nor expected, and he was still finding his way. Part of his duties, according to his immediate superior, Sultan Petrus, was to make himself known to Manatas society. His name was already associated with such events as the public shooting of a Franchen innkeeper and the even more public drowning of a fleeing woman. His exploits had been rendered into verse, and sung by the popular entertainer Willem of Cos so that most of Manatas now knew him as "The Stranger Who Faced the Sekonk."

None of this added to his status with the intelligentsia of the Manatas Madrassa, whose voices now filled the Assembly Room with a babble of tongues that grew louder as the party progressed.

He scanned the room, trying to find a face he recognized. There were a few youngsters at the edges of the crowd, among them his fervent follower Salomey, the sultan's daughter, who preferred to be called Selim and wore the embroidered silk jacket and trousers of a pampered teenaged boy. Most of the other guests were unknown to him, men decked in garments ranging from the dark-green kaftans and turbans of graduates of the Ulema of Baghdad to the black gowns that covered the breeches and jackets of the few Bretains and Danes who had managed to escape the clutches of the Questioners in lands conquered by Imperator Lovis.

Almost all were bearded—neatly-trimmed pointed goatees and mustaches for the Bretains and Franchen and flowing bushes adorning the chins of the Islim imams and Yehudit ravs. Only one face was scraped clean, and that was the one Halvar most detested of all the inhabitants of Manatas; it belonged to the former Leon di Vicenza, now known as Frater Leonidas.

Three persons he had least expected to see at such a gathering emerged from the crowd to partake of the refreshments laid out on the table.

3

"Devallon." Halvar acknowledged the Franchen ex-musketman who had arrived in the ship *Belle Fleur*, whose hulk lay across the bay on the shore of the Long Island. "What brings you to the madrassa? Free food and drink?"

"Not my idea, to be sure," the dapper veteran replied, scanning the table for something that looked remotely familiar. "Blame Master Edgar Norris."

He nodded at the slender man clad in the sober black breeches and coat favored by Franchen servants who hovered protectively behind his gaudily-clad master. Milord Summersby had chosen to wear his most elaborate green coat, embellished with silver braid, worn over a red waistcoat. He stood out like a burning coal in a dying fire.

"Milord is unhappy that he can find no one worthy of his company in Manatas Town. I thought he might find someone of suitable status among the students, but apparently not." Edgar, who had overheard their discussion, said as he scanned the room. "I met Master Albrecht LaPierre while I was buying food in the souk. He was at the Oxenbridge Collegium when Milord and I were studying there. I dared to speak to him, and he suggested Milord might find someone of his own rank among the masters."

"He won't find any Bretain milords at this party," Halvar observed. "As far as I can tell, this lot are mostly Andalusian and Yehudit teachers, ravs and imams. The Bretains and Franchen are sons of tradesmen who have lifted themselves into a higher place in life through their scholarship.

"Still, whatever their rank was when they entered the madrassa, once they get their status as professors, they're accorded the respect due an imam. At least, that's what they claim. If you're looking for sociable Bretains, you'd do better to go to the gathering for Redeemer's Nativity Watch-night later tonight at the Gardens of Paradise in Green Village, beyond the open field where the Feria is held. Most of the Bretains and other Oropans who live in Manatas wind up there, no matter what their rank was over the water. Everyone's welcome at the Gardens of Paradise, especially if they throw silver around."

"I'm still trying to get the hang of this place," Devallon complained. "There's the souk, over past the Broad Way, and there are small houses north of the souk that folk live in. I saw some big villas at the north end of the Broad Way that look empty. What's this Green Village?"

"It's the settlement beyond the town wall," Halvar explained. "Until two months ago, it was under Local control, but once the calif got here, the Local sachems and our own sultan decided to combine the two settlements into one. Easier to keep the peace, since they'd be under one law.

"As for those empty villas, they belong to the Afrikan merchants who sell at the feria. They go south for the winter, like the birds. Then they come back for the Spring Feria and spend the summer here, or even farther north, in the mountains, trading for furs with the Locals. They sell what they've bought at the Fall Feria, then go back south, according to my associates in the Guards.

"Green Village is where the Bretains and Oropans settled. They don't have big houses there—it's cabins and cottages, unless you count the Gardens of Paradise."

Before Halvar could explain the status of Green Village further, Milord Summersby spoke up from the far end of the table.

"What is this stuff? Why don't they have any meat? Sausages? Roasts? Fowls? And what is there to drink?" He regarded the delicacies before him with contempt.

"It's all halal," Halvar reminded him. "And with Yehudit present, no meat is served with cheese and yoghurt on the table. Plenty of sweet cakes, though."

"Fit for women!" Milord sneered, scooping up a handful and cramming them into his mouth. "I don't see any here."

"Most of the students are men, although I believe some women are allowed into the medical lectures, under the

5

supervision of Eva Hakim and the Sisters of Fatima." Halvar refrained from asking about Milady Summersby. As far as he knew, she was still across the bay among the Pure Sect in Brook-line Settlement. Instead, he said, "Devallon was asking about the housing here on Manatas. I understand you are unhappy with your cottage, Milord."

"There are no inns of any size on this island, and the house we have been allotted on Pearl Street is not what we are used to," Edgar said. "We were told there is some kind of annual fair. Where do the folk who attend that stay?"

"With their friends," Halvar said. "Or in the sailors' lodging-houses. Or they set up tents. What's wrong with your cottage? Seems comfortable to me."

"The place is far too small," Milord declared loudly. "There must be something larger in this benighted place."

"Those empty villas…" Devallon began.

"Belong to the Afrikans, and Sultan Petrus won't commandeer any of them," Halvar said firmly.

"But surely, some of those people stay for the winter?" Edgar suggested. "Or the servants of those who have left might not mind if we use the facilities, at least until we can arrange transport to Bella Mara? To whom may we direct our inquiries?"

"There's one or two merchants still in Manatas," Halvar admitted grudgingly. "There's Samuel Igbo, and his neighbor, Lady Tekla. She's the widow of a recently-deceased merchant, She stays here on the island year 'round. Her house is certainly large enough to accommodate your party, if she's of a mind to allow you to stay in it. Unfortunately, she does not speak Franchen, only Arabi and some Erse, so you may have some difficulty in getting her permission to quarter yourself on her. And without it, you are likely to be arrested for trespassing."

"And you would be glad to do it, I'm sure. I am fluent enough in Erse, and I've picked up some Arabi, so I am sure I can come to some kind of agreement with the lady," Devallon said with a sly wink. "When would be a good time to call on her? I'm not familiar with the protocols of Al-Andalus."

Halvar suppressed a smile. Lady Tekla was a formidable woman who would undoubtedly show this Franchen upstart just how unpleasant an Afrikan could be when provoked.

"Fasting Month is over," he said. "You might call on her tomorrow, between mid-morning and mid-afternoon prayers. You can tell when that is because the muezzin will call from the muskat, and the bells will ring at the waterfront chapel. You should hear both at your cottage."

"I shall take your advice on both counts, Capitán." Devallon made a sweeping bow and escorted his Bretain charges from the room, leaving Halvar to wonder just how long the unwanted trio was going to stay in Manatas.

The ships from the south weren't due for at least another two months, by which time almost anything might happen. He only hoped Devallon would be able to control the irascible Milord Summersby and his insufferable servant, and that the pair would manage to stay out of trouble until they could be sent off the island.

Alone once more, he tried to catch some scraps of conversation, but it was difficult enough for him to follow ordinary speech in Arabi, the language of Al-Andalus. The lingo of Manatas sounded like Arabi, but it was spoken at a brisk rate, with a nasal accent, and laced with colorful metaphors that referred to events and places the Dane had never heard of. As for the learned teachers, their Arabi was precise and pedantic, but what they were saying was so abstruse he couldn't understand half of what they were fighting about.

He leaned against the wall and wished he could be almost anywhere else. He was not a solitary sort; he'd spent half his life with the Free Company of Danes, marching here and there across Oropa. He liked the easy camaraderie of soldiers like himself. He enjoyed an evening spent around a campfire or in a tavern, telling war stories and singing old ballads. Here in Manatas, he'd made a temporary home at the Mermaid Taberna, where he could find a game of tables and a drink of ale, catch up on the news of the marketplace and the surrounding settlements, and retreat to a room of his own up the stairs.

When can I take my leave? he wondered, sipping from a mug of fruit-flavored drink. It smelled of apples, but he tasted no alcohol, which was probably a good thing, from the tone the conversation at the other end of the table was taking.

"No, no! You are wrong, you are completely wrong!" That was a rotund personage in the black gown and white neckband of a Pure Sect Erse Rite Kristo, his bald head covered by a felt skullcap, his gray wisp of a chin-beard waggling fiercely as he spat out his condemnation at the shorter man in front of him. "It is clearly written in the Holy Book! There is the incident when the Prophet Moshe commanded the sun to be still…"

"It was the Battle-lord Yeshua, and it was a metaphor for a battle that seemed to last all the day and the night!"

His opponent was Yehudit, round-faced with a short black beard and whose long black coat and broad-brimmed felt hat trimmed with fur marked him as Ashkenat, one of those Yehudit who had settled in the lands east of the Dane-March.

"I can prove it mathematically. The sun does not go around the Earth, but the Earth goes around the Sun. It is a fact, not a metaphor. "

"Mathematics is numbers. You can make numbers dance to any tune you like, Master Kupernik, but the Holy Book is the Word, and the Word is of the Almighty One!" the Kristo pronounced.

"Numbers do not lie, Master Boyle!" Kupernik repeated "One can quote any book written by men…"

"By the hand of the Almighty…!"

Halvar sighed. "How long is this going on?" he muttered aloud in Danic.

"Oh, they can argue in circles all day and all night," someone drawled at his elbow in the affected Arabi of Corduva. "It doesn't really matter, does it, whether the Earth circles the sun, or the other way 'round."

Halvar turned to the one person in the room he did not want to talk to.

"Leon, I didn't think Abbas Mikhail ever let you out of the Fratery on your own."

"He didn't. I have a pair of bodyguards to make sure I return to the sanctuary." Leon di Vicenza nodded towards the door, where two stalwart fraters in undyed wool robes like his own stood, arms folded, not partaking of any of the delicacies laid out before them.

"I suppose you're here to give your Seekers of Truth some words of wisdom at the season of the Redeemer's Nativity?"

Leon shrugged. "Benyamin asked me to come, and I decided to do so to remind certain people that I was once rather well-known for my views in academic circles. Even when I was a mere tutor in the sultan's household, my merit was recognized. I was allowed the honor of attending lectures and responding in debates here at the Madrassa. And, as you say, I had my little meetings at the Mermaid Taberna." He nodded smugly, recalling past triumphs. "They were very well attended."

"So I heard," Halvar said. His predecessor, the late and unlamented Tenente Gomez, had hinted those discussions could get fierce, leading to brawls that brought the Town Guard out in force. "Who's the Yehudit in the middle of the argument?" Halvar nodded towards Kupernik. "One of your mentors?"

"Master Kupernik? Hardly! He claims to be from Muscovy. According to him, he studied and then taught mathematics at the Collegium in Parigi but was forced out when Lovis started playing hail-stranger with Episcopus Innocente. Who, by the way, has now declared he is the Papa, the Holy Father of all Kristos, whether Roumi or Greco or Erse Rite; and that all Kristos therefore owe their allegiance to him, personally, and to the Roumi Rite religiously. You can imagine how well that sits with Abbas Mikhail!

"As for Kupernik, I've read his treatise on the movements of celestial bodies," Leon continued, with another dismissive sniff. "He may be right. I'm not a mathematician, myself, so I can't check his figures. He deigned to argue them at one of my debates at the Mermaid Taberna last summer. That was before you arrived in Manatas."

"I'm surprised you admit there's something you can't do."

"My field is natural philosophy," Leon said with affronted dignity. "Of course, I am adept at simple mathematics, but Master Kupernik's advanced theories are quite beyond the comprehension of a mere painter like myself. Or so he says," he added bitterly.

"Frater Leonidas!" Benyamin had found his way through the crowd to seize his leader by the arm. "What is your opinion of Master Kupernik's theories?"

"I've been telling our noble capitán that I am not an expert on the movements of celestial bodies. I am far more conversant with the world below, that of natural philosophy and the origins and uses of what has been given to us here on this earth."

Leon allowed himself to be drawn into the circle of intellectuals gathering at Halvar's end of the table.

"Of course, the son of an apothecary would know all about such matters as plants and minerals." Kupernik sneered as he caught sight of a new opponent.

Leon's mouth tightened, but he kept his voice even as he replied, "Just as the son of a landowner's agent would be conversant with numbers. May I remind you, Master Kupernik, that we are in the territory of Al-Andalus, and at the madrassa, where one's ancestry is to be considered of no account. The only achievements that matter are one's own. In my case, I admit to a lack of knowledge in the field of numbers, but I make up for it as a designer of bridges, one of which is even now under construction."

"Then you agree that the material world has merit?" another voice chimed into the discussion, a stout young man in the striped robes and blue cap of the Sefarat Yehudit whose beard had barely reached the chin-covering stage.

"Of course it does! We have to live in it, don't we?" Leon waved his hands at the refreshments. "Look about you! This place, this Nova Mundum, has proven there are more different plants and animals than the Holy Book described. On this very table, we see not only the grains and vegetables and fruits we brought from Oropa but the maiz and beans and nuts grown here by the Locals. We have cheese and butter from the cows and goats imported from Oropa, but also these cakes made from yams, which were brought here by Afrikans. And these white cakes…I haven't seen these before…"

"Batatas, from the far south, beyond Mechico," Benyamin stepped in to explain. "One of my friends who lives at the Afrikan Hostel gave them to me. He says they must be carefully cooked because the raw plant is poisonous, but cooking removes the element that makes it dangerous. Our cook grated them together with onions and cooked them in olive oil, to recall the sacred lamp that burned for eight days—the Great Miracle."

"How can the plant be poisonous only when eaten raw? How does heat change it" the Sefarat asked, instantly curious. "I am an alchemist and a student of medicine," he added, flushing at the sudden attention. "I am interested in all things material. I leave the theories to the mathematicians."

"Another facet of natural philosophy," Leon pointed out. "The exploration of the mixtures of minerals and plants."

"Cookery!" Kupernik sneered. "You talk of alchemy as if it were something based on reality, Efrem Russo. It is not. You have no idea what you are doing. You mix a little of this, a little of that, add a little of something else, and boom!" He flung up his hands expressively. "That is not what one would call *scientia*—science! It's accidental! True science is to logically devise a theory and use numbers to prove it."

"Do not be so scornful of cookery, Master Kupernik," Leon warned him. "It's more precise than you think. Take salt, for instance. Not enough, and the meal is tasteless; too much, and it's inedible. And there are substances which are quite innocuous by themselves but dangerous when combined."

"As in alchemy," another voice added, that of a wild-haired young man in a shaggy woolen over-tunic whose bushy mustache rivaled Halvar's, speaking in Arabi that, like Halvar's, had Danic overtones. "One must get the ingredients in correct proportion, as you have noted in your review of my recent lecture."

"Your *recipe*, you mean, Master LaPierre?" Kupernik sneered. "Have you completed your so-called experiments? Have you managed to perfect your smokeless gunpowder? You should not offer your theories until you can prove them mathematically, and reproduce the results every time. That, Master La Pierre, is science! As for your experimentation with dangerous materials, I suggest you do it farther up-the-hills, or you will set all Manatas ablaze. As it is, your alchemical explosions are enough to keep us in terror of our lives."

Halvar had had enough of this. He had to find some excuse to get out of this tedious party and go somewhere he could do some good.

A knock at the door turned out to be his release.

"Capitán!"

He turned to greet the scarred and black-bearded face of Tenente Flores, the chief remnant of the previous administration under Tenentes Gomez and Ruiz.

"What is it?"

"Come with me, Capitán. The Locals have found a body"

Halvar waved eagerly to the youngest person in the room.

"Selim! With me!" He turned to Benyamin, trying hard not to grin. "I fear I must leave this delightful gathering, Heer Benyamin. I thank you for inviting me, but duty calls. Selim, you are needed!"

With that, he fairly ran out into the Broad Way, took a deep breath of icy air, and turned to Flores.

"Show me this body!" he ordered. He had never been so glad to hear about a corpse in his life!

Chapter 2

HALVAR'S LONG LEGS FAIRLY ATE UP THE MILE
or so along the Broad Way between the madrassa and the
wall. Flores scurried beside him while Selim trotted behind,
her loose trousers flapping in the rising wind.

"This body, it was found by the Mahak Firebrand and
his team of Watchmen," Flores panted as they passed from
the district of shops and offices to that of the elegant villas of the Afrikan and Andalusian merchants. "They sent
one of their runners to the Rabat to find you, and I told
them to go back to the body while I got you from that
gathering at the madrassa. What a crew those professors
are! Hifalutin' know-it-alls! I'd bet wumpum to silver you
were glad to get out of there."

Halvar stopped to let Selim catch up with them, sti-
fling a grin. Flores might not be the cleverest of men, but
he certainly understood a soldier's mind.

"Firebrand's men? What are they doing at the wall?
That's Donal's charge. The Locals are supposed to be guard-

14

ing the shores, keeping their eyes open for Huron and Franchen invaders."

"Seems they found tracks of one of the big cats come down from the hills." Flores explained."They were following the animal when they spotted the body."

"A cat?" Halvar considered this new addition to his knowledge of the wildlife of Manatas. "Just how big is this wild cat?" He imagined something like the lynx that lurked in the woodlands of the Dane-march where he had spent his childhood.

Selim and Flores exchanged looks. Halvar had already met one of Manatas's more unusual animals, but the mountain cat was considerably larger and fiercer than the relatively mild-mannered sekonk.

"It's very big," Selim said, spreading her arms as far as they would go. "Big enough to kill deer."

"Dangerous, then."

"Very," Flores said. "It's known to kill donkeys and goats left out overnight."

"Then I hope Firebrand and his men find it and kill it before it does too much damage," Halvar said. "Where's this body?"

"Just past the gate." Flores steered him past the gate guardsman, who had come out of his tiny shed to stand at attention, his halberd properly grounded.

Halvar nodded approvingly. Perhaps his drilling and chiding and surprise strolls through Manatas were having an effect on the ragtag assemblage of out-of-work artisans, landless farmers, and former soldiers who had answered his call for recruits to the Manatas Town Guard. In the two months since he had been given the charge, he had tried to bring some kind of order to the disorderly gang that was still smarting from the loss of their former leaders. At least this fellow knew how to behave when his superior officers passed by.

Flores ignored the guard and hurried to where Firebrand and his band of Locals, Tenente Donal of the Green

Village Constabulary, and the inevitable donkey cart were standing next to something huddled beside the stone wall that divided Manatas Town from the rest of the island.

"What cheer?" Halvar greeted the tall Mahak, whom he had appointed one of his tenentes.

"No cheer," Firebrand answered, pointing to the object at his feet. "My man Muskrat found this when we were tracking the cougar."

"That's their name for the mountain cat," Selim explained from her usual post at Halvar's elbow.

"Has the cat been at this body?" Halvar asked, turning to the tall Afrikan bending over the corpse.

"Not so that I can tell." Dr. Moise, the resident medico attached to Sultan Petrus's Andalusian force straightened his lanky frame and rose to face Halvar.

"How long has he been there?" Halvar asked, looking at the assembled Bretains and Locals.

"I should say, by the laxness of the limbs, perhaps two days, perhaps three," Dr. Moise eyed the Green Village constable. "The first rigor has passed, but the flesh is frozen, thanks to the snowfall and the cold. He should have been found long before this!"

"He was covered with snow," Donal protested. "And in the shadow of the wall. And my men aren't used to patrolling the wall—they never had to before." He glared at the Mahak. "That's *their* job."

"True," Firebrand said. "But Capitán Halvar has given us the duty of watching the water. You are supposed to watch the land."

Halvar broke into the squabble. "Whoever he is, he's bound to be missed." This constant bickering and jockeying for position was getting annoying, but he had no idea how to stop it, short of punishments he didn't want to impose. "Has anyone reported a missing person at the Rabat?"

"Not this one," Flores said with disdain. "Look at his clothes. Worn-out macassins, patched trousers, ragged jacket. Scavenger, I'd say. Probably knifed in some petty dispute over a dice game or a woman. Tenente Gomez would not have given him a second thought. Why send for Capitán Don Alvaro? If he's a Scavenger, you should notify Emir Achmet. If he's not, why bother with him at all?"

"Because of this." Firebrand pointed to a large jagged hole in the middle of the body's back. "That's why we called you, Capitán. This is what must have killed him, and it is not a knife that made this wound."

"Quite right," Dr. Moise said. "It is my opinion this wound was made by some sort of firearm—probably a pistoia, from the size of the wound—fired at a distance of some ten paces. Any closer, and there would be burn marks on the body."

"But not here," Halvar said. He'd knelt beside the body and brushed the melting snow aside. "No blood. No blood on the wall, either." He frowned at two marks in the rapidly-thawing earth beside the body. "This wasn't made by a donkey cart, but somebody moved this body from somewhere else. Turn him over, and let's have a better look at him."

The two guardsmen gingerly poked the body with their halberds, rolling it over to reveal the pallid face of a young man just past the teen years, with a face marked by acne and sporting the beginnings of a fair beard. He had straggling fair hair, and his eyes had already been taken by crows. As his head fell back, the collar of his jacket opened, revealing a small crux on a string around his neck. Below the crux was another dark-brown patch, presumably where the bullet had left his body.

"Anyone recognize him?" Halvar scanned the group, then frowned down at the dead lad. "He looks familiar…"

Donal took one look and turned away, muttering a formula against evil spirits. Selim steeled herself to look closer.

"Maybe…" she quavered.

"Maybe what?"

"I think I've seen someone like him on the waterfront. He might be one of Prester Nicodemus's boys, the ones who carry messages and packages around town. He's wearing a crux, so he's a Kristo."

Halvar thought this over. "Dr. Moise, take this lad to the Rabat. There's blood on his front as well as his back, so we have to find the bullet that killed him."

"You won't find it here," Dr. Moise said firmly. "By the way the limbs were arranged, I would agree this body was definitely moved. You will have to find out where he was killed before I can say definitely what the weapon was that did it."

Halvar grimace. "That won't be easy. We have to find out who he was first, then trace his movements." He considered for a moment, "Tenente Donal, you and your men go to Green Village. Ask around, see if anyone remembers a youngster like this fellow hanging about just before the storm. And tell that fellow Simon to print up another issue of the *Gazetta* with information about this poor boy.

"But don't say exactly how he was killed, just that he was found dead. Maybe someone will read it and know who he is. Might as well get some use out of that wretched printing press." He turned to the Mahak. "Tenente Firebrand, what do you know of this animal—this cougar, or mountain cat, or whatever it's called? How dangerous is it? Will it stop folk from going to the Nativity Watch-night festivities in Green Village?"

Firebrand consulted with his men in Munsi then turned back to Halvar.

"We've seen the tracks, but so far, no cougar. It could be denning for the winter, up-the-hills." He gestured toward the pile of rocks in the distance that formed the northernmost end of Manatas Island. "I suggest all goats and donkeys be kept in sheds at night, and a watch put on the Feria grounds where they graze.

"Cougars generally do not come into the open during the day, but prefer to do their hunting at night. We will keep watch for it. It's not likely to come close to a place where there are many people, so your Kristos can have their Holy Meal when they will."

"Let me know if you see any more signs of it." Halvar turned to Flores. "Tenente Flores, you and Selim come with me. We'll see if any of Prester Nicodemus's lads are missing."

"Why bother?" Flores shrugged. "Those boys are nothing but trouble. They call themselves Waterfront Rats. They're always fighting with Emir Achmet's Scavenger lads, they steal from respectable waterfront peddlers, and they're all Kristos, too."

"They are people of Manatas, and they deserve protection," Halvar stated firmly. "Someone took this lad's life, and that is not right. Come along, Selim, Tenente Flores. We have work to do!"

The donkey-driver and two of Donal's men heaved the body into the cart and covered it with a piece of coarse sacking. Dr. Moise took his seat next to the driver. Selim looked longingly at the cart. She would have preferred to ride, but her self-appointed place was with Halvar.

For his part, Halvar wanted to stretch his legs again. He needed the fresh air against his face after the fug of that detestable party.

He headed back to town, shoulders squared, happy to have something to do besides shuffle papers and instruct underlings in the skills they ought to have learned as children. He would find out who'd killed this lad, and show the people of Manatas their capitán was looking out for their welfare, in the name of the Calif Don Felipe.

Chapter 3

THE AFTERNOON DARKENED AS THE WINTER
sun dipped towards the Great River. A fresh breeze gave promise of stronger winds to come, ruffling the surging waves.

Flores followed his leader as the donkey-cart and its
solemn burden plodded along the Broad Way. A gang of
young men in colorful jackets and wide-brimmed hats
trimmed with feathers from local birds stood aside to let
the cart pass.

Halvar waved to the tallest of them.

"Halloo, Stephane Mercier!" He waved his hand at the
tall Franchen, one of the devotees of the Local contest
known as the Peace Game, and a leader among the Kristo students at the madrassa. "Where are you fellows off
to, this Watch-night Eve? I thought you'd be at the Roumi Rite chapel on the waterfront."

The young Franchen student stopped in mid-stride.

"Capitán Don Alvaro Danico! The hero of the game!"
He took off his hat and bowed with a flourish. "We're no

friends of Papa Innocente. It's Green Village for us. We'll attend the Holy Meal at the Erse Rite chapel near the fratery later, after we've had something to eat and drink that isn't madrassa refectory fare." He noticed the body in the donkey cart. "What's this? Some poor soul frozen to death in the snow? May the Redeemer and his Mother Mara have mercy upon him." He made the sign of the crux.

"Not frozen, but sent to his end by something else," Halvar said. "He's about your age, but not one of the madrassa students by the look of his clothes. Selim, here, thinks he might have been one of those messenger lads who run about with letters and packages. If you don't mind, take a look and tell me if perhaps you have seen him somewhere."

Stephane grimaced, but nodded.

"I'll take a look, if you think it may do any good."

The donkey-driver pulled the cover off the corpse far enough to reveal the face. Stephane shuddered and made the sign of the crux again.

"I don't think I can give him a name, but I've seen him around. I just can't recall where or when."

"Not a madrassa student, then," Halvar mused.

"Oh, not at all," Stephane assured him. "Whoever he was, he wasn't one of us. None of us would wear such miserable garments, especially not now, during the Nativity season."

"Off to the Watch-night feasting at the Gardens of Paradise, are you?" Halvar eyed the assorted finery sported by the young elite of Manatas.

"After we work the lard off with a good game of kick-the-bladder." Stephane's friend, Albert, hefted a leather object. "Care to join us?"

Halvar laughed ruefully. "My kick-the-bladder days are well behind me. And how can you speak of lard in halal Manatas?" The witticism got a knowing laugh from the sportsmen. "Keep your eyes open as it gets dark. The Mahak tell me there's a nasty beast afoot, some kind of wild cat."

"A cougar?" one of the other students called out. "We should get our fowling-pieces and go after it."

"Fowling-pieces won't bring down a cougar," another student, clad in the dark suit and tall-crowned hat of the Pure Sect, asserted.

"You know this how? Halvar asked. "You've seen this cougar, fought it, brought it down?"

"They're all over the mountains in West Caster," the Bretain said soberly. "One of them got my uncle. It took a musket to bring it down. The Locals claim cougars are the spirits of the dead, and stay far away from them. "

Halvar frowned. "These fowling-pieces…I thought firearms are banned in Manatas."

Stephane shrugged expressively. "Sultan Petrus has ruled that guns are not permitted in Manatas Town, but one must be prepared for any disturbance. It's not as if we're stupid enough to carry the things about in public. Mine is heavy as a club, and that's all it's good for without powder and shot. A pity about poor Owen—his father sells the stuff, and he could have arranged for us to get some. But he is not available, so our fowling-pieces are useless."

"Owen…the lad who was killed at the Feria?" Halvar recalled the youngster whose love for the Peace Game had led to his recognizing a Huron player, who had clubbed the lad to death.

"The same." Stephane sighed, then looked at the sky, judging how much daylight remained. "We have perhaps an hour to get a good game going," he announced. "A blessed Nativity to you, Capitán."

Albert hefted the bladder once again, and Stephane led his team northward towards the wall.

Halvar grinned as the youngsters headed north. He'd seen students like these during his years as Don Felipe's bodyguard, when he'd lurked in the lecture-rooms of the Corduva Madrassa and stood in corners in rough taverns, watching for the knife that might take the life of the future ruler of Al-Andalus. Now, Don Roderigo ibn Petrus, Sultan Petrus's son, stood beside Don Felipe, while Halvar was left here on this island.

He suppressed the pangs of jealousy, and reminded himself he was only a Hireling, and his job now was to keep Manatas safe.

He stopped to let Flores and Selim catch up to the donkey cart. Daoud, the leather-lunged news-crier, joined them, proclaiming the discovery of yet another body to the populace of Manatas. A crowd gathered as news of the find spread, and a procession of curious onlookers started to straggle after the cart, chattering in the Manatas dialect.

"Tenente Flores, a word, if you please."

"Eh?" Tenente Flores looked about him, to see if anyone was doing something they shouldn't.

They had reached the Grand Muskat, the largest building in Manatas after the Rabat. Halvar beckoned Flores into the shelter of the pillars framing the doorway that led to the sacred space within.

"Something I've been meaning to say, outside the Rabat, where no one can listen to us." Halvar tried to frame his speech in the most neutral words he knew in Arabi. "It's no secret that you've come far and fast these last two months. With Gomez and Ruiz gone, the sultan could have picked anyone to fill their shoes, and you were the closest. You agree?"

Flores shrugged. "It's true. I never thought to be tenente. I was happy to have a bowl of soup twice a day and a place to lay my head in the barracks."

"And so was I, when I was in Al-Andalus," Halvar told him. "But I am the hireling of the Calif Don Felipe, may he have long life, and he placed me where I am now. And he told me to keep Manatas safe before he left for his tour of Al-Andalus-in-Exile."

Flores said nothing, but Halvar could feel the unspoken query: *What has this to do with me?*

"I'm not a man for pretty speeches. I don't have the Arabi for it. But to my mind, what keeping Manatas safe

23

means is that a shopkeeper can put his goods out and not worry that some thief will take them when he's not looking and sell them in the next street. A woman can hang her washing out to dry and not worry someone will take her few clothes to the used-clothing dealer in the souk. A pious Yehudit can go to the study house and not be set upon if he comes home after dark. A good Islim or Yehudit woman can go to the souk and not be accosted by some lout in a green coat with a cudgel at his belt.

"In short, ordinary folk can go about their daily lives without fear of being struck down or robbed. Do I make myself clear, Tenente Flores?"

Flores glowered back at him. "You're thinking that the Town Guard should be the protectors of the poor. That's not what Tenente Gomez was about. And if you've heard something about Zoltan chatting up the girls in the souk, well, you're the one who took him off the waterfront, where he was used to the free ways of the Bretain and Oropan and Local women. You think you know it all, Capitán? You don't know Manatas, and you don't know how we do things here."

"I don't," Halvar admitted. "But I do know how a city should be run, and making shopkeepers pay an extra fee for not being robbed isn't the way it's done in Corduva or Savilla. That's what the Town Guard is for, to stop that kind of thing. I suppose Gomez and that rascally emir split the take, and gave some to their underlings—including you, Tenente Flores."

"Well, let your people know those days are gone. If I find anyone taking money from shopkeepers or mokka-shops or even whores for protection, I will see them beaten and removed from the Town Guard. Islim, Kristo, Yehudit—they are all under the protection of the Town Guard; it's what they pay the town tax for. I'm not going to say this again, Tenente Flores. I will not have this petty thievery. It must stop! Am I clear? Do you understand my Arabi?" He glared fiercely down at the squat Andalusian.

Flores scratched at his beard.

"Oh, I hear you, Capitán, and I understand your Arabi. But I tell you this, since you like plain speaking: This will not go over well with the men who used to get a small bit of what Gomez took in. It wasn't much, but it was more than we got from the town treasury. This isn't Savilla or Corduva, it's Nova Mundum, where we have our own ways of doing things. You may have to bend that stiff back of yours, Capitán, before you leave Manatas.

"As for Zoltan, I can tell him to keep his tongue in his head, and not to jolly the Islim and Yehudit women the way he did the Locals and Oropans, but I can't make him stop doing it if it's the way he is."

"Just keep your men in order, Tenente. I want to show our calif a clean and prosperous Manatas when he returns for the Spring Feria." Halvar strode back into the street. "Come along, Tenente! Enough resting for you! We have a murder to solve!"

The donkey cart proceeded down the Broad Way to the Rabat, while Halvar, Selim, Flores and two guardsmen veered off, taking the path that led to Maiden Lane and the waterfront. There, the Roumi Rite chapel and its one prester tried to bring the word of the Redeemer to the sailors who washed up on the shores of Manatas and the whores and tavernkeepers who served them.

Chapter 4

THE VOICE OF THE MUEZZIN AT THE WATER-
front muskat joined the sound of the the bells of the Roumi
Rite chapel announcing the time for evening prayers as
Halvar and his group arrived at Maiden Lane. Selim, Flores, and the two guardsmen bowed, knelt, prostrated themselves and recited the prayers to Ilha that would see them
through the night. Halvar clutched his amulet that could
have been either a crux or Thor's hammer and thanked the
Redeemer, Mother Mara, and Thor for getting him through
another day without being attacked. That done, the delegation approached the tiny wooden shack that served as the
Roumi Rite chapel.

Prester Nicodemus, the tall, lean clergyman who served
the Oropan community on the waterfront, greeted them
at the door. Three boys about Selim's age were hanging
strings of bright-red berries around the doorway while
two younger lads placed candles in the two small windows

26

at the front of the wooden building. Their lights flickered through panes of colored glass that let in what little daylight was left in the rapidly-fading sunset.

Halvar stepped over the threshold, but the others halted outside, reluctant to enter the Kristo sanctuary.

"A blessed Watch-Night to you, Capitán Don Alvaro." Prester Nicodemus bowed and made the sign of the crux over his most reluctant congregant. "We have not seen you at the Holy Meal for some time."

"I've been busy," Halvar muttered. "And I'm more inclined to the Erse Rite."

"Heretics," Prester Nicodemus sniffed. "And Green Village is a distance away, whereas you are now residing at the Mermaid Taberna, just a short walk from here. You should think of your soul, Capitán, and come to the Holy Meal more often."

"I'll consider it, but right now, Prester, there's another matter I wanted to consult you about. I see you give house-room to young boys, who I'm told serve at the Holy Meal, and who carry messages here and there in Manatas. Have any of them gone missing?"

Prester Nicodemus looked startled.

"Why do you ask?"

Halvar raised his voice, and the various lads stopped their work to gather around him.

"I ask again, is anyone missing? We found the body of a young man, old enough to grow a beard but not old enough to make a full one, on the far side of the town wall. He looked familiar to me, but I don't know his name. I thought of you fellows, the ones who run here and there carrying messages and small packages. So, I ask a third time, is anyone missing?"

"Snake." A red-headed teenager, with sharp features and a dimple in his chin spoke up. "He went out on the day of the snowstorm, when there was all the commotion on the docks. You were fighting some fellow in a fancy suit and hat."

27

"And the ship that was in the bay tried to sail out, and crashed on the rocks against the Long Island," the smallest of the boys piped up.

"And Snake saw it all, and he ran away," the redhead completed the tale.

"This Snake...what does he look like?" Halvar directed his question to Prester Nicodemus.

The prester frowned. "Tall, but not as tall as you, Don Alvaro. Fair. He was growing a beard, but he was not, as you described, quite old enough for a full one. He wore macassins, trousers, jacket."

"Hat?" Almost everyone, male and female, in Manatas, covered their heads, as much for religious reasons as for warmth.

"Wool cap, the kind the whores knit for sailors," the redhead said. "What happened to him?"

"We're not sure," Halvar said. "We're not even sure if the poor lad we've found is him. One of you should go to the Rabat and see if you can identify him."

"Eh?" the smallest boy blinked at the long word.

"Tell us if it's Snake or not," the redhead interpreted.

"Foxy? You were closest to Snake, you should go." another of the boys said, turning to him.

"I've got to serve the Holy Meal," Foxy protested. "Besides, Snake was closer to Mouse. Mouse, you go to the Rabat, and tell them if it's Snake. Then you come back in time for Holy Meal. You got that?"

A blast of cold air made the flames of the candles in the windows dance as a tall youth flung the door open and strode into the room, bearing down on the redheaded boy.

"What's this about? Why is the Town Guard standing in front of the chapel? What's going on?" he demanded.

"The Capitán says they've found Snake," Foxy said before anyone else could.

"Found him? Where?"

"In the snow, on the other side of the wall," Halvar told him.

"What? But..." The tall boy stopped. Then he glared at Foxy. "It's not for you to say who goes where. With Snake gone, I'm the oldest. It's my turn to be the Big Rat."

"So you say, but I'm smarter than you. I can read better, and go faster, and I do more runs than you."

"I'm bigger and stronger!"

Prester Nicodemus intervened before the two could resort to blows.

"That will do! There must be no dissension in this chapel. Mouse, you go with the capitán. Bull, you and Foxy finish decorating our chapel. We must be prepared, in case the Redeemer decides this is the time he will come to us again. The image of Mother Mara must be given these flowers, too. There will be an extra portion of soup tonight, and we have some cakes from the women who come to the Holy Meal."

The boys went back to their tasks as Halvar led Prester Nicodemus aside, nearer the door, and out of the boys' earshot.

"Who was this fellow Snake? What can you tell me about him?" he asked.

"Very little. You may have noticed, Capitán, that here in Manatas, folk are somewhat careful not to reveal their past lives. It is as if coming to Nova Mundum is a chance at a new life as well as a new world. I think Snake came from Oropan stock, in that he was fair rather than dark, not like the Andalusians or Afrikans. Possibly Danic, possibly Bretain.

"He came to me as a half-grown boy, said his mother was dead, didn't know who his father was. I assumed she was one of those unfortunate women who serve the sailors, or a maidservant to one of the merchants who had lost her place for some reason or another. In any case, Snake earned his name by his cunning. A very clever lad, he took to learning quite well. You know I have a small school here. I try to teach these lads their numbers and the Roumi letters."

"Roumi letters don't do much good given the signs in Manatas are written in Arabi and Ogham," Halvar pointed out.

"Alas, my knowledge of Arabi is limited to what is spoken," Prester Nicodemus admitted. "The letters are beyond my grasp. I am familiar with the Ogham used by the Erse Rite, but I will not teach that heresy. Numbers, however, those are universal, since even Oropans use the ones devised by Arabi merchants."

Halvar nodded. He was barely able to read Rune, the square letters used to transcribe Danic, and the round Ogham letters used for Erse were as alien to him as the swirls and curls of written Arabi. But he could read numbers, and knew enough arithmetic to calculate how much he should be paid, and how much to pay for his meals, his clothes, and the roof over his head.

"Your lads, the messengers—they run all over Manatas, right? They have to be able to read the directions on the letters and packages they deliver."

Prester Nicodemus frowned in thought.

"Quite so, Capitán, but usually those directions are simply told to them by the ones whose packages were being delivered. And the messages are not generally written but spoken." He struggled inwardly, then said, "I am most distressed at this news, Capitán. I try not to play favorites among the lads, but Snake had a thirst for knowledge quite remarkable in these boys. Most of them are content to struggle along, living from day to day, but Snake had ambitions beyond the waterfront and this chapel.

"You may have been told that, before you came to Manatas, the painter Leon di Vicenza held court at the Mermaid Taberna, inviting students from the Manatas Madrassa to debate their theories concerning the natural world, the place of the Divine in it, the movements of the stars, and so forth."

"According to Tenente Gomez, there were fights that broke out after these debates."

Prester Nicodemus sighed. "Alas, such heretical theories could not go unchallenged."

"And Snake was at these debates?" Halvar considered what he knew of Leon and his taste for handsome young men. Would he have been interested in a ragged, skinny youngster who was trying unsuccessfully to grow a beard?

"He was." Nicodemus said. "I cannot say what was discussed. I did not attend such meetings. I told him not to do so, but he insisted on going. He would come back afire with what he had heard. It led to ambition, and pride —sinful pride. I cannot but wonder if that is what led him into paths that were…unfortunate."

Halvar put aside the personal angle and tried the professional.

"Tell me about these messages your boys carry, Prester. How is that arranged? Do the lads hang about the tabernas and the mokka-shops on the Broad Way, waiting for someone to call them, or are they hired by one or another of the merchants on a permanent basis?

"When I first came here, it was as you said—the lads would hang about waiting to be called. But Snake had a clever idea and put it into practice this summer. Instead of the lads simply running about town on their own, he organized them into districts and set up a schedule, so that each lad had his own territory. They would call at certain places at certain times to see if anyone needed messages or packages delivered, and were paid a regular sum by some of those who had such messages and packages besides whatever gratuities the boys got from the recipients of the letters and packages.

"According to Snake, this was a more efficient way of managing things. People knew they could be sure a lad would appear at a certain time, and that the message or package would be delivered quickly. The lads put their earnings into a common store, which I manage for them, and so helped provide our food and other necessities— wood for the fire, water, candles for lighting, and so on."

31

"Enterprising fellow, this Snake," Halvar commented. "I'm sorry I didn't get to know him."

"He certainly wanted to know you, Capitán!" Prester Nicodemus assured him. "You were something of a hero to him, especially after you dealt so handily with the nest of assassins at the Mermaid Taberna. He said that if a lout like you could become the calif's hireling and then Capitán of the Town Guard, there was certainly hope for him to rise in the world. All he needed was the learning and the luck, and he could do the rest."

"I didn't get the learning, unless it was at what they call the Collegium of Living Hard," Halvar said. "But I had the blessings of the Redeemer and Mother Mara, and the Three Old Women were on my side. Fate, luck—call it what you will," he added, seeing Prester Nicodemus's confused look.

"Snake was eager for learning, but alas, he did not have the luck," Prester Nicodemus sighed again. "His death is a great loss to our little community, Capitán. I hope when you find his killer, you see to it he is condemned to an evil death. Snake was not loved by all the boys, but he was kind to the younger ones like Mouse, and he would have become a great man, I am sure of it. And he was a devoted follower of the Roumi Rite." Once again, Prester Nicodemus made the sign of the crux.

Halvar looked around the small chapel. The clothes the boys wore were ragged, but they were clean and sufficiently patched to keep out the cold. He could smell something savory cooking in the kitchen of the chapter house next to the chapel, where the boys could be sure of a warm bed and a full belly. Prester Nicodemus was giving these lads a home and family and an honest living, which was more than could be said for the Islim Emir Achmet across the island, whose hand lay heavily on the youngsters in his gang of Scavengers.

Halvar stopped beside the small box that had been set beside the holy water-stoup and dropped in a purple wumpum bead from the string that hung from his belt.

"For the sake of the Redeemer and his Mother Mara, at Watch-Night," he murmured.

He strode off, trailing Selim, Flores, and his guardsmen, into the deepening murk of the winter twilight. He needed some answers—and a change of garments—before he could finish his chores for the day, and head to the celebrations at the Gardens of Paradise. He hoped to find both at the Mermaid Taberna.

Chapter 5

SELIM AND FLORES FOLLOWED HALVAR DOWN
Maiden Lane to the waterfront plaza and the welcoming
light of the Mermaid Taberna. A small market had been set
up under a brace of torches in front of the pawnbroker's shop,
with crude tables where Local women hawked beaded macassins and other finery and Danic and Bretain sailors offered carved wood and ivory toys, made during the rare mo-
ments aboard when they were not on duty. Andalusian Kristo and Yehudit buyers of both sexes browsed among the
hastily built stands, looking for small items to be handed out
to children, as was the custom for both Nativity and Festival of Lights. Wooden whistles, deerskin poppets, bead neck-
laces, small knives—all were offered for sale on this, the eve
of both festivals.

The air was brisk but not bitter as the wind off the bay
made the torches flicker and sent eerie shadows across the
plaza in the gathering dusk. The doors of the Mermaid

Taberna stood open, and its host, Hannes Zilberstam, stood just within, his round face beaming at potential customers.

"A hearty blessing to all on the Redeemer's Nativity!" he called out. "And a good Festival as well. May all the gods be gracious to us at the Turning of the Year!" He waved to Halvar. "Good Yule to you, Landsman! I have a fine salmon, fresh from the river, and a gobbler roasting in its juices, ready to carve. Fru Marta has outdone herself! She's made a pastry log with something very special from the Mechicans, something no one else in Manatas has! Wait till you taste it!"

Halvar looked longingly at the cheerful crowd within the taberna. He wanted nothing more than to join them in their merriment, to have a mug of mulled ale and to partake of the mouthwatering delicacies waiting for him.

Then he looked across the bay, where the hulk of the round-ship *Belle Fleur* was barely visible against the shore. There were matters to deal with before he could enjoy the holy day.

"Would that I could, Heer Hannes, but duty before pleasure. Have any of the Franchen from that ship come across the bay?" Halvar peered into the taberna, where a mixed gang of sailors and Afrikan workers were already making inroads on the food and drink.

"Come inside, Capitán, and talk to them for yourself."

Halvar turned Selim and Flores.

"I want to change my jacket," he told them. To Hannes, he said, "Give my assistants something to cut the cold and keep them from starvation."

As Selim followed Flores into the taberna, Firebrand emerged from the growing crowd in the plaza.

"Good cheer!" he greeted Halvar. "I have news."

"About the ship?" Halvar turned to face his Mahak ally. "What do you hear about it?"

"My men have been across the bay," Firebrand said. "They were there when the things were taken from the bottom of the ship, where the cargo is carried. There were large stones, and among them, wooden boxes."

"Stones are for ballast," Halvar said. "To keep the ship steady in the water, not like your flimsy canoe. Dhows and longships are built differently, don't need so much ballast, but a round-ship will founder if it's not properly loaded. But most round-ships carry stones or bricks for ballast, not wooden boxes. Those are properly placed in the hold."

"These were not. They were under a layer of stones."

"Hidden, then." Halvar considered this oddity. "Smuggling? What was in them?"

"The messenger was not able to see what was in the box when Sachem Mahmoud ordered it opened," Firebrand admitted. "But I will send Muskrat and Seulemon out tomorrow, at first light, to bring back whatever was in the box."

"Good work," Halvar said. "Any other news? What of the woman, Charlotte, Lady Summersby?"

Firebrand grinned. "She is not happy. She has not been allowed to use the things she brought with her from Franchenland—the creams and paints that Oropan women put on their faces and hands—and she complains that she is growing ugly. She must wear the plain clothes of the Pure Sect, not the soft dresses from the trunks she brought with her, and she says that the wool is making her skin itch.

"She has been set to sewing, since that is the only skill she has. She does not want to go across the bay with my people in a canoe, and no one will row across the bay until the water is calmer. If the wind changes, maybe someone can sail across, but certainly not for at least another day."

Halvar's grin matched Firebrand's. "That gives her husband at least one more day of peace." His grin faded. "I don't like the idea of a Franchen ship smuggling something into Andalusian territory. I have a very bad feeling about this. Make sure your men bring whatever they find in those crates directly to the Rabat. If what I think is true, Sultan Petrus will not be pleased."

"What do you think?"

"I'm thinking about how the Franchen took Al-Andalus in less than a year, and the weapons they used to do it."

"Cannons, you said. And muskets." Firebrand's face turned stony. "I will tell my people to keep careful watch tonight. We should be in the lodge, telling the Winter Tales and lighting the Council fire, but we will keep watch while you Oropans have your festival."

"And I, for one, am glad you are doing it," Halvar said, not knowing whether to pat Firebrand on the shoulder or shake his hand.

Firebrand drifted back into the shadows as Halvar entered the noisy taberna. He accepted a mug of warmed ale from one of Hannes's halfling servers and joined Flores and Selim at one of the small tables ranged around the central open area. One of the Franchen was delivering an old song, a legend about the Redeemer's birth, and how the humble shepherds met the great kings in an ox's stall.

"What next?" Flores asked, eying a platter of fowl pieces that had been dipped in maiz-meal and fried in a pan with bits of onion and other herbs.

"You two stay here. I'm going to change my jacket. This coat's not right for a Nativity feast."

Halvar headed for the stairs.

"We have to meet with Dr. Moise at the Rabat," Selim called after him. "You can leave off primping for your Yehudit fancy woman."

Halvar continued up the stairs to his private quarters. He had added a few extra touches to his rooms—a second chair, a bit of cloth to cover the window and keep the drafts out, and a small glass mirror. He peered into this, stroking his mustache, and wondered if he was becoming vain. No, he decided. He owed it to Don Felipe to present a good appearance, well-groomed and in the best garments he could afford. In his mind, he could hear the voice of Old Sergeant Olaf: *A good soldier is a clean soldier. Respect your gear, and folk will respect you!*

As for Dani Glick...

He shrugged mentally and hooked the silver frogs that closed his Andalusian-style black jacket. He admired her courage and her wit, and she was still good to look at, but he couldn't trust her, not entirely.

And he would have to do something about Selim's attitude! That girl was taking far too much on herself.

Halvar took one last look in the mirror. He adjusted his Danic cap, placed his aroughoun fur hat over it, and decided he was fit for a Nativity Festival. That done, he had one more duty to perform.

He rejoined Flores and Selim downstairs and led them and the boy called Mouse away from the waterfront.

"To the Rabat," he ordered, and strode out into the winter night.

Chapter 6

THE LANTERNS HAD BEEN LIT ALL THE WAY UP
the Broad Way so the Kristos could get to their chapels and
the Yehudit to their study house in relative safety for their
respective festivals. Inside the walls of the Rabat, more torches
sent shadows flickering off the massive walls of the fortress
that dominated the skyline of Manatas Island.

Halvar, Flores, Selim, and Mouse were admitted by the
guardsman on duty. They headed across the courtyard,
where a Local woman had set up her tiny brazier to grill
ears of maiz and Afrikan yams and keep a small pot of
chickory-laced mokka warm.

Dr. Moise stopped the group before they could approach the main tower, where Sultan Petrus lurked in Andalusian splendor.

"I suppose you want to know more about that poor
lad." The lanky Afrikan had added an embroidered woolen
caftan to his usual striped kutton garb, and wound a
knitted scarf around his neck to combat the cold.

"What have you found out? Was the bullet inside him?"

"Come inside, out of this wind." Dr. Moise beckoned Halvar into his sanctuary.

"Tenente Flores," Halvar said before his subordinate could follow him, "you go up to tell the sultan what we found. Tell him I'll be along shortly, as soon as I have more information for him. And wish him a good End-of-Fast. He seemed to be a little out-of-sorts when I gave him my report this morning."

Flores salaamed and ambled off, glad that he was not going to have to observe another autopsy.

Halvar and Selim were not so lucky. Mouse hung back until Selim grabbed his arm and shoved him into the chilly shack where Dr. Moise had his medical practice. Rugs had been hung on the walls, but they did little to mitigate the wind that blew through the spaces between the wooden slats, and the coals in the brazier in the corner could not ease the cold that permeated the rough building.

"You should get the sultan to give you one of his new stoves," Halvar commented as he approached the table where the body of the young man lay naked. His clothes had been placed in a neat pile near his feet.

"Malik the Smith is being kept busy making them for rich Afrikans," Dr. Moise said with a shrug. "A mere medico like me must make do with coals in an open brazier."

"Bring the lantern closer," Halvar ordered. "You, boy —Mouse? Is that your name?"

"It's what they call me," the boy admitted. "Mama called me Moshie, but Mama died, and Prester Nicodemus put the water on me, so now I'm Mouse and I'm Kristo."

"Typical Roumi Rite aggression," Dr. Moise sniffed. "The lad may have been born Yehudit, but he's being raised Kristo."

Halvar ignored the religious controversy.

"What about this lad? Kristo, Islim or Yehudit?"

"Oh, Kristo, to be sure." Dr. Moise lifted the cloth that gave the dead youth some slight degree of dignity. "Definitely not Islim or Yehudit."

40

Halvar drew Mouse towards the table.

"Is this the one you fellows call Snake?"

Mouse blinked back tears as he looked at the face of his one-time leader.

"It's him. It's Snake. At least, that's what we called him. Prester Nicodemus said his Kristo name was Stephen, because that was the Good Man's Day when he came to the chapel and took the water." He made the sign of the crux. "He took care of me when I first came to the chapel, and he wouldn't let the big boys hurt me."

"Selim!" Halvar ordered. "Write this down. 'The body of Stephen, called Snake, was found on the day before Nativity, at the Manatas Wall'." He turned back to Mouse, who had shrunk away from the table. "When did you last see Snake?"

"I told you—three days ago." The boy edged closer to the door. "Can I go back to Prester Nicodemus now? I'm cold, and hungry, and he's got our Nativity feast ready."

Halvar's long arm intercepted Mouse's escape.

"Not so fast, boy. Did Snake say where he was going? What was he doing before he left?"

"I don't know where he was going. He didn't say."

"What about the day the ship came in. Do you know anything about that?"

Mouse shrank back against Selim.

"I don't know anything. I didn't hear anything. Bull said—"

"Bull? What does he have to do with any of this?" Halvar demanded.

"He followed Snake when he went out, when all of us went to see the fight on the docks, when the woman fell into the water, just as the snow started. And when he came back, he said that he was the Big Rat, and we had to do what he said."

Halvar considered this piece of news.

"What do you know about the Franchen, the one who sailed the ship into the harbor? He came in nearly a week ago, went to the chapel, and talked with Prester Nicodemus, then sent Snake off on an errand. All this I already know—you're not telling any secrets. Did you hear or see anything that night that was wrong, or odd?"

"The Franchen captain came to the chapel for the Holy Meal," Mouse said, with an understanding nod. "And he told Prester Nicodemus he needed someone to carry his message, someone he could trust. And Snake said that he would go. And Snake went out that night, and he came back very late, he missed night prayers. And when they found the captain dead behind the whore's crib the next morning, Snake was went out on his rounds, and when he came back, he said he was going to be rich.

"And then, the next day, just after they found the woman on Maiden Lane, he went out again, and when he didn't come back I was worried, and I asked Prester Nicodemus if we should go after Snake, but Prester Nicodemus said that Snake probably went to Green Village and stayed there, because of the snow." Mouse stopped for breath and wiped his running nose on his sleeve. "That's all I know. Please, can I go back now?"

"Not just yet. Selim, fetch this fine lad one of those hot yams and something warm to wash it down with." Halvar slid several white wumpum off the string and handed them to her. He turned back to Dr. Moise as she went off on her errand. "Have you found the bullet yet?"

"I don't think I will," Dr. Moise said. "The shot reached his heart and went right through him. Not as much blood as you'd think under him, most of it sopped up by his jacket and shirt. Some odd bruises on his arms and legs, postmortem. I do not doubt he was moved after death, possibly strapped or tied to some kind of litter."

"What else can you tell me about him?"

Dr. Moise might enjoy descriptions of wounds, but Halvar had seen enough of them not to want to learn more than he had to.

"Not much. I'd guess his age as eighteen or nineteen, at most. He had good leg muscles—"

"All that running errands," Halvar interjected.

"His feet were callused, but not heavily." Dr. Moise ignored the interruption. "Not fat, but not malnourished, either. I have not opened his stomach—there's no reason to suspect poison in this case—but I'd say he had been eating the usual stuff: maiz, fowl, sallet greenery, fish. No signs of scurvy, so he must have had some fruit and cabbage."

"What about his clothes?" Halvar looked around for his expert. Selim might wear boy's garb, but she had a girl's eye for fashion. She had returned from her errand munching on a yam, while Mouse had an ear of maiz. Now, she inspected the dead lad's garments.

"Well-made cast-offs," she pronounced. "Prester Nicodemus came to the Rabat from time to time to ask for alms, and my father gave him some of the clothes our servants didn't want any more. This jacket was cut down from one of the guardsmen's coats, and the trousers are Bretain-made, maybe sailor's gear. The shirt is linen—Franchen, I think, because of the way the collar is gathered, very tiny stitches. The macassins are plain, no beads, the kind the Algonkin trade for iron pots on the waterfront or at the feria. And there's this." She held up a plain wooden crux, strung on a twisted linen cord.

"Well, that's nothing unusual. We know he was Kristo."

"But there's something on the back, in Ogham letters. Not the Redeemer's name, but something I can't make out." Selim held the crux closer to the lantern.

"You can read Ogham?" Mouse gazed at her in awe.

"And Arabi and Franchen," Selim replied. "Leon might not be a very good person, but he's a very good teacher."

She put down the crux and lifted the jacket.

"There's something sewn into the lining," she said, rubbing her fingers over the hem of the garment. "Something round...wait a minute...Dr. Moise, can I have one of your knives?" She cut the stitches of the hem and carefully extracted three coins.

"What have we here?" Halvar took the coins and held them up to the lantern.

43

"That's a Bretain penny," Selim pointed out. "And that's one of those Franchen imperials. But what's that square one? I've never seen anything like that, not even at the souk or at the Feria."

"I have," Halvar said. "It's Afrikan, it's iron, and it's from the Ashanti territory. They use them to pay the mercenaries who go into the forests to round up the souls who are to be transported to Nova Mundum, to work the big farms as slaves."

"How did Snake get that?" Selim wondered.

"And what was he going to do with it?" Halvar added.

Mouse tried once again to get out the door, but Flores blocked his way.

"Capitán! I have a message from the sultan. He wants to see you...now!"

Halvar sighed. "Selim, take Mouse back to the Waterfront; one of the guards can light your way. While you're there, see what you can find out about Snake and his rounds. Maybe the lads will talk to you more willingly than they'll talk to me."

Selim nodded and picked up the jacket again. Something else caught her eye.

"What's this?" She pointed at a red smudge on the shoulder. "This can't be blood, he wasn't hit in the shoulder."

"Not blood," Dr. Moise agreed, sniffing at it. "Wrong color, for one thing, and the wrong place for another." He sniffed at the smudge again and rubbed his finger over it. "Do you know, I think this is red paint, the kind made from earth and urine."

Halvar's nose wrinkled at the thought.

"Who paints their house in the middle of winter?"

"Some Afrikans decorate their villas for End-of-Fast," Dr. Moise pointed out. "The Ashanti, for instance, and some of the Yoruba."

"Do they, indeed?" Halvar said thoughtfully. "Then perhaps it's time to take a better look at some of those villas up-the-hills on the Street of Afrikans."

44

"But not tonight," Selim reminded him. "You have to report to my father. And then you wanted to go to Green Village for the Nativity Festival. I'll go to the waterfront chapel, and the boys will tell me everything you want to know about Snake."

"Maybe not," Mouse quavered. "We all know who you are. You're Selim ibn Petrus, you're the Sultan's son, and you follow Capitán Halvar Danske all over Manatas. And we don't talk to the Town Guards. They're all in the pay of the Scavengers, and us Waterfront Rats, we won't deal with Scavengers."

Selim thought this over, then said, "I can change what I look like. I can put on a woman's dress and let my hair show, and be Sally the Serving Maid from the Mermaid Taberna." She undid her turban, to let her braids drop to her shoulders.

Mouse gaped at her. "You're a girl!"

"And it might do me some good for a change," Selim said with a gleeful grin.

"What are you thinking, laddie?"

Selim's grin grew larger. "You know how it is. No one looks at the face of a serving girl. *You* didn't even know it was me until I tried to pass you a message. I can put some of Ayesha's cream on my lip to hide the hairs, and Mouse can say he met me on the way back from the Rabat. I'll say I was serving at a mokka-shop, and they let me go because I was Kristo, and Mullah Abadul is being strict about Kristos and Yehudit working for Islim."

"Prester Nicodemus doesn't take in girls," Mouse objected. "You might wind up with one of the whores instead."

"But I'll still find things out," Selim persisted. "Come on, Mouse. First, we'll go to my quarters at the Rabat, and then, we'll go to the waterfront. I've always wanted to see what the Nativity Holy Meal was like!"

"Before you go off on this little adventure, draw me a picture of this poor lad." Halvar ordered. "I'll take it with me to Green Village and ask if anyone there saw him around. We have to find out who the message from Girard was for, and whether Snake had an answer to deliver."

Selim sketched hurriedly, tore the sheet out of her notebook, and on her way across the courtyard before Halvar could stop her. Once again, the headstrong girl was off on her own adventure, without thinking of consequences. He could only hope her love of excitement wouldn't lead her into danger, and that, if it did, he could get her out of it before her father found out!

He headed towards Sultan Petrus's lair. The old man was already in a testy mood, and the news there had been another murder in Manatas wouldn't make him any sweeter.

Chapter 7

HALVAR CROSSED THE COURTYARD TO THE CENtral tower of the Rabat by the fitful light of the torches in their sockets on the inside of the surrounding wall. Overhead, stars were beginning to glimmer in the night sky. There was a smell of salt water from the bay as gulls wheeled, getting their last meal before settling down for the night on one of the many islets that dotted the bay that made Manatas so attractive as a port.

Sultan Petrus was seated in his armchair, his ivory leg propped up on a footstool. He had removed his elaborate silk robes in favor of a simple woolen caftan and a colorful wrapper; his turban was a plain length of cloth, pinned with a gold brooch. A small table near his right hand held his favorite brass mokka-pot and cups, and a sheaf of papers tied with red string. The new stove had been lit, and the room was tolerably warm.

"So, you're finally here!" he snarled as soon as Halvar stepped over the threshold.

Halvar salaamed.

"I had matters to attend to. A body has been found…"

"One of the Waterfront beggars. Tenente Flores told me about it." The sultan sipped mokka. "You're spending a lot of time on this boy. Why?"

"Because he was killed with a pistoia," Halvar said bluntly. "And because the body was moved. I want to know who moved it, and why, and where the boy died to begin with. I thought no one in Manatas had firearms. Now, I find out some of the students at the madrassa have them."

"Fowling-pieces." Sultan Petrus snorted. "Good for shooting pigeons, not people."

"A bullet doesn't care why it's fired, or from what. It can kill a man as well as a pigeon," Halvar countered. "And I've seen at least one musket in Green Village, and one is carried by the Dane who has a cottage on Pearl Street."

The sultan's scowl deepened into a frown.

"I can't collect every firearm in Manatas. The best I can do is try to stop new ones coming in." He shifted uneasily in his chair, closed his eyes, and stifled a grunt of pain. "And I make sure gunpowder is not manufactured on Manatas Island. The feria grounds were under Local control until this year, and the Mahak permit gunpowder to be sold, but I do not want the stuff made here. Too dangerous!"

"Quite right," Halvar agreed, trying to ignore the signs of fatigue on the older man's face, signs that the sultan was feeling the after-effects of too much rich food and drink. He eyed the pile of papers next to the mokka-pot on the sultan's table. "What do you hear from Bella Mara?"

"The snowstorm delayed the usual dhow, but one of the servants tells me the fishermen who brings a catch from the long bay says that Don Felipe, may he reign long, has been meeting with Afrikans from the southern territories, trying to make alliances in case Imperator Lovis and his

48

sons decide to bring their war over the seas. And one of the fishing boats had some letters from Bel'Mar."

"Not a bad idea, to ally with the Afrikans." Halvar nodded.

"Perhaps. But there's a small catch in the negotiations." Sultan Petrus glanced at the letters on his table. "According to Roderigo, the Afrikans will help us, but we're going to have to help them in their wars with the Locals. And they're bringing in more and more people captured in Afrika to work on the tabac and kutton farms."

Halvar tugged at his mustache as he considered the implications of such an alliance.

"Does Don Felipe really want to get mixed up in that kind of war? The Locals are defending their lands, and they're not as nice about it as Oropans. I've heard some hair-raising stories from the guards about what they do to prisoners."

"And some of them may be true," Petrus said. "My son writes that the Afrikans are claiming lands on the far side of the mountains, where the Cherokee people live."

"That's because they've heard there's gold there," Halvar said. "The merchant who died at the Feria, Ochiye Aboutiye, had gold ornaments for sale. There were gold nuggets among the amulets I saw on his stand at the feria. Some of the Afrikans have already taken steps to find where the gold nuggets come from. If they do find the source of the gold, they will go after it. And then the fat will truly be in the fire, and the Locals will be the targets. The Afrikans have already brought in Oropan soldiers, the ones who don't want to join Lovis's army, to fight the Locals for them."

"And they pay them with land," Petrus finished for him. "A farm, and the Afrikans to work it, for their service. So says Roderigo, and I believe him."

"Not a bad bargain for a penniless soldier," Halvar said. "All you have to do is go into the mountains, kill a bunch of Locals, and take what they have."

Sultan Petrus muttered a curse.

"Not honorable." He took another sip of mokka. "What about this dead lad? What makes you think his death means anything other than a falling-out between beggars for a few coins or a scrap of bread?"

"Beggars don't shoot each other," Halvar stated. "They don't have the weapons, and they can't afford the ball and powder. If this were a matter of beggars, he'd have been knifed. What's more, he's got an Afrikan coin sewn into his jacket. There's Afrikan paint on his jacket, too. Tomorrow I'll take a walk to the Street of Afrikans and see whether one of their houses has a fresh coat of red paint. It may be that the Afrikans are behind this death."

"I thought those houses were empty. That Franchen fellow, Devallon, wanted me to allow him to put the Bretain milord in one of them for the winter, or at least, until they could get a ship out of Manatas."

"The Widow Tekla is in one of them—she stays all year long." Halvar thought this over. "I've said as much to Sieur Devallon. It's up to him whether to approach her about renting rooms in her house. Until then…"

"The Bretain milord can sit in the cottage," the sultan finished, with another grunt. "What about that wife of his? The one who flaunts her hair?"

"She's in Brook-line, across the bay," Halvar reported. "And as far as I know, she's going to stay there."

"Good!" Sultan Petrus sneezed. "I don't want her anywhere near Lady Ayesha. She's a menace!"

"She's Franchen," Halvar pointed out. "And Kristo, Roumi Rite at that. They treat their women differently." He salaamed again. "If that is all, excellent sultan…"

Sultan Petrus shifted in his chair again.

"You'll be wanting to go to your Nativity festival, I suppose. Well, go and pay my respects to the Yehudit houri."

"I thought you were planning to attend the feast yourself."

"Not tonight. I've had too much rich food, too much festival. If young Selim wants to go, she's welcome to do so. Where *is* Selim? I thought she was with you at the party at the madrassa."

"Selim is pursuing a certain line of inquiry," Halvar said. "I've given her something to look into regarding this lad we found."

"She's an interesting girl, is Salomey. She's not a beauty, but she's got her mother's spirit." Petrus stroked his beard thoughtfully. "She'd make someone a fine wife, once he got past her height and her temper. And she'll have a good dowry, too."

"I thought your first wife, Lady Mariyam, had already picked out a husband for her." Selim had been so distraught at the thought she had run away from the Rabat, an act that had led to Halvar's discovering her true gender.

"Mariyam's got her own troubles, and she's not here. I am the girl's father, and I shall decide who her husband shall be."

And it won't be me! Halvar said silently. Aloud, he said, "I value Selim as an amanuensis and as a student, but she is still very young."

"Ayesha was just as young when we were married," Petrus pointed out. "But you may be right. The girl is still very headstrong. Just like her mother!." He sneezed again.

Halvar backed away from possible infection as two women descended from the stairs at the side of the room.

Sultan Petrus looked up at the younger of the two.

"My lady wife, what are you doing out of the harem? You see I have a visitor." He indicated Halvar, who bowed without looking directly at the sultan's third and youngest wife.

"My dear husband, you are not well!" Lady Ayesha hurried to his side. "I could hear you sneezing from the harem!" She ignored Halvar, who edged closer to the door and freedom.

Eva Hakim, a tall woman in the brown robe and green hijab of the Sisters of Fatima, joined her in fussing over the old soldier.

"Forgive me, excellent sultan, but your health is important to all who live in Manatas, and especially those of your household. You have had far too much excitement and rich food. You must rest and eat more sparingly. I shall make you a tonic of roots which the Local women tell me will strengthen your constitution against the rigors of winter."

"Dr. Moise has already given me some kind of potion made of willow bark," the sultan protested.

"Hot herb tea. I know just how to make it." Ayesha hovered over her aging husband.

Halvar eased out of the room. With the old man in the hands of his loving spouse and a good physician, he could leave for Green Village knowing all would be well… at least, for one night.

But the implications of what he had seen lingered. Perhaps his venal predecessor, Tenente Gomez, had a good reason to take the reins of governing Manatas into his own hands. If the sultan, the representative of the calif, was not able to function, then who could rule in his place?

Halvar shrugged. That wasn't his concern. He would go to Green Village and celebrate the birth of the Redeemer with the rest of the Erse Rite Kristos. And perhaps no one else would get killed until tomorrow.

Chapter 8

HALVAR MADE HIS WAY ACROSS THE COURT-
yard to the gate and acquired a donkey cart to carry him to
Green Village. He nodded to the guard and pointedly ignored the two who slipped out of the Rabat behind him—a
small boy and a tall girl. They headed to the waterfront,
while he ordered Avaram, his designated donkey-driver, "To
Green Village!"

The cold wind didn't seem to have driven anyone indoors. Knots of men huddled outside the mokka-shops,
whose windows were fogged with steam from the heat
within. Yehudit in fur-trimmed hats and long black coats
were headed to their study-house just south of the souk,
while a steady stream of Kristos in the distinctive trews
and smocks of Bretains were headed north toward the town
wall and Green Village. A few Franchen in tight breeches
and coats with nipped-in waists made their way eastward
to the Roumi Rite chapel on the waterfront.

Halvar passed the Grand Muskat, where Mullah Abadul glared at the passing throng from the doorway. The Islim leader could not remove the offending infidels—the Convivencia, the unwritten law of Al-Andalus that permitted Kristos and Yehudit freedom to worship as their conscience dictated, still held in Manatas; but he could make his disapproval known to all who heard his sermons. Halvar could only hope that, with the coming of winter, the mullah would preach indoors instead of trumpeting his hatred of all who were not Islim from the muskat steps, where all the passers-by on the Broad Way could hear him.

The crowd thickened as more and more people joined the procession towards Green Village. Now there were women within it, stout Danic and Bretain wives in woolen skirts and jackets, wrapped in furs and shawls against the growing cold, accompanied by their husbands or fathers. A laughing gang of students from the madrassa cut in front of Halvar's donkey-cart.

"A blessed Nativity to you, Capitán!" One of them waved at Halvar, who nodded and waved back. Maybe there was something to be said for making oneself known outside the Rabat. If he could only persuade these people the calif had their best interests at heart, his job would be easier.

He passed a trio of Kristos fraters in their dull woolen robes.

"Hold up!" he ordered Avaram. "Frater Leonidas? I thought you'd be at your fratery by now."

Leon di Vicenza looked up at him.

"I stayed to continue my conversation with Master Kupernik and his followers. And to partake of some better refreshment than I am likely to get at the fratery table. And to have a word or two with Imam Mustafa, who leads the department of natural philosophy, to suggest that I might give some lectures on the subject, with Abbas Mikhail's permission, of course. Now I must step lively if I'm to get to the fratery before the prayers start. Abbas Mikhail

was kind enough to let me leave my pris—that is, the fratery
—and I must not test his forbearance."

"Step into my cart," Halvar offered. "This donkey's
not the swiftest, but it's faster than walking. Easier on the
feet, too."

Leon glanced at his companions.

"I am not alone," he reminded Halvar. "My brothers
in religion are always at my side."

"Making sure you don't escape," Halvar murmured.
Louder, he said, "Of course, they are welcome to join us.
It's a bit of a step to Green Village, and it's a cold night."

Leon heaved himself onto the cart, followed by the
two bodyguards, whose weight made the vehicle lurch
wildly. The driver gripped the reins as the donkey brayed
with indignation about his added burden. Once the bodyguards were settled, the donkey pacified, and the driver
assured that they would not overturn, the cart moved forward again.

"What makes you so generous, Don Alvaro?" Leon
asked once he was seated on the crude board that consti-
tuted a bench in the cart. "I thought you had no liking for
me. I can't think why."

"I wanted to have a chat with you, and this is as good
a time as any." Halvar glanced back at the two fraters,
who were on the floor of the cart behind the bench. "Do
they speak Arabi?"

"Not very well." Leon shrugged. He continued in the
exaggerated accent of the Corduva elite. "What did you
need to ask me, noble Hireling, that you want to keep secret from my bodyguards?"

"I wanted to know how you were getting on," Halvar said in the same dialect. "How do you like being a
frater?"

"It is very…soothing," Leon said. "So…regular. The
bell rings, we rise. The bell rings, we pray. The bell rings,
we eat. The bell rings, we work." His voice grew shrill.
"The bell rings, we pray again, and again, and again. Always, when the bell rings, we must stop what we are do-

ing and do something else." He stopped, took a deep breath, and smiled, unconvincingly.

Halvar grinned under his mustache.

"As you say, very regulated. A change from your former way of life, Frater Leonidas. Obedience, poverty, that's the rule at the fratery."

"You forgot chastity," Leon grumbled.

"That's not my concern," Halvar shrugged. "I never bother anyone about their choice of playmates. Except when they get those playmates killed."

Leon drew a quick breath. "I did not want Otter Tail to die. I was very upset about that."

Halvar grimaced, The young Mahak had seen what he should not have seen, and paid a fatal price for it.

"What about the journal I sent you, the one the Franchen captain kept. What have you been able to find out?"

Leon glanced back at the two fraters, who sat with their backs against the sides of the cart, effectively barring him from exiting.

"It's not his logbook, if that's what you're looking for. Nothing about the position of the ship, or the weather or tide conditions. It's more of a personal record of his, um, amorous conquests. In fact…" Leon's tone lightened. "…it would probably sell quite well, especially if I illustrated some of the more, ah, provocative passages."

Halvar made an exasperated noise.

"Tcha! I don't care who he bedded or how! I want to know what he was up to in Kibbick and Bos-Town. Was there anything about that?"

"I didn't get that far," Leon confessed. "I began at the beginning, where he describes his encounters in Franchenland."

"Start from the back, then, and work your way forward. He was in Kibbick, where he picked up Milord Summersby and his bride…"

"I've heard about her from Dani Glick. According to Dani—a courtesan, and a very expensive one at that."

"With a harridan of a maidservant who wound up at the bottom of Manatas Bay," Halvar finished. "Milord also has two manservants, Edgar Norris and Andres Devallon. One Bretain, one Franchen."

"Those two fellows with Summersby at the madrassa gathering?"

"The same. Ever see either of them before?"

Leon frowned in thought. "I can't say that I have. Of course, I don't exactly travel in the sort of circles that a mercenary soldier would. I should think you'd know more about Devallon than I."

"I've met him," Halvar said, curtly. "What about Milord Summersby? And this fellow. Edgar Norris? There were plenty of young Bretains at the madrassa in Corduva. You had a few of them about you before you..."

"Were exiled? I did, but I can assure you, this Summersby person was not one of them. And neither was the servant. As for your friend Devallon..."

"No friend of mine," Halvar grunted. They had reached the gate in the town wall. "One more thing..." He reached under his jacket and pulled out the drawing of Snake. "Does this fellow look familiar?"

Leon held the drawing closer to the lantern that lit the gateway.

"I see Selim is using some the skills I taught her. It's a nice likeness. Do you know, I do think I've seen this fellow around the waterfront."

"Have you? Because he's the reason I was called out of the party," Halvar stated. "His body was found by the Mahak watchmen this afternoon. Dr. Moise thinks it was moved, where from we don't know; but best guess, he was killed two days ago, after we found the Franchen's body but before the snow started. The body was covered, was only found because the snow melted off. Look again..."

Leon shook his head. "I can't put a name to him, but I did see him once or twice at the symposia."

"The what?" Halvar took the drawing back and tucked it under his jacket again.

"The debates, if you will. When I was removed from the Rabat by that interfering Mullah Abadul and took refuge with the Taverniers at the Mermaid Taberna last year, I arranged for some of the students from the madrassa to have discussions on certain issues."

"And was Master Kupernik one of your madrassa lecturers?"

"Oh, yes. He arrived here in Manatas the year after I did, at which time I was employed at the Rabat, instructing young Selim. We met from time to time at formal functions, and I invited him to lecture when I took residence at the Mermaid Taberna. It was...most entertaining." Leon smirked, likely at the memory of the riot that had brought the Town Guards to the waterfront after the mathematician's speech.

"So Tenente Gomez told me. He also said those debates got so heated he had to break them up. Knives were drawn..."

"An exaggeration!" Leon scoffed. "Well, perhaps once or twice. Words, my dear Halvar, only words!"

"'Words can lead to actions,'" Halvar quoted from Old Sergeant Olaf. "What about this fellow? Was he at one of these debates?"

"Let me see that again..." Halvar obliged, and Leon handed the drawing back to him. "Now I remember him. Not a very good-looking youngster. Bad skin, dirty hair, big nose, and a whining tone to his voice. He hung about at the back of the room most of the time. He tried to get me to promote his bid for entrance in the madrassa."

"I heard he was ambitious," Halvar mused. "What happened?"

"He was stupid enough to try blackmail," Leon sniffed. "He said he'd go to the sultan and tell him about my, ah, relationship with Otter Tail."

"Was that supposed to be a secret?"

"It wasn't something I'd have Daoud the News-crier announce in the souk," Leon said. "But I have never pretended to be anything other than what I am, and so I told that silly boy...what was his name?"

"Stephen, but they called him Snake," Halvar said. "So, you turned him down."

"Of course I did. The fellow was not madrassa material, and so I told him. A waterfront beggar, a messenger, not the sort who would fit into the madrassa at all."

"But the calif's ruling is that anyone who can come up with the fees may attend the lectures," Halvar pointed out. "Even I, the calif's bodyguard, was admitted to the lecture-rooms at the Corduva Madrassa. It's how I learned Arabi, listening to those lecturers."

Leon sniffed again. "Oh, I don't say he couldn't have attended the lectures, if he had the money. And it's possible he might have made something of himself, in time. But I would have nothing to do with him. He was ugly."

"And a poor boy, no connections, not like Otter Tail, who was related to the sachem," Halvar said. "And here we are, in Green Village. I wish you a blessed Nativity, Frater Leonidas. You have given me something to think about. And please, continue your work on that journal. I want to know what Captain Girard has to say about the women of Bos-Town."

Leon's bodyguards followed him across the common ground to the Erse Rite fratery stockade. Halvar eased out of the cart and headed for the iron fence that enclosed the Gardens of Paradise. Lanterns lit the way through the now-bare trees to the open doorway, where light, music, food and companionship beckoned. He would celebrate the Nativity of the Redeemer and think about dead messengers tomorrow.

He slowed his purposeful stride as he realized the crowd around the entrance to the building wasn't as cheerful as he'd thought. Angry voices were spoiling the joyous mood of the night.

"I'll be a while," he told Avaram. "You can stay and enjoy the festival, if you like, or you can go back to Manatas."

"I'll stay. You may not be in a condition to walk when you get out of the Gardens of Paradise." The driver grinned as he turned the donkey loose to graze with the other animals on the common ground.

"I just hope it's from drinking and nothing worse," Halvar muttered as he approached what looked like a riot in the making.

Chapter 9

THE DOORS TO THE GARDENS OF PARADISE WERE
open to receive the Kristos of Manatas gathered to celebrate
the Redeemer's Nativity as well as the Yehudit who recalled
their victory over their Old Greco foes. As announced in the
Gazetta, there was a banquet table of succulent delicacies
ranging from tiny birds roasted in their juices and flavored
with expensive imported spices to sugar-topped cakes, all
to be washed down with liquids of varying degrees of al-
coholic intensity. Halvar smelled the delicious aromas, reminding him he had not eaten anything since sampling the
oddities at the madrassa party.

Dani Glick stood in the doorway. She had replaced
her "respectable Yehudit matron" skirt and bodice with a
Damascus-made silk tunic and loose trousers that revealed
her figure as much as covered it. A sheer silk scarf, the
least possible nod to the unwritten rule of Manatas society that any woman over the age of puberty should cover

her head, floated over her red hair. Gold chains glittered at her neck, gold bangles jingled on her arms. Revealed by the light of the lamps hung on the bare branches of the trees in the garden, she looked every inch the gracious hostess, ready to greet anyone who cared to join the festivities in Green Village instead of staying with the more sedate Islim in Manatas Town.

The revelers included every nationality found in Manatas, with the exception of the most pious of the Islim Andalusians and the most fanatic of the Roumi Rite Oropans. Halvar noted a party of Erse Rite Bretains in multi-colored trews and tartan-patterned smocks, and Egyptian Afrikans from the brickyards decked in gaudy caftans, heads topped with skullcaps sewn with gold thread that glittered in the lamplight. Behind them was a family of Danes, men in embroidered woolen jackets and caps, their wives in full skirts and tight bodices, hair neatly covered in lace caps.

He saw a group of Franchen, the men in blue or red coats, the women in striped skirts, proclaiming their adherence to the Erse Rite in defiance of Imperator Lovis's decree that all Franchen must worship according to the Roumi Rite or risk the fire. Sefarat Yehudit in long striped robes topped with embroidered caps, and Askenat Yehudit in dark coats and fur-garnished broad-brimmed hats joined the throng, preferring to celebrate in the warmth of the Gardens of Paradise instead of the more austere study house in the Yehudit quarter of Manatas Town.

Behind the Yehudit were the madrassa students in their sober over-gowns. Two Local women in deerskin skirts and bead-trimmed cloth blouses accompanied their Oropan men, artisans of some sort in well-worn coats and breeches. All were welcome at the Gardens of Paradise on this Watch-Night of the Redeemer's Nativity, in accordance with long-held Oropan custom.

Halvar joined the procession inching through the leafless shrubs and evergreens, only to be stopped by a trio of grim-faced Purist Bretains. Andrew MacAlan, the father of the murdered boy who had met his untimely end two months before, stood arms akimbo, exposing the butt of a pistoia thrust into the leather belt of his breeches. One of his cohorts, a gangly youth, held a long staff; the other, a stout older man, possibly the father of the young one, hefted a cudgel. They three took up all the space on the path between two prickly bushes. No one could pass them.

"Begone! This is an unholy assemblage!" MacAlan roared. "This is not a place for the godly!"

Tenente Donal emerged from the Gardens of Paradise. The Bretain had donned the green coat of the Town Guard over his checked trews to emphasize his position as representative of Law and Order on Manatas Island. Halvar shoved his way to the front of the line and glared at them.

"What's going on here?".

"The Pure Sect object to our rejoicing in the Redeemer's Nativity," Donal said from the doorway.

"Whatever for?" Halvar looked around at the crowd, who seemed to be a peaceful, joyous lot, none carrying visible weapons. "Why do you stop these good people from entering this place of entertainment?"

"It is a cesspit of vice and corruption!" the grim-faced man on the right spat out.

"It is not!" Padraig MacCormack the young apprentice printer, thrust forward, his father, Cormack MacCormack, the erstwhile leader of the Bretains of Green Village, close behind.

"Just because you are holy, MacAlan, does that make the rest of us evil? What right have you to disturb the peace?" Cormack demanded. "This is a time of rejoicing in the Redeemer's birth. Let us go and do it!"

"The Holy Book makes no mention of the date or time of the Redeemer's birth," MacAlan sneered. "This is pagan revelry, meant to distract True Believers from the meaning of the Redeemer's words. His birth is irrelevant. It is by his death the Redeemer saves us from sin."

"But it is of his life that we read in the Holy Book."
Padraig argued hotly. "And we should celebrate it. What's
wrong with that?"

"Let me pass!" a loud voice demanded from the back
of the crowd, punctuated by a shrill whinny.

Halvar turned to see Milord Summersby, mounted on
the sorriest nag he had ever see— an Arabian barb that
snapped at the crowd as if to say *I may not be much to look
at, but I am bigger and better than you!*

Devallon approached them, forcing the standers-by
off the path into the bushes and flower beds.

"Make way for Milord!"

Summersby rode along the path to the trio and stopped.

"Why do you not make way?" he demanded. "I am
Milord Summersby!"

"We are all damned souls, we should repent of our
sins!" MacAlan moaned. "In the eyes of Our Lord, you
and I are dust and ashes."

"How can we repent of sins if we don't have the chance
to commit them?" Milord countered, looking about for
confirmation.

Cormack obliged.

"Give over, MacAlan You're still grieving over what
happened to your boy at the feria. It's done with, the killer's
paid the price, and there's no blood-guilt on any of us.
Go back to Bos-Town, and take your grievance with you.
We're peaceable here, and we're going to stay that way."

"You've had your say, MacAlan," Donal said, moving to stand beside Halvar. "Now let these good people
pass!"

MacAlan would not be suppressed.

"You imperil their souls. You have sold yourself to the
Islim, you serve those who defile our laws—"

"He serves the people of Manatas!" Halvar had had
enough. "Tenente Donal is under my command, as part of
the Manatas Town Guard; and as such, he is being very
tolerant of this disturbance. Let these people pass, Mac-
Alan, or be arrested!"

64

"Is this your famous Convivencia?" MacAllan sneered. "I thought Manatas was a place where one could follow one's conscience in matters of religion."

"And so it is," Halvar stated. "But that means while you may practice whatever religion and worship whatever god suits you, you may not prevent another from doing the same. You may shout your sermons to the wind, even as Mullah Abadul does—"

"Do not compare me to that infidel!" MacAlan spat in contempt.

"By the same token, you may not prevent a lawful gathering of anyone else," Halvar continued, ignoring the interruption. "And this is a lawful gathering. So, take yourself and your friends off, and let us enjoy ourselves. Or you will find yourself in the Rabat!"

"For practicing my faith?" MacAlan looked around for supporters and found none.

"For inciting a riot." Halvar nodded to Donal. "Tenente, if these people give you any more trouble, you have my permission to remove them, as you will. But don't kill any of them," he added.

MacAlan glared at Halvar and Donal, then stepped aside to let the crowd pass through the doors.

Milord Summersby slid out of the saddle and handed the reins to Devallon.

"Take care of this animal, and join me inside after you do," he ordered grandly before strutting into the building.

Devallon looked about for someone to take the horse somewhere...anywhere! There was no groom or any other willing servant at hand. Halvar waved to Avaram, the donkey-driver from the Rabat, who lurked in the crowd.

"Turn this fine creature onto the common ground with the rest of the donkeys," he ordered, then turned to Devallon. "Where did you get it? The only horses I've seen on Manatas Island are the ones in the sultan's stable, and I don't think this beast came from that lot."

Devallon grinned. "Edgar's a resourceful fellow. He saw a farmer from up-the-hills with his cart and this beast selling vegetables in the street. He hired both the animal and its caretaker."

Halvar regarded the tack.

"Where did you find the saddle? Don't tell me Milord carried one with him when he came ashore."

Devallon's grin widened. "Edgar again. He went to that pawnshop on the waterfront and found the tackle. My thought? Someone, maybe one of those madrassa lads, came to Manatas with a horse, found no use for it, and sold the horse to the farmer and the tack to the pawnbroker.

"In any case, Edgar bought both horse and tack, and hired the farmer to look after both to add to Milord's consequence. It's not the finest beast in the world, but it didn't buck Milord off, which I don't know if it's a credit to the horse or to Milord. On the other hand, it's got an evil way of kicking when it's upset, and we have no idea what sets it off. And it doesn't seem to understand orders in Erse or Franchen, so Milord has had to learn a bit of Arabi to control it."

"Pity horses can't speak," Halvar mused as Avaram led both his donkey and the nameless horse to the common grazing-ground where the donkeys, goats and geese of Green Village foraged. "That one probably has quite a tale to tell."

Devallon stroked his neat mustache and beard.

"There seems to be quite a party doing on," he said. "Shall we join it?"

Halvar shrugged. "Why not?"

Together, they strolled into the main room and joined the joyous celebration. The long winter lay ahead, but this night, there would be laughter and music and good fellowship. The Redeemer and his Mother Mara would be pleased. Halvar thought, and Thor liked a good party, too. In any case, he decided, he'd have a better time at this party than the one he'd left at the madrassa.

Chapter 10

HALVAR PASSED THROUGH THE SMALL FOYER, where a halfling lad relieved patrons of their outer garments. He was stopped by another of Dani's servants, a girl who held a rush basket.

"One purple for a seat by the door, two for the middle of the room, three near the singers. All get you food and drink, but one gets you one plate, two gets you two, three is all you can hold." She thrust the basket, already filling with purple wumpum, at the two ex-mercenaries. Halvar slid the beads off the string that hung at his waist and jostled Devallon's elbow to do the same.

"You're paying?" Devallon raised an eyebrow. "You're the Capitán of Guards—that should count for something hereabouts."

"I always pay my shot," Halvar stated. "That way, no one can say I'm showing favoritism. Three purples is a week's wage for some of these folk." He accepted a wooden token that showed he had paid the maximum and was entitled to a seat in the middle of the room and as many trips to the food tables as he could manage.

In the main hall of the Gardens of Paradise, long tables had been set up against the walls, filled with platters of food and jugs of beverages. Small round tables and stools filled the rest of the room, with a space left in the middle of the floor for the entertainers. Bubble-pipes were in use at some of the tables, and their sickly-sweet aroma alerted Halvar to the possibility that not all the goodies at the Gardens of Paradise were edible. Two men at the back of the open space were sawing away at rebecs, adding their whining tones to the hubbub of chatter in various languages and dialects and the clatter of crockery.

Halvar and Devallon stood aside to let another group pass through the door. A buxom Danic girl checked their token and led them to one of the tables in the middle ranks, where Devallon sat on one of the backless stools and looked about, eagerly.

Dani Glick sauntered up to them.

"So, this is the famous musket-man," she cooed, with an appraising glance at Devallon.

The Franchen leapt to his feet, removed his hat and bowed, one leg forward.

"Andres, Sieur Devallon. And you must be the houri I have heard so much about."

"Fru Danella Glick." Halvar made the introduction. "One of the most notable persons of Manatas. Mind your manners, Musket-Man. Fru Glick is an adviser on the Town Council."

"Devallon!" A peremptory summons from the next table drew Dani's attention.

"Milord Summersby," Halvar told her. "The husband of that fine piece of goods you saw at the Rabat," he added, in an undertone. "A Bretain, with property in Terra Mara… or so he says."

"A Bretain milord?" Dani assessed the worth of this patron. "What's he doing here in Manatas?"

"He was a passenger on the ship that foundered in the bay two days ago. He's stuck here until the next one comes in."

" He's not happy at the Tavernier's cottage, or so I've been told," Dani said, her eyes bright with speculation. "Looking for new quarters?"

"He finds the accommodations too small for his consequence," Devallon said. "He's not too fond of the neighbors, either, and the proximity to a chicken-coop and goatshed is distracting. He's looking for a suitable lodging, and he's got plenty of silver." he added, with a meaningful lift of the eyebrows. "This place is quite large…"

"Not for sale," Halvar said. "Although there are rooms up those stairs." He nodded toward the balcony, where lanterns had been lit.

Devallon shrugged. "It's not quite what I had in mind. But it might do, as a way-station."

"That can be negotiated." Dani put on her most welcoming smile as she approached a source of revenue. "You must make me known to Milord, Sieur Devallon."

"With pleasure, Madame." As Halvar looked on, Devallon escorted Dani to the table where Summersby had stationed himself. "Milord, may I introduce to you the proprietor of this establishment."

"Fru Danella Glick." She dipped a curtsey in the Franchen manner.

Summersby looked her over.

"I understand this place has food and drink. "

"Most certainly, Milord. Roasted birds, a pudding of beans and maiz, sweetmeats. And as to drink…"

"I don't suppose you have anything but that foul cider." Summersby grumped.

"The Gardens of Paradise offers a broad range of pleasures, especially for those who are willing to pay for them. Unlike the Islim tabernas in Manatas Town, we have the dispensation to serve wine, rhum and uskebaugh."

Summersby's peevish frown eased into a look of anticipation.

"Wine?"

"From the grapes of Jerez, in the Kristo territory now called Hispania," Dani said smoothly. "Of course, we only have a few bottles…"

"I'll take them!"

"And those cost a great deal to bring in…"

"No matter. Bring me a bottle now, I'll have my man get the rest tomorrow." Summersby gestured grandly. "Devallon! The purse!"

The musket-man took a small pouch from inside his jacket and produced a gleaming silver coin.

"One silver imperial, fresh from Imperator Lovis's mint." He handed it to Dani.

"For this, Milord, you may have the best of our food and drink. And I wish you the blessings of your Redeemer's Nativity."

Dani bowed gracefully as she backed away, hiding a grin. Halvar suspected the wine in question was something no one but a Bretain Milord would think of drinking.

Donal stamped into the middle of the open space.

"My friends Kristo and Yehudit, we celebrate the turning of the year, the Nativity of the Redeemer and the Festival of Lights. To add to your pleasure, we have our own singer and teller of tales, Willem of Cos and his troupe, who have prepared both story and song, music and dancing!"

At that, Willem's drummer started a rhythmic beat. The trumpeter joined him, playing a cheerful tune, and the bagpiper added his notes. The girl busker began to jiggle, beating a tambourine to the beat.

A lanky youth in trews and smock swaggered into the center of the performance space and began a complex routine of heel-taps and kicks. He and the girl circled around each other, the girl eluding his eager grasp until, at the end, he caught her and tried to land a kiss…only to have her smack him resoundingly, to much laughter.

Devallon got to his feet and swaggered forward.

"That's no way to impress the lasses!" He started a dance of his own; the drummer and piper took up the rhythm and increased the tempo as the musket-man did. The lad took the challenge, and the two vied to see who could do the most complicated steps, leaps, and turns while the rest of the crowd clapped and shouted.

The music ended when both men had stamped themselves into a frenzy, and Devallon collapsed onto a stool, yielding the challenge-dance to his younger rival.

"Drinks all around!" Summersby ordered, flashing another of his silver imperials.

That led to more hubbub, which only stilled when Willem called for quiet.

"Silence, for Demozelle Renata!"

A slender girl, barely over the age of puberty, now stood in the center of the room, her pale brown braids framing a face dusted with freckles. She sang a sweet lullaby in Erse, claimed to have been the one sung by Mother Mara to the infant Chesu. Even Summersby fell under the spell of the silvery voice, reminding them why they were gathered in the first place.

Halvar felt tears prickling at the corners of his eyes. He had not heard this song since he'd left the Dane-march to follow the Free Company across Oropa and into Italia. It brought back memories of campfires, and unfamiliar chapels, and of one hideous Nativity spent in the Helvetian Mountains en route to the battlegrounds of Italia. He sniffled, and coughed, reminding himself he had to keep his composure for the dignity of his office and the reputation of the Town Guard.

The girl was replaced by an Askenat Yehudit, who insisted on performing a robust marching song, supposedly sung by the armies that had taken the Holy Places back from the Old Greco.

Then it was time for Willem to tell one of his funny stories, this one about the man who complained that his house was too small until a friend told him to bring the farm animals, one by one, into the house. Once he let them go, the man was delighted at how roomy the house now seemed. Halvar had heard the same tale two nights before, at the Mermaid Taberna. Then, the adviser was the Wise Hodja, a clever Islim preacher. This time, the advice came from the roguish jester Howleglass, but it was essentially the same story. Clearly, Willem shaped his act to his audience.

Halvar edged away from the crowd to stand by the wall. Dani joined him at his post.

"Not sitting, Halvar?"

"I like to see what's happening," he said. "And I'm not going to let you fuddle me again with food and drink."

"That was a mistake," Dani admitted. "I assure you, it won't happen again." She scanned the room with a practiced eye. "Everyone seems to be enjoying themselves. Even that Bretain milord."

"Where did you find that wine?"

"I got it from one of the Franchen merchants, who assured me his friends would drink it. What a mistake! The Franchen prefer their own wines, Islim can't drink it, and most of the Bretains here don't want it. This Devallon, what does he do for Milord?"

"Whatever Milord tells him to," Halvar said. "A hireling…like me."

"Not bad-looking, though." Dani smirked.

"I suppose." Halvar shrugged. He lowered his voice. "Dani, you've heard about the lad whose body was found by the town wall?"

"Poor boy," Dani said. "Frozen to death in the snow, they say."

'Not quite. He had a bullet hole in his back."

"Not good. Not good at all. What's it got to do with me?"

Halvar took the drawing out of his inside pocket.

"He was one of the messengers from the waterfront. I wondered if you'd ever seen him in Green Village."

Dani held the drawing up to the nearest lantern.

"Not a particularly pretty lad, with that nose and that skin...Donal!"

The erstwhile bouncer answered her call.

"Ever see this lad before?" She held the drawing out for him to examine.

"A time or two," Donal said, trying not to meet Halvar's accusing stare. "Is that the lad...?"

"It is. So, why didn't you say you knew him when we found him?"

Donal cleared his throat nervously.

"I didn't look closely at his face, Capitán. And if I had, I might not have recognized him, all frozen like he was. Remember, Capitán, until just recently, Green Village was separate from Manatas Town. We didn't send regular messengers back and forth, unless it was for business, and then merchants would send their own people. I wouldn't take any notice of them, not unless they made trouble, and a messenger's job is to carry messages, so they wouldn't want to make trouble, would they? This fellow..."

"They called him Snake."

"A likely name." Donal frowned at the picture. "You know, Capitán, now that I think on it, I do recall seeing him recently."

"When?"

"I can't recall offhand." One of the servers stopped by the table. "Hey, Johan, do you recall this fellow?" He thrust the paper under the server's nose.

The strapping youngster looked at the drawing.

"Aye, I've seen him.Two days ago? Maybe three?"

"Before or after the snowstorm?" Halvar demanded.

"Ummm." Johan screwed up his face in thought. "It must have been the night before, because it was the Long Night, and there was a bone-fire on the common ground. Tenente Donal was busy in Manatas Town, and he told us constables to make sure the sparks didn't reach the houses," he explained. "This lad came to the bone-fire, saw me, saw I was in the Town Guard coat and hat, and asked where he could find the Pure Sect folk from Bos-Town."

"He had a message for someone?"

"Why else would he ask after them? I told him which house they were lodged at and sent him on his way."

"Now, why would a Roumi Rite Franchen want to send a message to a Pure Sect Bretain?" Halvar mused aloud.

The clang of the chapel bell cut through his thoughts. He'd have to pursue this line of investigation later. It was time for the Holy Meal at the fratery chapel.

The crowd thinned as the Kristos reluctantly left the warmth of the Gardens of Paradise for the chilly chapel across the common ground, next to the high palisade that surrounded the fratery. Only the Yehudit remained.

Halvar hesitated at the door to see what was going to happen next.

Dani Glick beckoned to Johan, who carried a large eight-branched candlestick with one central holder from the back room to one of the tables. Five candles were laid in front of it. Dani put four into their cups, then used a tinderbox to light the fifth candle. Carefully, she touched the flame to the other four, then set the extra candle into its own holder while the assembled Yehudit murmured a blessing.

Halvar nodded to her and left for the chapel.

Chapter 11

THE MOOD OF THE CROWD CHANGED FROM raucous to subdued as the Kristos approached the wooden chapel with its bell tower and small glass windows. The fraters were already within, singing a hymn to the Redeemer, as the worshipers filed in to stand in place before the table where the Holy Meal would be offered.

Halvar grimaced. The Pure Sect were present in force, with Andrew MacAlan leading the pack again. This time his coat was drawn back to reveal not only a pistoia but a sword. This was a man prepared to fight for his religion!

He stepped forward to confront the fanatics.

"I thought I told you to leave off pestering these good people," he scolded MacAlan. "It's one thing to stop folks from enjoying themselves, but this is serious stuff. No one may prevent another from exercising his religion. So says the law of Al-Andalus, and so says the Calif Don Felipe, may he rule long, whether in Nova Mundum or in Al-Andalus. So, let us pass to make our prayers to the Redeemer and his Mother Mara, on the eve of his Nativity."

"This is an unholy congregation," MacAlan shot back. "There is no such festival in the Holy Book."

Abbas Mikhail had come outside to greet his flock. Now he turned on the Pure Sect.

"That is not so. Did not the Wise Men of the East and the shepherds of the fields come to see the newborn child that had been prophesied? Did they not offer gifts? So says the Follower Luke in the Holy Book. Therefore, we likewise join in praise and worship, and offer gifts to one another, and alms to the poor."

"There is no date given for His Nativity," MacAlan said stubbornly. "This festival of yours is nothing but a pagan ritual decked out in borrowed clothes, devised to distract the sinful from the True Fait, and the fate that awaits those who do evil."

Halvar had had enough theology for one day.

"It's cold, and we're tired," he stated. "MacAlan, if you keep on like this, you will find yourself in the Rabat. Not for exercising your religion, but for stopping these good people from exercising theirs. Tenente Donal!"

Donal hurried forward from the end of the line, where he had been hustling the laggards forward.

"Tenente, have you a lock-up in Green Village?"

"We do." Donal grinned. "It's the shed back of the Gardens of Paradise, next to the jakes."

"Not a pleasant place, on a cold night?"

"No fire, Capitán. Too dangerous on a windy night."

Halvar turned back to glare at the Pure Sect rebels.

"If these people do not allow the rest of us to give the Redeemer and his Mother Mara our praise and thanks, you may lock them up. They can keep themselves warm with their prayers!"

With that, he stepped forward, daring MacAlan to stop him.

The Bretain's hand hovered over the hilt of his sword. Then he stepped aside, and glowered at the procession as the Erse Rite Kristos of Manatas entered the chapel.

They filled the small room, which usually held a dozen fraters and a dozen more in the congregation. Now, Halvar was jostled into a corner by the crowd. A feather tickled his nose, and he realized Devallon was standing next to him. Milord Summersby had pushed to the front of the room, nearest to the Holy Table, clearly expecting to be seated. He would be disappointed—there were no benches, stools or chairs, other than the one behind the Holy Table where Abbas Mikhail was now enthroned.

"I'm surprised to find you here," Halvar murmured. "Milord's Bretain, so I suppose he's Erse Rite, but you? Franchen—that's Roumi Rite."

"I go where I'm told," Devallon said with a shrug. "Us hirelings have to follow where we're led. What surprises me is that you haven't gone Islim, after all those years in Al-Andalus."

"No need. There are a few chapels in Corduva, mostly for the madrassa lads from Bretain and the Dane March. Yehudit study-houses, too. The Convivencia works...mostly. Sshh! Abbas Mikhail's preaching!"

Abbas Mikhail's homily focused on the Redeemer's eternal love, and the need for peace in Manatas. He glared at the Pure Sect men who stood just inside the door to the chapel, daring them to refute his claim that the Redeemer had come in peace, and therefore, peace must be the watchword of all good Kristos. This should be a season of rejoicing that God the Father had sent his Son, the Redeemer, to save men's souls.

To which end, the fraters sang a joyous anthem, and all the congregants came to the Holy Table to receive a crumb of bread and a sip of wine. Then, one by one, two by two, they left the chapel, refreshed and fulfilled, some to their cottages and cabins in Green Village, the rest to form a torchlit procession across the now-barren feria ground back to Manatas Town and their lodgings in Andalusian-style villas and tenements.

Halvar was among the last to receive the blessings of the Redeemer and his Mother Mara. By the time he left the chapel, the torches could be seen across the field, a line of lights leading down the path to the Manatas Town Wall.

Avaram had brought the donkey cart from the common ground to the chapel.

"Shall we go now, Capitán? The moon is setting. Soon, it will be dark, and there's a ways to go. And the wind is picking up again."

Halvar took a deep breath of the crisp night air.

"I'll walk," he decided. "You can follow me to the Town Wall."

Behind him, he heard loud voices shouting in Erse and a whinny. It appeared Milord Summersby's horse was unhappy at having to leave Green Village and its tasty grass. Halvar grinned under his mustache. It had been a good Watch-Night. Tomorrow he'd have to get back to work and find out exactly what Snake's message had been, and who gotten it. He wondered whether Selim was enjoying her foray into "under-the-covers" work.

Then he set out across the feria grounds, following the last of the flickering torches towards Manatas Town.

The full moon cast eerie shadows over the bare ground that twice each year held the stands and tents of the feria. The torches that lined the path were beginning to sputter out, having burned through their twigs to the hardwood beneath. The stars above wheeled and sparkled, adding their dim light to that of the setting moon.

Halvar strode down the path, skirting patches of ice forming in puddles left by melting snow. He went over what he had learned of the messenger Snake and tried to make sense of the boy's death.

Snake had tried extortion at least once to get what he wanted. Had he tried it again with the wrong victim? With whom? And to what end?

It must have to do with that message, Halvar decided. The Pure Sect came from Bos-Town. The Franchen captain, Girard, had stopped at Bos-Town on his way to Manatas. According to Michel Primero, Girard's first mate, putting in at Manatas wasn't the plan at all, but a last-minute diversion from their route to get out of the way of bad weather—which, as it happened, had occurred just as Girard had predicted.

But the Franchen had sent a message to someone from Bos-Town living in Green Village, so he must have known he would be making port. And there was that tantalizing gap in the *Belle Fleur*'s voyage—the week in Bos-Town...

Halvar heard the jingling of harness and the clop-clop of hooves behind him. *Summersby's finally got mounted,* he thought. *Trust a Bretain milord to find the only riding horse on Manatas not in the sultan's stables.* The beast was probably sharing the goat's shed, and its groom housed in the cottage. Like the fellow in Willem's tale, the little house was getting smaller and smaller.

The last of the torches started to flicker out.

The stillness in the air was shattered by an unearthly screech. A deer sprinted across the open field, followed by something large and fast. Halvar was startled out of his rumination as the deer zigged and zagged across the path. The predator behind it sprang just as the deer put on a final burst of speed.

Halvar heard a pop and felt a stinging sensation in his left shoulder.

"Thor's Hammer!"

The large predator yowled again, and Halvar stared at the creature. It was a cat, to be sure, but larger than any he'd ever seen. He'd seen a lion's skin from Afrika; this animal seemed to be of a similar size. So, this must be the mountain cat he'd been warned about.

The animal bounded away as Avaram drove up beside Halvar with his cart, just visible by the light of the lantern hung on a pole jammed behind the driver's seat.

"Capitán! Are you all right?"

"Well enough...I think. Was that the mountain cat?"

"I didn't see it," Avaram confessed. "But you're bleeding. And your jacket's torn at the shoulder."

Halvar pressed a hand to his shoulder. It came away red.

"Thor's Hammer!" he swore again. "I've been shot!"

"Shot!" Avaram looked around the field. "By who?"

"That's the question, isn't it?" Halvar heaved himself onto the cart. "Get me to the Rabat, and hurry. I don't want to bleed to death on Watch-Night."

They started off with a jolt, only to be alerted by a flurry of hoofbeats behind them. Avaram turned the cart off the path just in time to avoid a major catastrophe. Milord Summersby hurtled past, clinging to the reins of his panicked steed. Devallon followed at a dead run, panting heavily.

"Can you take me up, Halvar Danske? That animal, whatever it was, spooked that Satan-bred horse, and Milord's going to get home sooner than expected." The musketman peered at Halvar's shoulder. "You're bleeding."

"So I should think. Someone's taken a shot at me. I don't suppose you saw anyone waving a musket or a pistoia around?" Halvar gritted out.

"I didn't see anything but that hideous creature." He peered at Halvar's shoulder. "This is serious! I don't suppose you carry anything so refined as a nose-wiper on you?"

"I wasn't expecting to need one." Halvar groaned.

"Lucky for you, I do carry one." He dug a wad of cloth out of his coat and pressed it to Halvar's shoulder.

"Get me to the doctor at the Rabat," Halvar ordered. "If there's a bullet in me, he can dig it out."

"I think the bullet missed you. This looks worse than it is. No bone broken?"

"It hurts like mad! Now's when I wish I'd had some of Fru Glick's uskebaugh."

Avaram tried to urge the donkey into a faster trot. Halvar struggled to retain consciousness as Devallon pressed his makeshift bandage onto the wound.

They passed through the gate and onto the Broad Way, and were halfway back to the Rabat when a figure erupted from one of the side streets leading to the waterfront.

"Stop! Stop!" A girl in a mid-length tunic worn over loose trousers waved wildly as she ran after the cart. "Is that you, Avaram? Take me up, before they catch me!"

"Hallo! Where did you come from?" Devallon snatched the scarf off her head. "Sorry, my dear, but my handkerchief is soaked, and we need this."

Selim took in the gory sight.

"What have you been up to, Don Alvaro? I thought you were going to the Holy Meal?'

"And I thought you were doing the same." Halvar stifled a shriek of pain as Devallon pressed on his wound. "What are you doing running about all by yourself?"

"Explanations can wait. " Devallon's eyes narrowed as he examined the new arrival. "Well, well. The last time I saw you, you were sitting in the Rabat taking notes for our good friend Halvar. And you weren't wearing a dress or a head-kerchief, either."

"This is Selim, and that's all you have to know right now. Get me to Dr. Moise." Halvar shivered in the cold wind as the cart proceeded down the Broad Way.

Avaram shouted as they approached the gates of the Rabat, to alert the guards within.

"Who goes there!" The guard emerged from his shed, yawning.

"Open the gate! It's Capitán Halvar Danske, and he's bleeding to death!"

The gate creaked open just wide enough to allow the cart and its passengers into the courtyard. Avaram and Devallon eased Halvar out of the cart, and the trio staggered into Dr. Moise's chilly sanctuary, Selim tagging behind.

Halvar's last coherent thought was, *I must be doing something right. Someone's tried to kill me. Again.*

Chapter 12

HALVAR CAME TO CONSCIOUSNESS IN A STARK cell in the Rabat, a grim chamber of bare walls whose one high window let in a sliver of light and a blast of cold air. He groaned and tried to sit up.

A firm hand restrained him. Selim had reverted to her masculine garb and now glared at him from a three-legged stool at the head of the bed.

"What happened to you?" she demanded. "I thought you'd be safe!"

Halvar tried moving his left shoulder and was rewarded with a stab of pain. A bandage had been wound around it, supporting his left arm.

"Someone shot me," he said. "I don't know who, but I know why. I'm getting too close for someone's comfort. Holy day or no, I've got to get up and get moving."

"No, you do not. You are supposed to stay put until Dr. Moise has a better look at you." Selim called out the door, "He's awake! Fetch the doctor."

"And just what were you doing, running through the streets?" Halvar tried to turn the discussion away from his injuries. "I thought you were supposed to get information from those Waterfront Rats."

"And I did. Mouse took me to the Prester, said I was a good girl who had lost her place and needed somewhere to stay until after the Nativity. Prester Nicodemus said he'd see if one of the women in his flock would take me in, because he had no place for a girl, and besides, girls were not welcome in a place for boys. So, I stood in the back of the chapel while they sang, and then I slipped away to the dormitory where Mouse said Snake had his bed. And I looked around where Snake kept what little he had, and I found something under his mattress, some papers with writing, but the big boy, the one they call Bull, came after me, and he was..."

Selim stopped, her face flushed.

"He thought you were just another street girl?"

"He tried to kiss me! And he put his hands right under my shirt!" She was nearly in tears.

Halvar was torn between laughter and rage. Between her high rank and her male disguise, no one had ever treated Selim as if she were easy prey for any boy or man eager for conquest.

"So, what did you do about it?"

"I kicked him," Selim said. "And I gave him a bloody nose. And he looked hard at me, and said he knew who I was. And he ran down to the chapel to tell, but I got out the door before he could alert the rest of them and ran to the Broad Way. And I was running back to the Rabat when I saw Avaram and the cart, and you and Devallon."

"What about Mouse? Where is he?"

"I don't know. Should I go back for him? I wouldn't want him to get into trouble for helping me..." Selim's voice trailed off.

"If he's thrown out of the chapel, he can come here," Halvar told her. "At least you're safe."

"And I found something." She reached under her jacket.

"So, you're awake?" Dr. Moise marched into the cell, interrupting the conversation. "I didn't know Kristo Watch-Night festivities got so violent."

"They don't, as a rule," Halvar said, struggling to inch higher on the bed. "What damage did the bullet do?"

"Oddly enough, not much," Dr. Moise told him as he examined the bandage. "Whoever shot at you didn't have very good aim, or perhaps it wasn't a good weapon. You've got a flesh wound, some skin taken off, but the bone wasn't hit. You've lost a bit of blood, though. Good thing you had that musket-man with you to staunch the bleeding."

"That was his idea, not mine," Halvar grumbled. "Where is he, anyway?"

"He took off after we got you into Dr. Moise's workroom," Selim said. "I suppose he went back to that cottage where he's staying with Milord Summersby."

"As long as he doesn't take over my quarters at the Mermaid Taberna, he can sleep in the streets!" Halvar said.

"What was the Franchen doing in Green Village, anyway?" Selim asked.

"Dancing attendance on Milord Summersby." Halvar stifled a scream as Dr. Moise dressed his wound and tightened the bandage. "Am I still bleeding?"

"No, and the wound is quite clean. You should be healed in a week if you rest and don't use that arm for anything more active than spooning broth," Dr. Moise assured him.

"I can't stay here for a week. There are things I have to do! I have to find out why that boy is lying on your table, for one, and what the Franchen captain was up to for another."

There was a flurry of action at the door to the cell.

"What's going on out there?" Halvar called.

"You can't go in…

A rough male voice was answered by a firm female one.

"I am the Sultan's physician. Of course I can enter!"
Eva Hakim strode into the room, nodded to Dr. Moise, and
peered anxiously at Halvar's wounded shoulder. "I see you
have bound it with spider web. I would have used honey."

Dr. Moise sniffed. "I have heard that is efficacious with
some wounds. The frater at Green Village uses moldy bread.
Clean rags are most efficacious in wounds of this type."

Before Halvar could say anything in his own defense,
Flores arrived, with a green coat over his arm.

"Better get dressed. Old Silver-leg wants you. Your Locals are here, and they've brought something from across
the bay."

Firebrand loomed up behind Flores.

"They have not been able to bring all of them," he said

"All of what?" Halvar stifled another scream as the two
doctors worked on his bandages.

"Some kind of weapon," Firebrand said.

"Weapons? Flores! Firebrand! Get me out of this bed
and into that coat!" Halvar pushed at up and swung his
long legs out of the bed.

"Are you mad? You'll open that wound again!" Dr. Moise scolded him.

"You are tempting Ilha's wrath." Eva Hakim added.

"I've fought battles with worse," Halvar declared. "Selim, get outside while I put on my trousers. Flores, Firebrand, just get me on my feet. Doctors both, if I start bleeding again, I'll come right to you, but there's something going on in Manatas, and I can't stop until I find out what
it is."

"At least, wear this sling, so there will be no pressure
on the shoulder," Dr. Moise fussed.

Between them, Flores and Firebrand got Halvar dressed
in his baggy woolen breeches and heavy green coat. Eva
Hakim tied the sling around his neck and eased his arm
into it. Firebrand added his belt and dagger. With his Danic
cap, and the araghoun fur hat on top of it, he felt ready

to take on whatever the Three Old Women wanted to throw at him.

Just to be on the safe side, though, Halvar murmured his daily prayer to the Redeemer and Mother Mara, with an extra plea to Thor. He had a feeling he would need all the help he could get to make it through the next few hours.

Chapter 13

HALVAR'S BREATH MADE LITTLE PUFFS OF STEAM
as he staggered across the courtyard, Firebrand and Flores
lending their support and Selim trailing them. They negotiated the steep stairs to the second floor, where the sultan
awaited them.

Halvar was nearly blinded by a sudden burst of sweat
dripping into his eyes as he entered the room, heated by
the iron stove to summer warmth. When his vision cleared,
he salaamed to the sultan, then focused on the two long-
barreled muskets laid across the small table that usually
held the sultan's mokka-pot and cups.

He shook off his assistants and strode to the table, his
eyes glued to the weapons.

"Where did those come from?"

The two Locals next to the table looked to Firebrand
for permission to speak. The Mahak Muskrat cleared his
throat nervously, but it was the Algonkin, Seulemon, who
spoke up.

"They were found among the stones at the bottom of the ship. In wooden boxes."

Halvar picked up one of the muskets for a better look. It was difficult to do one-handed, and he propped the stock under his arm as he tested the weight of the thing. He maneuvered the musket forward so he could check the firing mechanism.

"I've heard of these," he said, finishing his examination. "They're the new muskets Imperator Lovis has his manufactories turning out by the hundreds."

Sultan Petrus ran a hand over the remaining musket on the table next to him.

"Not a pretty thing," he stated. "No decoration on it at all. Not so much as a curl on the stock."

"They don't need to be fancy. They just need to shoot." Halvar's mouth tightened. "I watched at Salamanca when Lovis's troops were lined up against our archers. They were able to mow down our crossbowmen before they could rewind their winches after their first shot. These things are worse than cannons, because the musket-men can carry them forward, and the cannons have to be placed well behind the troops."

"Strategist, are you?" Sultan Petrus grunted.

"Observer only," Halvar demurred. "But it was a dreadful sight. It's how Lovis has taken Al-Andalus and turned it into Hispania in only three years. Look at the breech."

Sultan Petrus frowned at the weapon in his hands.

"How does this fire? There's no match, no fuse."

"There is no need. This isn't a wheel-lock or a matchlock. Some Bretain genius has found a way to adjust a little flint onto the firing-pin. You put your gunpowder in the pan, pull back this lever, let the hammer hit the flint. It makes a spark that lights the gunpowder, and that pushes the bullet out." Halvar pointed to the intricate mechanism.

Sultan Petrus tried the action. The hammer hit the flint and gave off a spark, but without powder in the pan, all he got for his trouble was a flash.

"And you say these were stowed in the ballast of that ship?" the sultan asked the two Locals. "Who has them now?

"The Canarsee, who live near where the ship went aground, have salvage rights," Firebrand explained. "They gave the boxes the guns came in to Sachem Mahmoud as part of their tribute. But the Bretains and Franchen who have the settlement called Brook-line also claim them, the Bretains because they also have salvage rights on certain parts of the shore, and the Franchen because the ship was Franchen, under the command of a Franchen."

Sultan Petrus thought this over while Halvar examined the muskets more closely to see if he could determine their origin.

"What does Mahmoud intend to do with these muskets?" Sultan Petrus asked.

"He has sent two to his ally, the Mahak Sachem Grey Goosefeather, as a Winter Gift," Muskrat said. "Two he keeps for himself, two he has sent to you."

"How many were there all together?" Selim asked.

Muskrat and Seulemon shrugged. Figures were not their strong point.

"How many boxes?" Selim tried again.

Seuleman held up one hand.

"Five boxes? And how many in each box?"

More consultation in Munsi. Muskrat held up both his hands.

"Ten muskets in each box, five boxes—that's fifty muskets!" Selim looked to Halvar for approval.

Halvar was too appalled to praise her arithmetic.

"Fifty of these *verdammitte* things loose in Manatas!"

"Not fifty," Selim consoled him. "If Mahmoud has two, Gray Goosefeather has two, and my father has two, that's six. Six from fifty leaves forty-four."

"So you've learned your numbers," Sultan Petrus grumbled. "That still leaves more of these things than I care to have in my territory."

89

"Of course, they're only large clubs unless and until there is powder and shot," Halvar reminded him. "That's what makes the difference." He turned to the two Locals. "When the Canarsee took over the ship, did they see any barrels with black powder in them?"

Muskrat and Seuleman consulted in Munsi again.

"I did not see any such thing," Muskrat said.

"But there may have been such before we got there," Seulemon added. "We only saw these muskets because Sachem Mahmoud wanted to give you these two, as his tribute, and as a gift to show that the Algonkin will stand with Al-Andalus, should the Huron attack. The rest he keeps on the Long Island, in his lodge."

"Where he can hold on to them, but he can't use them. Not unless he gets the powder and the shot." Halvar summed it up. "It's easy enough to make bullets by melting down iron or lead pellets. But gunpowder? That's another thing. Alchemists make it, but I don't know how they do it. The mullahs in Al-Andalus preached against it, so Andalusian alchemists wouldn't touch the stuff. More's the pity, because gunpowder's what armies run on these days."

"At least the Locals don't have any. That's a comforting thought." Sultan Petrus gave the musket one more look and laid it back on the table. "I'd better write to Calif Don Felipe, may he live long. He'll want to know about this."

"More to the point," Halvar said, "Where were these things supposed to go?"

"Eh?" Sultan Petrus slewed around in his chair.

"I wondered why the Franchen Captain Girard made port in Manatas when it wasn't feria time. What if it was to deliver these muskets?" "But they weren't delivered," Selim pointed out. "They were still hidden in the stones in the ballast."

"True." Halvar considered this. "But perhaps Girard was supposed to meet someone here in Manatas, a middle-man who was arranging the delivery."

"Delivery to who?" Flores broke into the discussion. "And for what? The Franchen aren't here, they're miles away in Kibbick. And we're not at war with the Mahak or the Algonkin. At least, not now."

"Not now? Then, when?" Halvar wanted to know.

"My predecessor,'" Petrus said. "He had an argument with one of the minor Mahak sachems. It got ugly. It resulted in a vicious massacre and led to his death. I had to do some fast talking to make peace with the Mahak." He frowned at the weapons. "Of course, if the Huron are on the march, it's only natural Grey Goosefeather should get the muskets, the better to defend the Mahak villages up north."

Halvar started to pace. "It still doesn't make sense for him to come here, storm or no storm. According to my old acquaintance Devallon, the *Belle Fleur* set sail from Franchenland, went to Kibbick, then stopped at Bos-Town before coming here." He stopped in mid-stride. "Muskrat, Seulemon, when the *Belle Fleur* was salvaged, were there books, papers, maps?"

The two locals shrugged.

"We weren't there, Capitán. We can't say what was found and what was not. And there were some of the Pure Sect who objected to some of the things the Franchen captain had and burned them."

"Surely not the maps!" Halvar howled. "And his log! And the fine instruments for navigation, the sextant and the spying-glass? What about them?"

Again, the two Locals shrugged.

"Those we did not see. If they are good for finding one's way on the sea, it is possible one of the Bretain seamen claimed them," Muskrat offered.

"He had his private journal," Selim said. "Did I copy that whole thing for nothing?"

"Not quite nothing," Halvar said with a grin. "Leon di Vicenza—I mean, Frater Leonidas—says it's quite racy reading. He's already planning to have it set in type and sold in Mendel the Bookseller's stall in the souk."

"I don't care about that Franchen's love life," Sultan Petrus growled. "What's this about Bos-Town? It's a hotbed of radicals and religious fanatics."

91

"And merchants and manufactories," Halvar reminded him. "And they were there for nearly a week. Devallon said it was because of Milady Summersby, but just suppose some of those Bos-Town manufactories were making these new muskets? Or the powder and shot to arm them? And some of these Pure Sect merchants were ready to sell them to whoever would buy?"

"They'd sell their own grannies for a dinar," Flores put in. "Pure Sect? Purely for cash!" He spat his disgust. "Money-grubbers, all of them, Shaitan take them to Gehenna!"

"They weren't the only ones," Halvar said. "Girard was out for money, too. He put in at Manatas not to get away from a storm but to make contact with someone here, someone who would act as middle-man between him and whoever wanted to buy the muskets. The question is, who is the middle-man? And where were the muskets bound for?"

"Another question." Firebrand spoke up. "You say this Girard was to make contact with someone. How did he know who the someone was if he hadn't been to Manatas since spring? Does this conspiracy go all the way back to the Spring Feria?"

Halvar tugged at his mustache and frowned.

"It just might. Thor's Hammer, this gets twistier by the minute."

"That's why he needed Snake!" Selim said. "Snake knew people, he went all over Manatas, even to Green Village."

"The lad went to Green Village on the Long Night," Halvar said. "He was seen by one of Donal's constables at their bone-fire."

"But the boys at Prester Nicodemus's said he came back that night and didn't go out again until he learned that Captain Girard was dead. Even then, he just did his usual round the next day and returned to the chapel. It was the day of the storm that he went out and didn't return."

"It's clear to me what happened." Sultan Petrus had been stroking the new weapon while he listened to the discussion swirling around the room. "This Snake, he's a messenger?"

Selim nodded.

"Well, then, he went to tell whoever it was the first message went to that the sender was dead, and that there would be no deal to be made with the Franchen."

"But where did he go?" Flores asked. "And who is this mysterious middle-man? And why keep it a secret?"

"If you were dealing weapons in Manatas, you'd keep it a secret, too," Selim retorted.

Halvar winced as his shoulder ached.

"There was paint on the lad's coat," he recalled. "The Afrikans paint their houses for the Fasting Month and the new year. With your permission, Excellent Sultan, I will look at some of those houses and see where there is smeared fresh pains. Then, perhaps, we will be able to find some answers to these questions."

"Go, then." Sultan Petrus waved them away. "Find out where these weapons came from, and who was supposed to receive them. Report back to me as soon as you have answers. And one more thing," he called out as Halvar started through the doorway. "I've had a delegation from Emir Achmet. Make sure you give him his donation for the turn of the year. Otherwise, we'll have trouble from the Scavengers. One war at a time, Don Alvaro! One war at a time."

The sultan chortled happily as he contemplated his new toys, while Halvar and his troupe headed down the stairs, back into the crisp chill of a Nativity morning.

Chapter 14

AFTER A BRIEF STOP AT THE BARRACKS FOR A
quick break-the-fast of maiz mush and mokka, Halvar was
ready to lead his squad forward. The muezzin was calling mid-
morning prayers as they left the Rabat. Halvar clutched his
amulet and murmured his standard prayer, and added a brief
apology to the Redeemer and Mother Mara for working on
Nativity Day. Thor, at least, would understand it was a matter of some urgency that took Halvar to the Street of the Afrikans instead of staying relatively warm in the chapel.

Avaram was waiting with the donkey cart, but Halvar
waved him away.

"I think better when I'm walking. Selim, you're with
me. Flores, Firebrand, you can take the cart if you like, and
meet me at the Street of the Afrikans."

Firebrand dismissed the idea of riding with a contemp-
tuous shrug.

"If a wounded man can walk it, I can," Flores sneered, propping himself up on his trusty halberd.

Selim merely snuggled further into her padded jacket and trotted breathlessly after the other three, doggedly determined to keep up.

They marched northward on the Broad Way, through the morning traffic. Madrassa students hurried to classes, while artisans and small merchants of the souk headed to their stalls. A lad in gaudy trews topped with a knitted tunic waved copies of the *Gazetta*, shrilly informing anyone who stopped to hand him a white wumpum bead that this issue had all the details of the body found on the Local side of the wall. Local women trudged alongside large dogs pulling braziers of coals, ready to set up shop to provide hot yams and roasted maiz ears to anyone who needed refreshment.

All this activity brought Mullah Abadul out of the Grand Muskat.

"It is Rest Day!" he bellowed. "You must put aside your business and praise Ilha the All-Merciful, and his Prophet!"

His words were lost in the cold wind that blew across the island, sending the students, at least, indoors. Steam coated the small windows of the mokka-shops along the Broad Way, where those merchants who had elected to remain in Manatas for the winter sat over their hot beverages, discussing the latest news from Al-Andalus, which was now to be called Hispania. Reports were trickling in by way of coastal boats and riders from both the Bretain settlements of West Caster and Bos-Town and the southern sultanates of Sequannok and Terra Mara, of raids by Franchen ships on outlying islands and incursions of Local tribes into Afrikan territories.

Halvar stopped the ragged vendor, paid one white wumpum bead, and passed the *Gazetta* news-sheet to Selim.

"What has Padraig got to stay about last night's disturbance at the fratery? And what do they say about finding the body"

Selim scanned the side of the paper printed in Arabi.

"Only that there was an attempt made to stop the worshipers from their lawful exercise of religion, and that the noble Capitán Halvar Danske, with the assistance of Tenente Donal, put aside the protesters, and the law of Al-Andalus was obeyed."

"Nothing about the mountain cat? Nothing about my being shot at?"

"Not yet." Selim checked the Ogham side of the paper. "I suppose it happened too late to make the morning paper. And there's the notice of the body being found, but nothing else, not who or what he was, or how he died. 'Anyone with information must give it to Tenente Donal at the Gardens of Paradise in Green Village or Capitán Halvar Danske at the Rabat in Manatas Town'," she read.

"Just as well. I don't want whoever shot me to know I'm up and about, thanks to that musket-man." Halvar stepped aside to let a donkey cart go by. "Well, well, one speaks of Shaitan, and here he is. That's Devallon, and where's he heading, I wonder?"

"Up-the-town," Flores surmised.

"To Green Village?" Halvar wondered. "Or to negotiate for one of the empty Afrikan villas? Milord Summersby wants more space," he told Flores,

"I don't doubt it. The Bretains think they can take over the world." Flores snorted his disgust. "And the Afrikans are willing to accommodate. Anything for silver!"

Halvar ignored the slur and concentrated on getting to the Street of the Afrikans without falling on his face. The snow that had fallen early in the week had melted and refrozen into icy puddles, treacherous underfoot. Piles of leaves made the brick walkway even more slippery, and the unpaved alleys between the blocks of buildings were melting into slushy muck that clung to shoes and the hems of cloaks.

They arrived at the row of villas known as the Street of the Afrikans. Halvar nodded toward a gap between the two largest houses on the street.

"That's the villa belonging to Samuel Igbo." He pointed to the two-story house, decorated with angular red and black lines. "The other one is house of the late Ochiye Aboutiye, now held by Widow Tekla. Which first?"

Selim squinted at the Igbo house.

"I think that red is a lot like what was on Snake's jacket," she observed.

"Let's take a closer look."

Halvar loped toward the alley. Flores followed him, with Selim close behind. Firebrand stayed back, one hand on the knife at his belt.

"Hoy!" he called out.

"What is it?" Halvar stopped in mid-stride.

"Marks." Firebrand pointed at two two ruts in the rapidly-thawing muck. "Like the ones near the body of Snake."

Halvar squatted for a closer look.

"Something came here, something heavy," he muttered. "Not a donkey cart—these are too small for wheels, too close together."

"Dog-pull," Firebrand decided. "Must be dog-pull."

Halvar recalled the Local women leading large dogs with a ladder-like contrivance strapped to their backs, the ends of the ladders dragging on the ground, and baskets thrust into the spaces between the rungs.

"Why would someone run a dog-pull on the Street of the Afrikans?" Selim wondered aloud. "Especially in this cold weather?"

"Maybe a Local woman selling vegetables? Maiz-cakes? Beaded trinkets for the festival days?" Flores offered.

Halvar tugged at his mustache.

"When were these marks made, do you think, Firebrand?"

The Mahak frowned. "Can't say. The snow made the ground wet, then it froze, then it went soft, then hard again. No dung, but dogs don't leave dung just anywhere, they have particular places where they go to put it."

Halvar nodded in agreement. He had some acquaintance with the habits of dogs.

"There's more!" Flores pointed to a discolored patch of mud. "Something bled here, I think."

Firebrand nodded assent. "Not today. Blood soaked in. But maybe, two, three days ago?"

Halvar tugged at his mustache again. "I think we've found our murder site, lads," he decided.

"Someone in one of these houses must have heard or seen something," Selim offered. She looked from one house to the other. "But who? And from which house?"

"Let's see what the folks who live there have to say," Halvar said.

He led his squad to the large front door of Samuel Igbo's villa and knocked briskly. A male servant in a woolen caftan opened it a crack to see who was calling in the middle of a business day.

"Capitán Danske?" The servant recognized the famous Hireling.

"We are here to speak with Samuel Igbo. Is he at home, or at his place of business?"

"This being the Rest Day, he is at the muskat."

"Frigg's Day already?" Halvar did a mental count of the calendar, and remembered Mullah Abadul's passionate demand for worshipers. The Nativity festivities had put him off. "When he returns, tell him I want to speak with him."

"And what shall I say is the matter on which you wish to speak?" The doorkeeper's voice dripped scorn.

"There was a disturbance reported," Halvar persisted. "It is possible that Heer Samuel Igbo might have information about it."

"This is a respectable street. We have no disturbances." The servant slammed the door.

Flores stepped forward, glowering at the closed portal. Halvar stopped him.

"Not yet, Tenente. Have another look at those walls. There's something odd about the pattern on the side near the alley."

Halvar pointed to a smudge that disturbed the evenness of the zigzag red line on the white wall. Selim went closer to examine it.

"Definitely smudged," she said. "About the height of Snake's shoulder, I'd say."

"And on Igbo's side of the alley," Flores declared. "He may not be so arrogant when we get through with him!"

"Not so fast, Tenente," Halvar chided him. "Let's see what Lady Tekla has to say about the events of the Longest Night."

He went back to the street and rapped on the door of the house to the left of Igbo's. A panel in the wooden door slid open, and a suspicious face peered out.

"Capitán Don Alvaro Danico, to speak with Lady Tekla," Flores announced. "And don't tell me she's at the muskat! I can see smoke rising from the chimney." The panel slid shut.

"I stay out here," Firebrand decided. "I will keep watch, to make sure no one disturbs this alley."

"It's too late for that," Halvar said. "Anyone and everyone could have passed by here in the last two days."

"Not everyone. I only see one set of footprints, near the marks of the dog-pull. This is not one of those passages that is used to shorten the distance from one street to another. Behind this house is the wall of the garden of another villa, one of the ones left empty for the winter. There are prints of dogs in the mud, but no shoes, except for the ones near the dog-pull." Firebrand pointed to the freezing muck.

"Stay outside, then, and if Igbo or his people come by, let them know I'll be along shortly."

The door opened just wide enough to let Halvar, Selim and Flores into the house. They stood in the vestibule, shivering.

"I will see if Lady Tekla wishes to see you." The servant pattered away.

An all-too-familiar voice boomed from inside the villa, speaking loudly in Franchen-accented Erse.

"We are travelers, stranded on this…"

"It seems Sieur Devallon is trying to find lodgings for Milord," Halvar said, with a grin. "Perhaps we should offer Selim's services as translator."

In defiance of all good manners, Halvar followed after the servant into the house before anyone could stop him. He made his way around the atrium, through the chilly feasting-room, and into the one room that might be insulated against the cold. Perhaps Lady Tekla would exchange information if he could rid her of this unwelcome visitor to her kitchen.

Chapter 15

LIKE MOST VILLAS CONSTRUCTED IN THE AN-
dalusian style, Lady Tekla's residence was built to withstand
extreme heat. The side windows were unglazed, opened to
facilitate the entry of the summer breezes. The pleasant garden within the brick walls made for a refreshing oasis, with
a fountain that cooled those who rested there.

These villas were well suited—to the climates of Al-
Andalus and Afrika, not the colder clime of Nova Mundum.
In winter, the bracing winds of Manatas whistled through
the barred windows, setting the leaves of the dead plants
in the atrium rustling and whirling with each blast. The
fountain was covered with ice.

Halvar shivered as he marched through the house,
wishing he had added a fur-trimmed cloak to his gear. If
Milord thought he could winter over in comfort in one
of these villas, he was in for a shock.

In the kitchen, an open fireplace and a tiled stove offered respite from the cold. Lady Tekla occupied a carved

stool next to a large table where bowls and beakers were set out, indicating a meal was in the making. Her bulk was swathed in woolen scarves, her head covered with an elaborately tied kutton kerchief. Behind her stood her muscular and pugnacious Afrikan cook, who had been involved in the investigation into Lady Tekla's late husband's untimely death. Two maids cowered in one corner, a scrawny lad huddled by the fireplace, and the largest male in the place glowered from the back door, his hand on a lethal-looking knife.

Before her stood the Franchen musket-man Devallon, his broad-brimmed hat in his hand.

"Lady Tekla, Capitán Don Alvaro Danico requests…" the doorkeeper began.

"My good friend Halvar! Capitán Danske!" Devallon interrupted, greeting Halvar with the air of the prisoner who sees deliverance from a dire fate. "Can you, perhaps, explain to this fine lady that my employer, a most noble lord in his own country, desires to use her residence temporarily as a stopping place? Surely, the laws of hospitality apply here in Manatas? I was told that among Islim this is a paramount dictum, that hospitality must be offered to the traveler…"

Halvar held up a hand to stop the spate of flowery Franchen-flavored Erse.

"I'll see what I can do." He turned to Lady Tekla, salaamed, and greeted her in Arabi. "Salaam Aleikum, Lady Tekla. I hope your End-of-Fast was a good and joyous one."

The generously proportioned Afrikan woman inclined her head to acknowledge Halvar's presence in her home.

"Permit me to explain that this gentleman, Sieur Andres Devallon, is trying to find better lodgings for his patron, Milord Summersby, than the ones they now inhabit, which are in one of the small cottages on Pearl Street, near the waterfront."

"I have heard of this Bretain milord," she said in Arabi, with the musical intonation found in Afrikans. "It is in the *Gazetta* that he comes to Manatas with his wife and his servant." She patted the paper on the table next to her.

Halvar nodded back. "Milord Summersby and his wife paid a visit to Sultan Petrus. They suggested to him that they wanted to use one of the empty villas on the Street of the Afrikans until they can continue their journey to Bel-la Mara. Sultan Petrus reminded them that, in Manatas, one does not occupy an empty villa without the consent of the owner. If you know the owner of one of the villas, perhaps you could act for them, at least until they return for the Spring Feria." He switched to Erse and repeated this offer to Devallon.

Lady Tekla eyed Devallon with loathing.

"I do not like Bretains," she declared in passable Erse. "They come to our country. They take our people away to work on the Ashanti farms."

"Lady Tekla is Yoruba," Halvar explained before De-vallon could protest. "Her husband was poisoned by a con-cubine two months ago at the Fall Feria, so perhaps she's not as amenable to having strangers in her house as some-one else might be. There's a fellow next door, Samuel Igbo…"

"Igbo!" Lady Tekla burst out in Arabi. "A vile man! He consorts with the Oropans! He would do anything for their silver pieces. He goes to the muskat, he pretends to be good Islim, but he deals with the Infidel. Bah!"

She snorted loudly. Behind her, the cook nodded, and the male servant added an imprecation in a dialect whose exact words were unclear but whose meaning was obvi-ous. Samuel Igbo was not liked by Lady Tekla's household staff.

"You have seen Oropans in Heer Samuel's house?" Halvar asked.

"With my own eyes, I see them! They wear tall hats, they speak loudly in Erse." Lady Tekla scowled. "He con-sidered marrying his daughter to my son. Ha! I put a stop to that idea! Yakub went back to Savana Port with the son of the Cherokee woman. He will find a good Yoruba woman there. There will be no Igbo in this house!"

"And Milord?" Devallon asked eagerly

Before Lady Tekla could answer, Halvar stepped in.

"I don't think he'd be comfortable here. There's no heating except in this room. At least at the cottage you've got the fireplaces in the front and back rooms, and the chimney to keep the smoke where it belongs."

Devallon swore in Franchen under his breath.

"I've got to find Milord somewhere to live until the ships come back in the spring."

"You could try Samuel Igbo," Halvar suggested. "If, as Lady Tekla thinks, he's that greedy, and does business with Bretains, perhaps some of those silver Imperials will persuade him to put braziers in his bedrooms. Selim can do the translating, he's good at it."

"He?" Devallon raised his eyebrows at Selim.

"In public," Halvar murmured. He turned back to his reluctant hostess. "Lady Tekla, I do not like to disturb you on the Rest Day, but I have some questions regarding a disturbance that may have occurred two, perhaps three days ago. The End-of-Fast feast day, the day of the snowstorm."

"Disturbance?" Lady Tekla frowned. "There was no disturbance in this house."

"Not here, but outside. Perhaps in the alley between this house and Igbo's?"

"I do not bother with what happens in that house," Lady Tekla said loftily. "I held the End-of-Fast feast here, in this kitchen, with my loyal servants, who have chosen to stay with me here in Manatas instead of running away with the Cherokee woman to Savana Port."

"They don't like the cold?" Selim ventured.

"They fear the spirit of Ochiye," Lady Tekla sneered. "I told them—there is no ghost in this house. He did not die here. It is my house, and I will live in it!" She nodded firmly, setting the ends of her headpiece bobbing.

"And may you do so in good health, for many years," Halvar added politely. "So, you heard nothing during the storm? No sounds of fighting, for instance? Nothing unusual?"

"In this kitchen? I hear nothing besides my own people."

"No shots? No explosions? No one fighting, arguing?" Flores persisted.

Lady Tekla regarded the guardsman with scorn.

"I heard nothing like that. The winds were very loud, and there was much snow. I do not go out in the snow."

"What about the servants?" Flores asked, turning his attention to them. "Any of you hear or see anything in the alley that shouldn't be there?"

"Nothing," the cook declared. "All was as it should be. What is this about? We have done nothing wrong."

"We think there may have been a death during the snowstorm," Halvar said. "Did none of you hear anything? A large boom or bang?"

There was a consultation in Afrikan between the cook and the doorkeeper.

"I may have heard a loud noise, a bang," the cook admitted. "But it was snowing very hard, and the wind was very strong. I did not want to look outside until the wind was down, and when I did, I saw nothing but the snow. I thought perhaps one of the jars that hold waste for the scavenger was blown over in the storm."

"That's possible," Halvar said. "Was the jar on its side when you looked out, after the storm was over?"

"Not at all. It was standing where it should be." The cook nodded firmly. "I saw nothing amiss in the alley. The scavenger had been through, I suppose, and put the jar straight."

Halvar salaamed again.

"I thank you for your time, Lady Tekla, and for what you have told us." He started to leave, then turned around again. "One thing more, Lady Tekla. You do business in the souk, do you not? Your son has a stall there, to sell whatever was not sold at the feria. Who takes care of the stall when he is in Savana Port?"

"I have two servants, good people I can trust, who go to the stall," Lady Tekla said.

"And do you send messengers to them, to tell them what goods to sell, and for how much?"

Lady Tekla frowned. "Of course I do. I have a good lad, he runs fast, he carries messages for me."

Halvar thought this over.

"So, you wouldn't know anything about the boys who carry messages and small packages from one business to another in Manatas? The ones they call the Waterfront Rats?"

"Those lads? The captains send them to all of us when their ships off-load, to let us know what goods are for sale. Ochiye would sail with his own merchandise, so I had no need of messengers. When Yakub comes back in the spring, he will do as his father did and bring his own shipload. I do not have to bribe the Kristo who runs the messengers to send word before anyone else, the way Igbo does."

"You are fortunate, Lady Tekla, in having such an enterprising son." Halvar said, with another salaam.

This time he followed Flores, Selim and Devallon back through the house and out to the street, where Firebrand waited with an Afrikan servant.

"Samuel Igbo is on his way back from the muskat," Firebrand announced, indicating a procession approaching from the end of the street. "And that smeared paint is exactly the same as what is on Snake's shoulder."

"Then I think we'll have a word with Samuel Igbo," Halvar said. "I'm starting to understand what happened in this alley. What I don't understand is why it happened, and how our poor fellow wound up on the wrong side of the wall."

He strode back to Igbo's door. This time, he'd get some answers.

Chapter 16

SAMUEL IGBO WAS BOUND FOR HOME FROM
the muskat at the end of the Street of the Afrikans near the
East Channel, picking his way carefully around iced-over puddles and patches of snow. Behind him came several other
Afrikan men, presumably merchants like himself, accompanied by their servants, all huddled in fur-trimmed cloaks.
Bringing up the rear of the parade was a party of women,
presumably the wives, daughters, and concubines of the male
worshipers, now headed for whatever warmth they could
find in their own houses.

Halvar watched the parade with a critical eye.

"Tenente Flores, what can you tell me of Heer Samuel
Igbo?" Halvar turned to the Andalusian, who had been
one of the infamous Tenente Gomez's underlings before
the Dane's arrival on Manatas. Was it only three months before?

"A merchant," Flores said dismissively. "He buys and
sells."

"Buys what, and sells what? Buys from whom and sells to whom?" Halvar persisted.

"Who knows?" Flores shrugged. "He can usually be found in the Blue Parrot Mokka-shop on the Broad Way. It's opposite the Alchemist's School at the madrassa," he added, seeing Halvar's puzzled look.

"Lucky he's a devout Islim, then, or we'd have to chase him down," Halvar observed. "Anything else known about him? Aside from his dispute with Ochiye, or his being an Ashanti snob?"

Firebrand frowned. "He trades with the Oropans who go into Mahak territory to hunt for furs. Our sachem, Gray Goose-feather, has spoken about this in council. The Oropans take too many beaver and fox; they trap them in the winter, when their fur is thickest. This is not good, because that is when the she-foxes have their kits."

"But Samuel doesn't trap the animals himself," Halvar pointed out. "And it's not his fault if Andalusians want furs to keep warm in the winter. What about you, Tenente Flores? Has this Samuel ever been in trouble with the Manatas Town Guard?"

"Nothing I ever had to deal with," Flores said. "Tenente Gomez and Emir Achmet kept order on this street between them. Rich Afrikans can afford to pay for extra attention from Scavengers and Town Guard."

By this time, Samuel Igbo had come close enough for Halvar to greet him.

"*Salaam aleikum*, Samuel Igbo." He stood in the path, flanked by Flores and Firebrand, with Selim behind him and the big musket-man preventing anyone from proceeding toward the Broad Way.

Samuel returned the greeting with a brief nod.

"*Aleikum salaam*, Capitán. What brings you to this street on such a cold morning? Is it not your feast-day? Your Redeemer's Nativity? I would think you would be in the chapel, giving thanks for his appearance on this earth."

"Alas, Heer Samuel, it is a sad task I have. The body of a young man has been found, and there are indications he met his death near your villa." Halvar sighed.

"Near *my* villa?" Samuel echoed. "What sort of indications?"

"There is a smear of paint on his clothing that matches that used on the side of your house. And there is a stain that might be blood in the mud between the two houses." Flores stated. "What have you to say about that?"

Samuel Igbo shrugged. "If someone chooses to lean against a wall with fresh paint on it, it is of no concern to me. As for blood, there are people who bring meat to the kitchen. It could be something dripped. I had nothing to do with this messenger. Now, if you will permit me to return to my own house..." He tried to get past the guardsmen.

Halvar would not be moved.

"Heer Samuel, I have some more questions. We would be more private inside."

Devallon coughed, meaningfully, behind him. Halvar took the hint.

"And Sieur Devallon, this Franchen musket-man, may have a business proposition for you," he added. "So, if you please, may we enter your house and continue this discussion in a place that is more comfortable for all of us?"

Samuel Igbo looked around at his followers.

"If you insist," he said ungraciously. "Let us complete this business indoors. The wind is picking up. I think we shall have more snow, and that very soon."

With this, Samuel led Halvar into his villa, Devallon, Selim and Flores crowded behind him. Firebrand was left outside once again when the Afrikan servant sneered and slammed the door shut before the Mahak could enter.

Halvar pretended not to notice the slight to the Local. Instead, he observed how the villa had been adapted to the rigorous climate of Manatas by the addition of wooden panels set between the brick pillars that formed the arcade around the central atrium. Bits of glass had been set into the narrow outside windows so that light filtered into the otherwise dark rooms.

"A most ingenious renovation," Halvar remarked as Samuel allowed himself to be divested of his outer wrappings by his steward. "Lady Tekla's house is not so well adapted to the cold."

"Indeed, it is ingenious," Devallon agreed. "Why, even as noble a traveler as Milord Summersby would be delighted to sojourn in a place so well-built as this one."

"Then he should build one for himself, as I did," Samuel told him as the women slipped past the unwelcome visitors into the private quarters, where no stranger was allowed to penetrate.

"I could not stop the Oropan," the servant mumbled. "Capitán Don Alvaro…"

Samuel waved the old man away.

"I understand, you do not have to apologize. Capitán Don Alvaro is doing what he is bound to do, by his oath to our beloved calif and the excellent Sultan Petrus. It is necessary for me to answer his questions, even on the Rest Day," he told the steward, "Send mokka and a fire-pot to my study."

The servant scurried away, and Samuel led Halvar and his party to the room next to the vestibule that served as his business office. The small square room's outside windows had also been fitted with small panes of glass.

The meager furnishings included a small table on which were stacked ledgers and scrolls whose contents Halvar could only guess at along with pens made from reeds and quills, an inkpot, and a stool on which Samuel placed himself with the air of a monarch ascending his throne. This was Samuel Igbo's kingdom, and he was secure in it.

A servant trotted in with a wheeled platform on which was set a large clay jar that gave off enough heat so no one's' breath was visible as they spoke. Another servant carried a tray with the inevitable mokka-pot and cups. A third servant bore a lamp, which lightened the room further but did nothing to ease the cold.

Mokka was poured into cups. Servants handed one to Samuel, one to Halvar. Devallon, Flores and Selim were ignored. Halvar murmured the requisite blessing and sipped from his cup. The mokka was barely drinkable, thick with honey and spices, and the temperature of the room.

Once the amenities were done, the servants withdrew. Samuel looked Halvar over.

"You say you have questions for me?"

"I do. Have you read the *Gazetta* this morning?"

"I do not read the *Gazetta*," Samuel said loftily. "I hear the news-criers, and I have my own sources of information concerning business matters. The rest is of no use to me. I do not listen to idle gossip."

"Then you know nothing of the body that was found yesterday, beside the wall?"

"Only what you told me. What makes you think I have anything to do with it?"

"There is the paint on the man's clothes that matches the paint on your wall, and we have found a place where blood was spilled," Flores said. "He was found beyond Manatas Town, but we think he was killed right outside your door, Samuel Igbo. Now you tell us you don't know anything about it? I don't think so!" He stepped forward to tower over the seated man.

Halvar held a hand up to stop Flores's advance.

"Tenente, we do not want to imply that this honorable gentleman killed the unfortunate lad himself. But I am curious, Heer Samuel. If you didn't know anything about him, how did you know he was a waterfront messenger? You say you do not read the *Gazetta*, but it is readily available. Even your neighbor, Lady Tekla, had a copy."

"And it didn't say who or what the dead youth was in any case," Selim put in. "We didn't know ourselves until quite late last evening, when we could put a name to him. And we didn't tell anyone from the *Gazetta*." She looked to Halvar for confirmation. "Did we?"

"I certainly did not," Halvar said. "So, Samuel Igbo, how did you know it was a messenger? Did you send or receive a message using one of those waterfront lads recently? And don't try to lie, because we're going to ask your servants, and one or the other of them is bound to recall him."

Samuel chewed on his lower lip.

"Very well, I admit I got a message delivered by one of the Waterfront Rats," he said reluctantly.

"When?"

"It was three, maybe four days ago. The evening of the day before the snowstorm."

"The day of the Longest Night. Who was the message from?"

"A person with whom I do business."

"His name?" Halvar was relentless.

"I cannot say."

"Cannot, or will not?" Flores stepped forward again with a menacing scowl. Once more Halvar had to restrain his impetuous underling.

"I understand these things," he said, in what he hoped was a soothing tone. "Heer Samuel's business is confidential. However, I think I should warn you, Heer Samuel, that certain merchandise has come to light that is both dangerous and illegal, and if we discover that you, Heer Samuel Igbo, were involved in its transport, there will be very unpleasant consequences."

"I don't know what you're talking about!" Samuel blustered. "I am a middle-man, I direct merchandise from one person to another. If there is something illegal about it, I know nothing!"

"From one to another," Halvar mused. "As, for instance, from a Franchen sea captain to, let us say, a Bretain in Green Village? According to Lady Tekla, you have been observed dealing with the Pure Sect Bretains. The ones who wear the tall hats," he added, to differentiate them from the Bretains who preferred woolen or araghoun fur caps.

"Do you refer to the unfortunate man found murdered in Maiden Lane? The Franchen sea-captain? I thought he was killed by some whore he'd betrayed," Samuel burst out.

"That's true enough, but I had a few questions about his surprise visit to this island that he never got to answer," Halvar said. "One of them being, what brought him here in the first place? His first mate and passengers thought it was a whim, but I'm not so sure."

"I don't understand what any of this has to do with me," the Afrikan whined. "I admit that a messenger came to me late on the evening of the End-of-Fast, well after evening prayers, with a written message, which I read. I gave it back to the lad and told him to take it to a person in Green Village, which, as far as I know, he did."

"What about the day after that? The day we found the Franchen dead? How did you you find out about that? And what about your business contact in Green Village? Did you inform him about that?" Halvar pursued.

"I should think everyone on Manatas Island knew about the murder," Samuel sniffed. "Daoud the News-crier made sure of that. And the discovery of the Afrikan Scavenger in the latrine, and the fight on the docks, and the wreck of the round-ship. That ship is still sitting there for all to see, across the bay. When this news got to Green Village, and how it did, I cannot tell you. I assumed the people in Green Village would hear of it in the usual way, from the news-criers."

"True," Halvar mused. "Gossip runs faster than the *Gazetta* sometimes, and the ship's still there. Of course, its cargo has been taken off."

"Its cargo?" Samuel repeated.

"The ship had a clandestine cargo—hidden in the ballast, of all places. Five crates of brand-new muskets. What do you think of that?"

"What has this to do with me?" Samuel quavered, looking from Halvar to Flores. "I know nothing about muskets. The message said nothing about muskets, only that Captain Girard had some business he wanted to negotiate, and would I put him in contact with a certain merchant, who he said would be living at Green Village. That's all I know. I sent the boy on and did not speak with him again."

Halvar nodded. "You were the middle-man, only that. So, Heer Samuel Igbo, who was the other party in this business transaction? Who was the one Girard was supposed to meet?'

"I do not know," Samuel stammered.

"Where did you send Snake?" Halvar persisted.

"To the house used by the Pure Sect Bretains," Samuel said. "If there was a particular person involved, I do not know who it was. I tell you, I know nothing at all! Nothing!" His voice rose to a shriek.

"Then I will bother you no further, Heer Samuel. But think very hard, and you may recall something that will help us find this murderer, for murder was done, right outside your back door. Think well, Heer Samuel."

"I think I have heard enough," Samuel said. "It is Islim Rest Day, and it is your Redeemer's Nativity. Neither of us should be pursuing business. As for this unfortunate young man, I repeat: I received the message, I sent him on to Green Village. What he did after that, I cannot tell you.

"As for the paint on his coat? The lad could have stopped between the two houses to take breath, or to warm himself before proceeding elsewhere, with another message. He could have leaned against the wall and got paint on his coat that way. The stain and the blood in the alley? There may be, as I said, other reasons for its appearance. Some meat may have dripped, or one of the dogs that lurk in the alleys could have been in a fight. Kemal, see these people out! *Salaam aleikum!*"

The steward appeared, accompanied by two burly Afrikans who could have been porters or bodyguards. It was clear to Halvar he was being dismissed.

Devallon stepped forward to postpone their departure, but Halvar forestalled him.

"I don't think Heer Samuel is in a mood to rent out his villa," Halvar told him. "Better you should go back to the cottage and tell Milord he's going to have to wait out the winter in inferior quarters."

Devallon shook his head. "There has to be somewhere better," he stated. "And I am going to find it."

Out in the street , Halvar and Devallon found themselves the object of interested attention, while Flores and Selim conferred behind them.

"That Afrikan knows more than he's telling," Flores grumbled. "We should take him to the Rabat. A day or three in a cold cell will have him talking."

"He must have known about the muskets," added Selim. "Girard needed someone to arrange their sale. Who better than someone like Samuel Igbo, who can read and write in Franchen as well as Arabi and Erse?"

"And the buyer was one of those Pure Sect infidels," Flores finished for her. "They can't hide from Manatas law anymore. We can go after them—"

"Not yet." A movement in the alley caught Halvar's eye."Hoy! Stop!" He trotted through the alley and skidded on a patch of ice. Only Devallon's strong arm under his hurt shoulder stopped him from a disgraceful fall into the slimy muck.

"What was that?" Devallon stared at the corner, where two ruts had cut into the muck of the street.

"There's a Scavenger with a dog-pull. That's how the body got from here to there," Halvar said. "Follow that Scavenger!"

Chapter 17

AT THE END OF THE ALLEY, A FIGURE SWATHED in voluminous wrappings led a large dog around the corner onto the Broad Way.

"Who's that?" Flores asked.

"Can't tell whether it's a man or woman, but it's definitely a dog." Halvar pointed to a paw print in the muck underfoot.

"A Scavenger with a dog-pull," Firebrand commented.

"Obviously," Halvar retorted.

The dog and its owner trotted across the Broad Way toward the Great River winking in the midday sunlight. Halvar and the rest of his squad followed.

"Hoy! Stop!" Flores shouted.

Firebrand added something in Munsi.

It did no good. The Scavenger ignored the cries and plodded onward, picking up jars and depositing the con-

116

tents in one or the other of the two receptacles jammed into the spaces of the dog-pull.

"Why can't we catch up to him?" Flores asked. "He's not going that fast."

"Where's he going?" Devallon panted.

Halvar turned to face his one-time enemy.

"At a guess? The Scavengers' Pit. Don't you have anything better to do, Musket-man? Why follow me on my rounds?"

"I told you, I've been given a mission. Find Milord Summersby better quarters. Which, I may tell you, I'd prefer as well. I'm now bedding down with the horse-tender, who stinks of the stables."

"You've done worse," Halvar reminded him.

"Not recently," Devallon countered. "And I'm not about to bring the horse, the chickens and the goat into the cottage to make it seem larger when I get them out."

Halvar grinned, recalling the tale Willem of Cos had told.

"How does Milord this morning?"

"He's nursing a bad headache," Devallon said with a grimace. "That wine at the Gardens of Paradise was quite... interesting. And so was the dame who supplied it. An old flame of yours, or so the gossip goes."

"That is none of your affair," Halvar huffed. "Aha! I was right! The Scavenger is heading towards the Scavengers' Pit. Just as well—I have to give Emir Achmet his alms, and I want a word with him in any case." He strode forward, Devallon still at his heels.

"This Emir...?"

"In Parigi, I suppose you'd call him King of the Beggars. He runs the Scavengers, who clean the streets and get rid of the, um, waste. They also pick up odd things that are unattended, so keep your hand on your purse when you meet him." Halvar hustled forward, a clear sign the discussion was at an end.

Selim caught up to him as Devallon fell back.

"I wanted to show you something, but that Franchen took all your time," she groused. "What does he want?"

"To take my place, I think," Halvar muttered. "What have you got?"

"When I was in the dormitory, before that awful Bull boy got hold of me, I found something in Snake's bedding." She reached under her jacket and pulled out a sheaf of folded papers. "I haven't had much chance to look at this."

The Scavenger stopped to tip something into each of the large jars on the dog-pull, Halvar took shelter behind the corner of the nearest building to unfold the paper.

"This looks like the *Gazetta*," he said. "What's this?" He pointed to marks in the margins of the printed sheet.

"I think Snake was practicing Arabi writing," Selim said, examining the scrawl. "He's underlined some things in Arabi print and repeated them in the margins, next to some in Roumi letters. Ordinary words, and some names."

"So he has," Halvar mused. "And what's more, he's made a squiggle, like the Rune S. Marking his own copy?"

Selim turned the page over.

"He's done the same with the Ogham letters on the Erse side."

"Prester Nicodemus teaches Roumi letters, the ones used by Franchen," Halvar said. "This lad Snake was trying to learn Arabi letters. Why?"

"So he could read the messages he was carrying?" Selim considered the possibility. "The messengers are told when and where to deliver their letters. They aren't expected to open them or read them, or understand what they're carrying. In fact, I think the Waterfront Rats were deliberately told not to learn Arabi so they can't read the messages they deliver."

"But Snake wanted to know," Halvar finished the thought. "And then..."

"He'd use what he knew," Selim said slowly. "But why? For what?"

"For money," Halvar said. "Those coins in his coat. He didn't put those into the common purse." He peered around the corner. "What's the beggar doing now?"

The Scavenger continued along the alleys, oblivious to the group following his dog and its reeking cargo. The procession wound around more villas—smaller ones, each with a pine bough over the door—and past a small chapel. Halvar stopped briefly, listening to a hymn of praise for the Redeemer's Nativity, sung in Danic. He murmured an apology to the Redeemer and Mother Mara. He had to finish what he started before he could attend to his salvation.

They were now in the district settled by Oropan artisans and shopkeepers, who preferred not to live in the souk. Workshops were closed on this, the festival day, but some of the bakeries were still functioning. Halvar sniffed hungrily. Someone was cooking something tasty! He wished he had the time to sample some of the wares, but the Scavenger plodded on, and so must he.

The muddy alley ended at the path along the riverbank that led to the ramshackle settlement at the end of the Town Wall. Halvar stopped to let Firebrand and Flores catch up with him.

"You two, stay with me," he ordered. "Selim, keep behind them. Devallon…"

"If you please, Capitán, an introduction to this emir might be useful. It's possible he knows someone who has a larger house than the one we occupy who would be willing to, ah, trade quarters?" Devallon smiled unconvincingly.

"Once I finish my business, you can do what you like," Halvar told him. "But don't say I didn't warn you."

He approached the settlement where Emir Achmet held court in front of his stone hut, sitting on a throne-like chair taken from some burning house next to a large brazier whose coals gave off enticing heat. A large pot placed on the grill above the coals emitted the aroma of roasted mokka-beans steeping in water.

"*Salaam aleikum*, Capitán Halvar Danske!" the rotund emir greeted them, with a genial wave of his hand. He had added several furs to his usual array of woolen caftans and shawls, and his turban was pinned with a gaudy broach that might have been a ruby. Behind him stood his two lieutenants, Osman and Rachav, one with only one hand, the other missing several fingers. Both were wearing coats in the Oropan style, with set-in sleeves and large cuffs, and had furry caps on their heads.

"*Aleikum salaam*, Honored Emir," Halvar responded. "As is the custom, I come bringing alms to the poor on the Nativity Day of the Redeemer Chesu." He held out a small leather bag trimmed with Local-style dyed quills that gave out a tuneful clink when Emir Achmet accepted it.

"Your alms are accepted, with gratitude," Emir Achmet said, tucking the sack of coins into his sash. "And what else can I do for the noble capitán on this fine day?"

"You can tell that fellow to stop what he'd doing." Flores snarled, pointing to the dog-pull and its owner, who was tipping the contents of one of the jars into a wooden vat. Presumably, the other jar would go into the reeking pit next to it.

"Fellow?" Emir Achmet looked towards the revolting pit. "Oh, no!" He started to laugh. "That is no fellow, that is Lula! What do you want with her?" He took in Devallon's finery and sneered. "I know Franchen have odd tastes, but Lula?"

Devallon's face turned red. He gripped the hilt of his rapier. Halvar stepped in before blood could be spilled.

"Lula, is it? It's hard to be sure, what with all the wrappings in this hard weather."

Osman returned, leading Lula, who now was revealed to be a stocky copper-skinned woman wrapped in odd bits and pieces of tacked-together clothing, and whose broad nose and wide lips betrayed an Afrikan somewhere in her family tree. Her dog, whose head nearly reached her waist, stayed with her, the ladder still strapped to its back, the two ends dragging in the mire of the Scavengers' settlement.

She stared from Halvar to Firebrand to Flores and back to Halvar, then peered questioningly at Oman.

"Wha?"

"Lula don't speak much," Osman explained. "Except to me, and that only because I can understand her. It's the hearing," he added. "Maybe when she was little, someone hit her upside the head too hard, so she don't hear so good."

"We have to look at her dog-pull," Firebrand said.

"Eh?" Lula stepped back as Firebrand stepped forward. Her dog growled, daring anyone to get near its mistress.

Firebrand stepped back, and the dog relaxed as Lula stroked its neck.

"You heard Daoud the News-crier? A lad was found dead beside the wall, on the Mahak side," Halvar said, emphasizing each word. "But he did not die there. Someone moved the body, someone with a dog-pull. If it was you, Lula, you must tell us. It is a bad thing, to move a body that is dead. This one was killed, he did not die of cold, and we must find the one who killed him. So, you must tell us if you found the body, and where you found it."

Lula's broad face twisted in confusion as she stared first at Halvar, then at Osman.

Emir Achmet's face had grown redder with each revelation.

"A lad, killed? What lad? Why was I not told of this? And who told Lula to move this lad?"

Halvar explained, "One of the Waterfront Rats, a young man called Snake, was shot—"

"Shot!" Emir Achmet exploded with wrath. "*Shot?* With gunpowder?"

"That's how it's usually done," Devallon said.

"Who? Why?" Emir Achmet sputtered.

"That's what I'm here to find out," Halvar said. He turned back to Osman. "Tell her to hold the beast and let Firebrand have a look at that dog-pull."

Osman made a sign to Lula, who shied away from Firebrand as he stepped forward once again. This time, she

121

gripped the harness and murmured soothingly to her dog as Firebrand examined the odd apparatus.

"Dark marks here. Could be blood."

Lula stared at Osman, her eyes filled with fear.

"Nah!" Tears filled her eyes. "Bah!"

"She didn't kill him," Osman burst out. "We didn't know he was shot. All we saw was the blood, all over his front and back. We didn't know he was shot. We didn't kill him!"

"Nah, nah!" She shook her head vigorously. "Nah mah!"

"Of course you didn't kill him," Halvar said to soothe the frightened woman. "All you did was move him from where he was. Isn't that right? Did you move him because you saw him lying there?"

"Nah mah!" Lula said vigorously.

Osman glanced at his leader.

"Not Lula. Me," he confessed.

Emir Achmet glared at him in righteous wrath.

"Without notifying me!"

"Or me!" Halvar put in. "I thought I'd made it clear any untoward death was to be reported to the Rabat."

"But this was just a Waterfront Rat," Osman protested. "Nobody important. See, Lula saw him when she was making her rounds, and she come to me, like she does when she has a problem, and I went with her and saw him lying there."

`"How did you know who it was?" Halvar demanded. "Was he on his front or his back when you saw him?"

Osman shrank under Halvar's gaze. He stared wildly at his usual confederate, but this time he got no help from Rachev.

"He was lying on his front," Osman said at last. "But I looked at his face when we put him on the dog-pull. He was stiff by then, and the blood was all gummy-like. I thought I'd seen him here and there, a time or two, when he come with a message from Tenente Gomez about something on the waterfront. I didn't know his name."

"Stephen, called Snake," Halvar said.

Emir Achmet nodded in sudden comprehension.

"Ah. That one. Now I recall him. Not one of your pretty boys, but a clever young fellow."

"Clever enough to challenge you?" Flores put in. "The kind who wants to go far? Perhaps this time, too far?"

"Too far for someone's comfort," Halvar agreed. He turned back to Osman. "Tell me what happened, and don't try to lie. You know I'll find out the truth sooner or later, and it's been a few days since he was killed, so I'd prefer it to be sooner."

"If this Snake fellow was killed during the snow, that was three days ago." Rachev counted on his fingers. "Three whole days, and you didn't tell me?" It was hard to tell whether his outrage was because of the murder or Osman's silence about it.

"Three days...that's right." Osman licked his dry lips. "It was the day after we found poor old Ibo and took him back here. Lula didn't know anything about that; she just went her rounds as always. There's new orders, when we do the Oropan villas, that the piss should be kept separate from the shit, two different jars."

Halvar thought this over. "Whose orders are those? Not the sultan's—all he wants is for the stuff to be off the streets. Getting it to the Pit, that's your business, Emir, not his."

"We got word there's some Bretain who'll pay for pee but not for poo, but it has to be Oropan pee, not Afrikan," Achmet explained. "So, we keep the one in the wooden vat for them to collect, and the rest goes into the pit, like always."

"Not Afrikan? Only Oropan pee?" Halvar put that odd notion at the back of his mind. "So, Lula was going along, and she comes upon this dead lad. Then what?"

"She comes to me," Osman said. "And she takes me to it."

"And you didn't think to notify the Rabat?" Halvar repeated.

"Or me!" Emir Achmet was still furious.

123

"Or me?" Rachev added.

"It was End-of-Fast," Osman whined. "I thought, Why bother either of you two noble persons with such a minor thing as the death of some Waterfront Rat? The one who owns the house where we found him, he come out, saw us, and said we should get the body away from there before the dogs got to it. I helped Lula load the lad onto her dog-pull, and we got him through the gate and dumped him against the wall. It was starting to snow, and I thought, well, he'd be hidden, and maybe the animals would eat him…" His voice trailed off.

"Osman, Osman, how many times do I tell you, you don't think, you let me do the thinking!" Rachev chided him. "You're not good at thinking. You should have come to me."

"Or me!" Emir Achmet scolded him. "Involving us in this business! " He turned to Halvar. "I regret this stupid man's interference in what was, after all, a minor matter. Of course, he should have informed the Rabat as soon as he saw the body, but it *was* the End-of-Fast day, and he must be excused for his zeal in protecting us from unwanted distraction from our celebrations."

"And maybe this Afrikan who owned the house where he fell might have given you a little something to get the body out of the way?" Flores glared at Osman and Lula.

The thought of payment aroused Emir Achmet's attention.

"Where, exactly, did you find this body?" he asked Lula

"In the Street of the Afrikans? Between two houses?" Halvar roared at her.

Lula turned from Achmet to Halvar, then to Osman, her face screwed into an expression of confusion.

Osman shrugged. "I don't know which house it was. The back alleys are all alike, just doors and walls, maybe a window."

"One of the houses was freshly painted—white-wash, with red and black zigzag stripes," Flores said. "Surely, you would notice that?"

"It was getting dark by the time I got there," Osman whined. "I only had a lantern to see by, didn't see which house it was."

Selim turned Lula to face her.

"Was it in the passage between the houses of Lady Tekla, whose man died in the feria, and Samuel Igbo, who is a trader?" she asked, articulating each word carefully in her best Arabi.

Lula's worried expression softened into comprehension.

"Yah, yah! she cried out.

Selim turned to Halvar.

"I think she can tell what people say by looking at their mouths. She can't see past your mustache, or Emir Achmet's beard. She may be deaf, but she's not stupid. She does what people tell her to do, that's all. And if Osman and Igbo told her to move the body, then the fault is theirs, not hers."

"Moving a body is a very severe offense," Halvar reminded the luckless Osman. "Especially if you've been given a bribe to do it."

"It wasn't a bribe," Osman insisted. "It was a...a token of respect. I was going to turn it in, but I needed a new coat..."

Emir Achmet's fury had grown with each admission.

"You've got the coat, now give me the rest of the money."

"More to the point, who gave it to you?" Flores demanded.

"The trader, Samuel Igbo," Osman confessed. "One of his servants must have heard us in the alley. He come out of the house and saw us, and he gave us two strings of purples. Said it was alms, and that I shouldn't worry about the dead one but should take him away, lest he bring bad luck to the house.

"I gave two of the purples to Lula, for the End-of-Fast, to get herself a nice hat, and I got a coat with the rest of the string in the souk." He scrabbled among his garments and came up with a string of purple wumpum beads, which he held out to Emir Achmet. "I was going to give these to you, but I forgot."

The Scavenger leader snatched the string away from his minion.

"Get away, and stay in your hut for the rest of the day. No soup for you tonight! Rachev, keep an eye on him from now on. Moving bodies! Bah!" Emir Achmet tucked the wumpum string into his belt, muttering to himself.

Halvar turned to Flores and Firebrand.

"Now we have something solid to grab that slimy trader for. If he told the Scavengers to move the body, he knew full well there was a death in that alley, and he should have notified the Rabat immediately, festival or no festival! Tenente Flores, when we get to the Rabat, find a couple of stout guardsmen and go back to Igbo's villa. Take him into custody—"

"He can't do that," Selim interrupted.

"Why not?" Halvar stopped to stare at the girl.

"Not without a firman, a warrant," she said firmly. "It's Bretain law, according to their own charter, that no one can be taken into custody without reason. It was part of the agreement they made when the two settlements merged, that the Bretain laws regarding personal rights were continued in both Green Village and Manatas Town. It was printed in the *Gazetta*."

"We have reason!"

"But my father has to sign the firman,"

Halvar made an exasperated noise.

"Very well, we'll get the firman. There shouldn't be too much trouble about it—the excellent sultan already knows we suspect Samuel Igbo of dealing in muskets. Now, we have a witness who can attest to his moving the body of the messenger who can identify his client.

"While we wait for the excellent sultan to give it to us, Firebrand, you go to Green Village and get Tenente Donal out of the chapel if you have to. Find out all you can about that Purist MacAlan. When did he get here? What's he been doing since he came?"

"I see why you want to question Igbo, but what does this Bretain Purist have to do with this Snake business?" Firebrand asked.

"According to Lady Tekla, Igbo was consorting with Pure Sect Bretains," Halvar reasoned aloud. "MacAlan is their leader. If he's not the one dealing with Igbo, he probably knows who is.

"And I'm curious as to why he's still here, long after his son's death. He said he came to Manatas to put the lad into the madrassa, but as far as I could tell, the only thing that fellow wanted to do was play the Peace Game. So, why come all this way to do something he could just as easily done in West Caster? And with far less trouble, too.

"Look into it, Tenente Firebrand, and if you have trouble with those Pure Sect bigots, put Tenente Donal onto them."

Halvar heard a gentle cough behind him.

"Hem. My dear friend Halvar, aren't you forgetting something? A small favor, if you will?"

"Aha! Devallon! I'd almost forgotten you were there, you were so quiet." He grabbed the musket-man by the arm, thrusting him forward to face Emir Achmet.

"Noble Emir, I present to you Sieur Devallon, who will, I am sure, have something to say regarding a matter of business. *Salaam aleikum!*"

Halvar retreated, leaving Devallon to deal with the emir on his own. At last he'd got rid of that pesty Franchen! Now he could get on with his own business. First on his agenda: finding somewhere more comfortable than the Scavengers' Pit to sit and go over what they had learned with Selim.

With this in mind, Halvar led his squad back to the Broad Way, where Firebrand headed for the gate in the wall and Flores looked for an unoccupied donkey cart to get them back to the Rabat.

Part 2

The Poisoned Professor

Chapter 18

THE MUEZZIN'S CRY ANNOUNCED THE TIME FOR midday prayers. Halvar clutched his amulet and thanked the Redeemer, Mother Mara, and Thor for their guidance and protection, while Selim and Flores found a dry spot on the brick path to perform the necessary prostrations. That done, Flores hailed one of the many donkey carts whose yellow flag indicated the driver was free to take passengers wherever they wished to go. The three clambered aboard.

"Where to?" the driver inquired.

"Rabat," Halvar ordered. "Tenente Flores, once we get there, you can ask Sultan Petrus for the firman. As soon as you have it in hand, go back to Igbo's villa, arrest him on the charge of moving the body, but don't make a great show of taking him. Use one of the donkey carts. We don't want every Afrikan in Manatas raging in front of the Rabat. You're right to think that after Samuel Igbo spends an hour or two in the cold cells, he'll tell us what we have to know, just to get back to his nice, warm, study."

"But what does he know? If Girard came into Manatas only a few days ago..." Flores objected.

"Samuel was the middleman in this deal. He had to know who was going to purchase the muskets. He might even know where they were supposed to go once they were in the buyer's hands." Halvar stopped short. "What's this?"

The donkey-man pulled his cart to the side of the road, where Benyamin ben Mendel stood waving his arms furiously.

"Capitán Don Alvaro!" the Yehudit gasped, his round face red with his exertions. "Thank the Almighty One I've found you! I've been looking for you all morning!They told me at the Rabat that you were going to the Street of the Afrikans to talk to Lady Tekla. I asked for you at her villa, but you'd gone somewhere else. Someone said they say you heading for the Scavengers' Pit, so I was on my way there, since you are on your way somewhere else..."

"Calm yourself, Benyamin. What do you want me for?"

"It's Master Kupernik!" Benyamin gasped. "We...that is, at the Yehudit House..." He took another gulp of air. "There's something very, very wrong. His door is ajar, but something is blocking it. We...that is, I...can see his foot, on the floor...I think he may be ill...or worse..."

"How is the door blocked?" Halvar asked.

"I'm not sure. His servant and I pushed it, but it only goes so far. The handle turns, but the door won't move when it's pushed."

Halvar frowned. "You say you saw Master Kupernik's foot? How far open is this door? Can someone slender and small get in?"

"It would have to be someone very slender," Benyamin said. "I tried to reach in with my arm and didn't get far."

"What prompted you to try to open the door in the first place?"

"Master Kupernik is always among the earliest risers," Benyamin said. "Even when he's been up all night, studying the motions of the stars, he always comes to the morning prayers before we have break-the-fast. He often leads the reading from the Holy Book, and takes part in the discussion of the portion while we have our mokka and mush. But he wasn't there this morning, and Oleg, his manservant, says he didn't answer the knock at the door."

"This sounds serious." Halvar turned to Flores. "Tenente, you proceed to the Rabat. Get the firman from the excellent sultan. As young Selim reminded us, we cannot flout the law ourselves if we mean to keep it in Manatas," he added before Flores could protest. "As I told you, arrest Igbo, but don't hurt him, and whatever you do, make sure he's alive when he gets to the Rabat! I don't want another death on my hands."

"As you say, Capitán. And what are you going to do?" Flores asked.

"I'm going to see what's wrong with Master Kupernik. I have a question or two to ask him, in any case. Something he said yesterday at that party intrigues me. You go ahead, Tenente. I'll find another cart." He eased himself out, with Selim behind him. Benyamin waved down another passing donkey cart, handed the driver two white wumpum beads, and ordered, "To the Yehudit House on the Madrassa Way."

Halvar and Selim joined Benyamin in the cart as the donkey plodded southward on the Broad Way past the district of villas to the part of of Manatas Town where business was conducted. Brick buildings in the Andalusian style rubbed shoulders with Oropan wooden ones; a flat roof would be next to a pitched one. Mokka-shops on the ground floors were open for business, their small windows fogged with the steamy breath of the men within. Beyond the Broad Way, Halvar could see the smoke rising from the houses of the Yehudit Quarter, strung along the bank of the Great River.

132

Between the brick houses and mokka-shops and the wooden cabins of the Yehudit Quarter lay the ramshackle sheds, tents, and shacks of the souk, where the ordinary inhabitants of Manatas could do their daily shopping.

They arrived at the wide place in the road where the stone minaret of the Grand Muskat faced the more sedate facade of the main hall of the Manatas Madrassa and the main path of the souk crossed the Broad Way. Both edifices owed their architecture to Al-Andalus, but the Grand Muskat's two minarets and tiled domes dominated the skyline of Manatas, rivaling the Rabat for the pride of place, whereas the Madrassa Assembly Hall was lower but wider, with round arches holding up an arcade that faced east. On either side of the main hall were the brick buildings that housed the lecture rooms and small classrooms where the professors instructed their students.

A muddy lane marked the northernmost edge of this complex, into which the donkey-man turned his cart towards the Great River. Several wooden houses lined the lane, each with its signboard in Arabi and Ogham letters. The lane bent around a large tree and continued north and south, where long, two-story brick buildings faced each other across a wide, unpaved road.

"Where are we?" Halvar muttered.

"Behind the Madrassa," Selim whispered. "It's where the students and masters live."

The donkey cart lurched as Benyamin climbed down and assisted Halvar to the street. Selim slid out of the cart, her eyes taking it all in. This was the part of Manatas she had never seen.

"This is the Masters' dormitory," Benyamin said, indicating the west-facing building whose facade was broken by three separate doorways. "There are three houses, separated by inner walls, each with its own assembly room for prayers. One is for Kristos, one for Yehudit, one for Islim, so that can each can have its own kitchen, to conform to dietary laws."

133

He waved at the east-facing buildings.

"This is the dormitory for the students who don't have the money to pay for private lodgings. For a small sum, they can live simply, several to a room, with a refectory for meals. Of course, some of the Bretains and Franchen, the Afrikans, have separate houses, with their own servants, paid for by themselves, more luxurious than the dormitory."

"Students like Stephane Mercier?" Halvar hinted.

"And like the Afrikans who wanted to play the Peace Game," Selim reminded him. "They have their own house. They can afford it," she added with a scornful sniff.

Benyamin rapped on the door to the Master's House. A worried face looked out.

"Shalom, Benyamin ibn Mendel. Have you found—"

"He's here." Benyamin gestured toward Halvar. "Capitán, this is Rav Eli, who is in charge of the Yehudit House. Eli, what word of Master Kupernik? Have they succeeded in waking him?"

Eil was a portly Sefarat Yehudit whose flowing gray beard covered most of his chest, clad in the typical gray-blue kaftan and blue kutton cap favored by those Yehudit who lived in Al-Andalus.

"He still does not answer," Eli said, allowing Benyamin, Halvar and Selim into the entry hall. Benyamin touched the small box affixed to the doorpost as he entered.

"Have you tried the door?" Halvar asked.

"Several times, but we did not wish to be too...vigorous." Eli looked embarrassed. "Master Kupernik can be somewhat, um, irascible when disturbed."

"Don't want to provoke him, eh?" Halvar took in his surroundings. The house was small, but pleasantly warm, a relief after the biting wind outside. The walls were paneled and varnished, the floor was wood. A staircase led up to the second level.

"The other masters are quite unhappy," Eli said. "They had to drag someone inside from the Broad Way to make a tenth for prayers. We could only suppose that Master Kupernik over-indulged at the party yesterday. He never oversleeps!"

Eli led them up the stairs to the landing, where several men stood, their voices raised in debate in a mixture of Arabi and Danic dialects.

"Masters!" Eli's sharp voice commanded silence. "Capitán Don Alvaro Danico has arrived to assist us in rousing Master Kupernik."

"Something has happened to Master Kolya!" said a large, shaggy-haired, red-bearded man in a linen shirt with a high collar that buttoned under one ear instead of in front who stood by the door in question.

"This is Oleg," Benyamin explained. "He came to Manatas with Master Kupernik."

Oleg spoke in heavily accented Arabi.

"Master Kolya never sleep late. There is something bad here."

Halvar frowned at the door, which was,, as reported slightly ajar. He tried to get his arm, then his leg into the gap. His boot caught on something at the edge of the doorjamb, but he could not budge the door. He tried to move whatever was stuck under the door with his toe; then he pushed against the door again. It gave slightly under the pressure and moved with a scraping noise.

"There's something blocking it," Halvar stated. "Benyamin, Oleg, can you help me here? And is there one of you gentlemen who will...?"

Eli shouted down the stairs. "Dan, Shmuel!"

Two well-muscled men bounded up the stairs, both in the sort of woolen jacket and breeches worn by common folk all over Oropa. They joined Halvar and Benyamin in their efforts.

Without warning, the door flew open, sending the rescue party staggering into the room; Oleg let out a howl of anguish.

At their feet was the body of the late Master Kupernik. He was obviously dead.

Chapter 19

HALVAR STEPPED CAREFULLY OVER THE BODY.

"So...now we know why Master Kupernik didn't come to morning prayers." He turned to the crowd of eminent scholars huddled in the hallway. "Oleg, Benyamin, Selim, you come in. The rest of you, stay out."

"Someone must notify Imam Gamaliel," Eli quavered. "He leads the Manatas Madrassa, he must know what has happened. And Rav Nahum, who is the most senior of the Yehudit at the madrassa, he is delivering a lecture at the Assembly Hall—he must be told."

"Go ahead and do it," Halvar agreed. He stared down at the body stretched out before them. "Benyamin, can you confirm this is, indeed, the body of Master Kupernik? Given name...? Halvar looked at Oleg.

"Nikolai, but he was called Kolya." The servant blubbered, "He is dead!"

"That he is," Halvar said. He turned the body over to observe its face. "He didn't die easy, either."

The dead man's mouth and eyes were open, his face twisted into an expression of anguish. His arms were outstretched, reaching for the door. He was clad in a wool caftan over a kutton undershift. His feet and legs were bare.

Benyamin looked at that face and turned away, his lips white under his growing beard.

"It's him. It's Master Kupernik."

"Not likely to be anyone else," Halvar muttered, "but we've been fooled before. " He searched the body for a wound and found none. "Master Eli, send one of your lads to the Rabat and tell Dr. Moise to come here, with a cart. I want this body examined as soon as possible."

Eli had recovered from the shock of seeing the body.

"An army bone-setter? What good can he do? This man is clearly beyond his help. Here at the madrassa, we have renowned physicians, learned doctors, masters of anatomy who can conduct whatever examination you feel necessary. Not that there is any doubt. Master Kupernik was of a choleric humor. He must have died of a seizure of the heart."

"And maybe he was poisoned, " Halvar countered. "I didn't know him, only met him at that gathering yesterday, but I take it he wasn't well liked by his colleagues."

"He could be...abrasive," Benyamin admitted. "And forceful, when his theories were challenged." His voice trailed off as he contemplated the corpse, murmuring phrases in Ivrit.

"As I heard," Halvar said. "Selim, draw me a picture of this body. And another that shows the room, where everything is. Benyamin!"

"Yes, Capitán?" The stout young Yehudit was jolted out of his reverie.

"Go with the messenger, and come back with Dr. Moise. If he makes a fuss, tell him the madrassa professors don't want him, that'll bring him here fast enough. And if you see Tenente Flores, tell him to keep watch over his prisoner. I don't want another death on our hands."

Benyamin shoved his fellow students out of the way in his eagerness. Selim squatted next beside the body, carefully drawing the face of the dead man.

Halvar stood in the middle of the room for a moment, then made a slow tour of the place, trying to understand the man who had inhabited it.

Except for the narrow bed jammed into the corner of the room farthest from the door and the bedside cabinet next to it, the room was filled with reading and writing materials. Shelves on brackets nailed into the wall held stacks of papers, neatly tied with string. More shelves in bookcases held larger tomes. Scrolls had been stuffed into the sections of a cabinet set on a small table. A large table, under the window, held more papers and books, as well as the learned man's writing-tools—quill and reed pens, jars of red and black ink, and blank sheets of paper.

A large lamp had been placed next to the inkstand. Halvar peered into it, frowned, and set it back down.

The wooden chair in front of the writing-desk was askew, as if Kupernik had pushed it aside when he stood up; two more chairs held yet more books.

Halvar hovered over the nightstand, which held a pottery jug and small cup. The inevitable chamberpot was placed on the lower shelf of the stand. He peered into the water-jug.

"Empty," he noted.

Selim scanned the titles of the books on the chairs.

"Maybe he got thirsty, found there was no water in his jug, and had an attack of the heart when he went to call for his servant."

"But he never got to the door," Halvar objected. He picked up the clay cup and sniffed at it. He put a finger inside and frowned. "Not wet."

"Water could have dried," Selim said.

"Maybe. We'll have to ask one of those alchemists their opinion of what killed him. Maybe one of them knows more about poisons than I do."

"Are there alchemists in the Yehudit House? I thought they were all teaching things like mathematics and philosophy."

"At least one of them's a physician," Halvar said. "He was at that party yesterday." He continued his examination of the room, running his hands over Master Kupernik's outer garments that hung on pegs rammed into the wall next to the door—a black cloak trimmed with fur, a broad-brimmed felt hat, and a black coat with silver buttons.

"His underthings are in here." Selim lifted the lid of the sea chest that stood at the foot of the bed. A quick search revealed linen shirts, woolen stockings, something that resembled Halvar's own braes, and some square items with fringes on the corners and a hole in the center for the head to poke through whose use Halvar could not determine. They were too large for nose-wipes; perhaps used as an extra layer against the cold?

The most elegant item in the chest was a velvet bag with letters in Ivrit embroidered on it that contained a large fringed shawl of Damascus silk with a gold-encrusted section on one edge, and an elaborate apparatus of straps attached to two small wooden boxes.

"He was no jack-a-dandy, that's for sure," Halvar commented as he fingered the plain shirt and stockings. "No ruffle around the neck, just a string to hold the neck together and keep the cold out. And what's this thing?" He held up the straps.

"It's what the Yehudit use to pray with," Selim told him. "Master Kupernik might proclaim himself a Free-thinker, and talk heresy, but he prayed like a Yehudit."

Halvar nodded and turned back to the largest piece of furniture in the room, the table that served at Master Kupernik's writing-desk. It was shoved under the window that looked out over the roofs of the souk towards the Great River. The sun was already sinking towards the formidable pink stone cliffs that kept the Locals on the other side of the Great River safe from Oropan or Andalusian invasion.

Once again, Halvar checked the lantern.

"Candle's burnt down to the wick," he observed. "No one blew it out. Leads me to think Master Kupernik was interrupted by someone last night." He sat down on the chair, then rose again. "He's doing something here, he gets up, he answers the door..."

"Who was there?"

"We'll have to find that out, won't we? What was he doing at the table? Writing, reading? I didn't see any ink on his hands, so he wasn't writing."

"Reading, then. A book?" Selim checked the table. "Not one of these, to be sure. Unless whoever was here closed the book or took it with him. But perhaps, one of these papers?" She nodded toward the piles that were neatly sorted in front of the chair.

"Don't move them," Halvar ordered. "Just pick them up, and put them back exactly where they were." He peered over her shoulder. "What are they? The letters look different."

"These are in different languages," Selim explained. "This pile is Arabi, this one in Ogham. This one seems to be some kind of Roumi, but I'm not very good at that, so I'm not sure what it says."

"What are they? Letters? Lists? What was he reading when he was struck down?"

"These are in different hands, with lots of numerals. I think they may be student's papers, examinations, that kind of thing. They are marked with red ink." She nodded towards the large inkwell, "He might have finished what he was doing, marking the papers and making notes. The notations in red ink are all in the same hand, but in different letters, depending on what the student wrote in."

"I don't read anything but Rune, and that not well," Halvar admitted. "Master Kupernick must have been a very learned man, indeed, if he could answer all these students in their own languages." He picked up the one paper that stood out because of its different shade and tex-

140

ture, coarser and darker than the rest. "What's this one? It's not on the same paper as these others. They're finer. "

"The paper is what's used in the souk to wrap food in sometimes, sometimes to send messages. The writing…it's Arabi, and it looks like…wait a minute!" She reached under her jacket and drew out the copies of the *Gazetta* she had taken from the Waterfront Rats' dormitory. "This is very odd. You know, I think this is a letter from Snake! See? He's tried to copy the Arabi words from the *Gazetta* to send a message to Master Kupernik. And he signed it with his S-mark."

Halvar snatched the two papers from her hand, held them to the light filtering through the windowpanes, one next to the other.

"You're right, laddie. This is definitely the same hand, so it must be Snake's. What does it say?"

"It's the same numbers, and Master Kupernik wrote something on it in Arabi."

Halvar's eye was drawn to a paper on the floor next to the writing-table.

"Here's something else, same paper, same hand. What's he say?"

Selim read slowly. "'Meet me tomorrow. Important news. Have money for fee.'"

"He had the money for the madrassa fee," Halvar said. "It was in his jacket. Why did he think Master Kupernik would meet with him? And what did he have to tell him? What connection can a Waterfront Rat have with an eminent professor of mathematics?

"And what does it have to do with his death?" Selim asked.

Before the question could be answered, another one was asked.

"Where is this body?" It was a female voice Halvar knew well.

"In here, but you cannot go—"

Another voice, that of Dr. Moise, the surgeon from the Rabat, countered the fussy servant.

141

"Of course she can. This may be a matter of poison, and Eva Hakim is an expert in such matters. We have been summoned by Capitán Don Alvaro Danico to examine a body. I assume it is within, so let us pass."

The gaunt Afrikan doctor had arrived, accompanied by the Nizim of the Sisters of Fatima, to the profound dismay of the noted physicians of the madrassa, who gathered in the hallway to protect their domain from the intrusion of a mere surgeon and a midwife.

"Let them in," Halvar ordered. "And the rest of you, stay out."

The young Sefarat who had challenged Master Kupernik at the party shoved through the crowd.

"I know alchemy, as well as medicine, " he declared. "If Master Kupernik died of poison, I will know which one."

Halvar looked to Dr. Moise. The medico nodded his approval.

"Very well, you can come in, but the rest of you lot stay back. But don't go away. I'll want to talk with you as soon as Dr. Moise and Eva Hakim, and this young fellow…?"

"He's Efrem Russo, he's a physician, but he also studies alchemy under Master Albrecht LaPierre." Benyamin struggled through the crowded hallway to enter the room. "If there's alchemical poison here, he'll know what it is. It's his specialty. And I have a message from Tenente Flores. He's still waiting to get the firman from the sultan, but as soon as he does, he'll get the official cart to take the prisoner back to the Rabat, so the Afrikans won't see one of their own being marched to jail by the Town Guards."

"Thor's Hammer!" Halvar swore. "Why the delay?"

"I think Sultan Petrus is not well. Eva Hakim was there to attend him, that's why she was able to come when I called for Dr. Moise."

"What's wrong with him?" Selim asked anxiously. "I know he's had a lot of excitement, and eaten things he shouldn't…"

"He's sleeping quietly, as far as I know," Benyamin assured her. "And as soon as he wakes up, Tenente Flores will get the warrant."

"What is this about a body?" Dr. Moise interrupted. "I have better things to do than be dragged all over Manatas to examine the dead when there are living souls that need my care."

"Then you might just as well go back to your army shed," Efrem Russo snapped. "Because I can do this as well, or better, than you and this…this midwife! I am an accredited physician, while you are—"

"One who has studied at the Madrassa in Corduva!" Dr. Moise informed him loftily.

"And Eva Hakim is an expert in poisonous plants," Selim put in.

Halvar stepped in before the argument got to the point of knives drawn.

"I don't care who went to school where. I want to know why this man is dead! Was it a natural death, or not? And if not, who did it?"

"The manner of his death we will try to ascertain," Eva Hakim said. "But whether it was a deliberate act or the Will of Ilha, that is another matter."

"I don't think Ilha had anything to do with this," Halvar muttered. "More likely Shaitan. Just…get on with it."

Chapter 20

DR. MOISE CAST A CRITICAL EYE OVER THE CORPSE
of Master Kupernik.

"Has he been moved?"

"Only to turn him over," Halvar said. "He was lying
facedown, his arm stretched out, as you see him. We could
just see his feet through the gap in the open door."

Dr. Moise squatted to test the corpse's limbs for flex-
ibility.

"Rigor has set in," he announced. "I place his death
at least twelve hours ago."

"Around midnight, then?" Selim had her notebook out,
recording everything.

"I should think so." Dr. Moise looked toward the door.
"I need someone to put this fellow where we can see him
better."

Oleg beckoned to Dan, and the two of them gently
lifted the late Master Kupernik onto the bed.

Efrem Russo lifted each hand and examined the nails. Dr. Moise frowned into the dead man's open mouth.

"He was calling out," Dr. Moise observed. "But I do not think he could make a sound. What do you think, Eva Hakim? Have you seen anything like this before?"

The Sister of Fatima's usually serene face creased into a frown under her green hijab.

"I have seen this, but not in a grown person. There have been cases of children who suffocated with no apparent cause."

"What kind of poison does this?" Halvar asked. "Was it something he ate?"

"Not exactly poison."

The two medical examiners stared at the student who'd spoken.

"But something that might be perfectly innocent to one person can be deadly to another."

"Indeed? How so?" Halvar asked.

Efrem Russo's round face turned bright-red in embarrassment at being the center of everyone's attention.

"It is something I have noticed, because it happened to my younger brother," he stammered. "In Franchenland, where I grew up, before Lovis's expulsions. My brother ate walnuts and choked on them, and died. It is why I wanted to study medicine—to find out why such a thing could happen. The rav said it was the Will of Adonai, but why should so simple a thing as a walnut make a child choke to death?"

"It is a sensitivity to certain foods," Eva Hakim said. "There are persons who, for some unknown reason, cannot eat foods that others will happily ingest. I have noted it myself when dealing with Locals. Some of them cannot digest foods that Oropans use in their daily diet, things like cheese and butter."

Halvar nodded. "Just as in the old tale I heard of the first ones who went a-Viking across the Storm Sea—Erik the Red One and Leif, Erik's son. They met some folk they

145

called Skraelings. They feasted them, gave them cheese, but the Skraelings took sick from it, claimed they had been poisoned, and there was a great battle. Leif decided there were too many Skraelings for him to fight, so he went back to his own lands. So runs the tale."

Dr. Moise nodded gravely. "It is an oddity, indeed. I, too, have seen it. Local children have no trouble with cheese or butter, whether from a cow or goat, but when they grow past a certain age, all such foods cause great distress."

Halvar looked at the body.

"So, what happened to this man? He was chipper enough at the party yesterday. I don't recall him eating or drinking anything in particular. Benyamin? Selim? You were there. Did you see Master Kupernik eating or drinking anything out of the ordinary?"

"He was too busy talking." Selim giggled. "And arguing with Master Boyle and Master LaPierre, and almost everyone else."

"And with Leon," Halvar added, his expression growing grimmer.

"But there couldn't have been anything bad for him at the party," Benyamin protested. "I was in charge of the arrangements, the food and the drink, and I made sure nothing was served that could not be eaten by all those present. It was halal and kosher, all dairy and grains, no meat. Cheese there was, cut into small pieces, and there were cakes—"

"Those batata things," Halvar recalled. "Yams, roots, —do any of these cause reaction to this kind of sensitivity?"

Eva Hakim considered, then shook her head.

"I have never heard of such. Of course, we cannot know what effect the more exotic spices have on the human system. Some of the peppers from the Mechicans are quite... potent."

"Whatever it was, it closed his throat," Dr. Moise stated, ending a prolonged examination of that very throat.

"So, if he had needed help, he could not cry out," Eva Hakim agreed.

"He might have tried to drink, but his water-jug was empty," Selim put in, pointing to the pottery ewer on the night table.

Dr. Moise strode over to the bed and like Halvar, peered into the ewer and the cup. He frowned at the chamberpot, lifted it out of its shelf, and sniffed the contents. His frown deepened as he tentatively touched a finger to what sloshed inside and raised it to his tongue.

"This is not urine," Dr. Moise declared. "It is plain water."

"Water?" Halvar cried out. "Someone poured the water out of the jug and into the chamberpot? Why?" He turned on Oleg, who cringed in the doorway. "Did you do this?"

"Not so! I fill water jug every night before Master Kolya go to bed. Water in jug, jug and cup on table next to bed, chamberpot on floor next to bed where Master Kolya can use it if he needs it."

"So, who put it onto the shelf?" Selim wondered. "And why bother?"

"A mistake," Halvar said. "He didn't want Master Kupernik to see that it had something in it. Oleg, Master Kupernik is in his nightclothes. Did you help him undress?"

Oleg's broad face screwed up as he reviewed his memory.

"Master Kolya come from the dinner room. He eat with the other Yehudit teachers and their students, they light the lights, they say the blessings. Then he come back here, he tell me to go to my own dinner, and he will write and read. I help him take off coat, I put it on peg. I leave robe for him to wear. I fill the water jug, I put chamberpot where he can find it, I go down to the kitchen. We have a good dinner, me and Dan and Shmuel, and eat what was left from party. I do not hear from Master Kolya anymore."

"Was that usual?" Halvar asked.

Oleg shrugged. "Most nights he stay up late, reading. Sometimes, on a clear night, he go up to the rooftop to look at stars. He was easy master, did not call me in the night for foolish reasons like some do. Every morning, I call him for morning prayers, but he usually is awake anyway. Today, he do not answer, so I go to Master Eli, and he summon Master Benyamin and..." Oleg began to snuffle. "He was kind master. He give me good place to live, he never beat me."

Halvar thought aloud. "Someone must have visited Master Kupernik after you set out the water jug. They may have given him something to eat or drink."

"With something in it that would cause him to choke?" Benyamin considered this with a growing look of horror. "But, if that someone poured the water out into the chamberpot, then they knew what it would do to him. They must have..." His voice dissolved into a sob.

Selim had gone back to rummaging among the papers on the table.

"What's this?" She pulled out a piece of paper that had been folded around something that had left splotches of dark stain. She passed it over to Halvar, who rubbed it between his fingers then sniffed at the stains.

"This looks the stuff Snake wrote his letter on. Smells odd, too, like the souk. Didn't you say the vendors use this kind of paper to wrap their goods in?" He sniffed again. "I've smelled this before..."

Dr. Moise took the paper, smelled it, and passed it to his colleague.

"What do you think?"

"I do believe this is *nguba*," Eva Hakim decided after repeating the process.

"*Nguba*?" Halvar echoed. "Those beans the Afrikan women sell in little rush baskets? Are they poisonous?"

"Not as far as I know," Selim said. Her voice took on the tone of one delivering instructions. "The Afrikans grow them in their own country, and they brought them here when they settled in the southern territories. They grow underground, like roots. The Afrikans use them in all kinds of ways. They can be roasted and salted, and eaten as a snack, or ground into flour, or mashed into paste to spread on bread. According to Leon, they only grow in the south because they die if the ground is too cold. They are supposed to be very nutritious."

"I don't know about nutritious, but they are tasty," Halvar commented. "I've had some myself, and they did me no harm. Might even have done some good." He turned to Eva Hakim. "These *nguba*…has anyone ever taken ill after eating them that you know of?"

"Not that I am aware of," Eva Hakim said. "But then, I am not always called on, especially if it is a child who is ill. Far too many women are willing to allow their children to go untreated. Sometimes it is a matter of ignorance, sometimes, alas, they do not have the few wumpum to pay a physician. Some women are afraid to question the will of Illha, may his name be blessed."

Halvar turned to the medical student.

"Efrem Russo, you knew Master Kupernik. Did he ever show this sensitivity, this difficulty, with *nguba*?"

"I did not know Master Kupernik very well," Efrem stammered. "But I knew he was somewhat, um, picky about food."

"True," Benyamin spoke up. "He was very wary of new foods, especially those from Nova Mundum. He would not taste anything he did not know, or that was not spoken of in the Holy Book. The nuts of the trees called hickory, for instance, or the ones from the Afrikan territories in the south of Nova Mundum that are called butter-nut or pecan. Some of his students brought some here with them after they had gone home for a visit and returned, to share with us at our Shabat dinners. Most of the students were eager to try new foods, also some of the masters, but not Master Kupernik."

"How many people knew about this, um, peculiarity of Master Kupernik's?" Halvar asked. "It's not something that would be made public, would it?"

149

"Hardly. You don't think…oh, no! Not one of us!" Benyamin cried out.

"Someone gave Master Kupernik something to eat that made his throat close up," Halvar stated. "That person must also have emptied the water jug so he couldn't wash the food out of his mouth. That person knew about Master Kupernik's, um, malady. It had to be someone living in this house."

He paced around the room then stopped by the door —something had caught his eye near the doorjamb. He stooped and picked up a small piece of wood.

"And he jammed this under the door, so even if someone heard him calling for it, Master Kupernik wouldn't get any help. This was no accident, nor was it an innocent mistake. This was malice. This was deliberate. This was murder."

Chapter 21

"MURDER!"

The crowd at the door parted as a tall man in the green turban and robes that marked him as an imam of the Ulema of Baghdad strode into the room, his dark eyes radiating anger over his full gray beard.

"Who calls this murder?"

"I do," Halvar stated. "And I thought I told everyone to stay out."

"I am Imam Gamaliel, the head of the Manatas Madrassa. Who allowed the Town Guard to invade these sacred precincts?" Imam Gamaliel glared at the two men behind him, one in the black gown over a simple black woolen jacket and trews favored by the Pure Sect of the Erse Rite Kristos, the other in the fur-trimmed coat and broad-brimmed hat of the Askenat Yehudit. Halvar recognized them as two of the many masters to whom he had been introduced at the fatal party the day before. He put names

151

to their faces—the Yehudit was Rav Nahum, a Master of Rhetoric; the Bretain, Master Artur Rufford, who taught law.

"Ahem." Rav Nahum coughed gently behind his neatly trimmed gay beard. "It was I, Revered Imam. When Master Kupernik did not appear for the morning prayers, I sent young Benyamin to his room. I thought he might have, um, over-indulged yesterday at the festival gathering."

Imam Gamaliel transferred his gaze to Benyamin, who reddened but said,"I was worried about Master Kupernik, too. "

"Then why did you not call for Rav Eli?"

"I did, and we tried to open the door, but it wouldn't budge, and Master Kupernik didn't answer, but I saw his foot, and I thought…that is…" Benyamin's voice faltered.

"You thought to avoid responsibility by foisting this… this…person upon us!" Imam Gamaliel sneered.

"Benyamin did the right thing." Halvar spoke up for his follower. "As it turns out, this death was no accident. Someone deliberately gave some kind of foodstuff to Master Kupernik, something that would close his throat so he could not breathe. Then he made sure Master Kupernik couldn't get help by pouring the water out of his jug, then inserting this piece of wood under the space between the door and the threshold so he could not open it. It took four of us to break in, and we found him lying in front of the door. Show him the drawing, Selim. This is exactly how we saw him." He offered the chip he had found near the door for Imam Gamaliel's inspection.

Selim presented her notebook to the enraged cleric, who glanced at it and raised an eyebrow.

"And in case you're wondering if this is all a story, I've got witnesses to attest that the dead man was right where I say he was." Halvar glared at Benyamin, Oleg and Rav Eli, daring them to refute him.

Imam Gamaliel sniffed. "This does not alter the fact that the madrassa is considered sacred ground, and that the law of Al-Andalus does not apply here. We obey only Sharia."

"Sacred ground?" Halvar repeated. "This is the first I've heard that"

"In Bretain and in Franchenland, the schools are considered a part of the religious sector." Master Rufford, a short, weedy man with a straggly gray wisp of a beard dangling from his chin, piped up. "The collegium at Oxenbridge and the one in Parigi do not follow the civil law but the religious."

"Well, here in Manatas, things are different," Halvar stated firmly. "Besides, this isn't some case of a student drinking too much uskebaugh in some waterfront taberna and getting roughed up in a brawl. This man is dead, and I was called in because that's my business, finding murderers."

"And mine," Dr. Moise put in. "We must take this man back to the Rabat for further examination. Whatever he ate is still inside him."

"The Rabat?" Efrem Russo asked. "Whatever for? We have a perfectly good examination room right here at the Madrassa. Well-heated, too," he added. "If you must continue the autopsy, you can do it there."

The African's habitual icy attitude seemed to melt at the thought of penetrating the hallowed space of the madrassa.

"I have heard of this examining room, but I have never actually been invited to attend the lectures held in it. Of course, my experience is more empirical than theoretical," he added as if in apology.

"Empirical experience is valuable," the Sepharat admitted. "But a mere surgeon is not to be considered the equal of a trained physician."

"I have had a year at the madrassa in Corduva," Dr. Moise retorted, back to his usual testy self. "But if you would permit me to use the facility here, I would like to attend to the autopsy on Master Kupernik."

Halvar stepped in once again.

"I don't care who does it, but I want this man cut into. Find that cake or whatever it was that killed him."

153

The Imam looked alarmed. "Are you saying the food in this house is tainted?"

"If no one else is ill, I think not," Eva Hakim declared. "Have any of the persons who partook of the refreshments at the gathering reported any difficulties?" She looked at the group muttering in the hall.

"I don't think so," Rav Eli reported.

"Then no one else is in danger," Dr. Moise announced. "Whatever did this, whether it was *nguba* or something else, it was meant for Master Kupernik and none other."

"That's comforting to know," Benyamin said sourly.

Selim had been examining the paper wrapping.

"Look here, Capitán. This is Snake's mark, here on the corner."

"So it is," Halvar agreed. "But Snake certainly didn't send this. He's been dead for three days."

"But someone sent the package in his name," Selim reasoned. "That means—"

"There was a connection between Snake and Master Kupernik. We already know that."

"But more, someone knew about it. Someone who could get at Snake's private stock of paper, and who knew about Master Kupernik's difficulty with certain foods."

"Someone who hated Master Kupernik? Who could convince someone, perhaps one of the madrassa servants, to deliver the food with the dangerous food in it, empty the water jug and jam the door? Someone who has a grudge against the madrassa itself?" Halvar's expression hardened. "Once I finish my investigation here, I think I will have to go back to Green Village and have another talk with Frater Leonidas."

Chapter 22

HALVAR LOOKED AROUND THE ROOM ONE MORE
time make sure he hadn't missed anything.

"Selim, we have to take these papers back to the Rabat,"
he ordered, gathering the loose items from Kupernik's desk.
"I want you and Benyamin to go over them carefully. It's
possible Master Kupernik left some kind of clue, something
to tell us who hated him so much as to wish him dead."

The imam began to speak, but Halvar went on without allowing him to say anything more.

"Revered Imam, learned masters, I must interview anyone who had anything to do with Master Kupernik—his
students, his colleagues, even the servants in this house.
Is there some place where I can do this in privacy?"

Eli wormed his way through the chattering crowd.

"If you please, Capitán, I have put a fire-pot in the library. You may conduct your business there."

Halvar followed the steward down the stairs to a small
room at the back of the house, Selim at his heels and the

155

rest of the company close behind them. The so-called library was little more than a pantry, located next to the kitchen, its built-in shelves filled with large and small bound books. More reading matter was stacked on the bookcases on either side of the door and made the room seem even smaller. There was no window to give light, but an oil lantern hung from the ceiling. Heat was provided by the coals that glowed in a brass foot-stove.

Halvar bent his head as he sidled through the small passage between two tables and the backless stool, which was jammed under the shelving. Selim wiggled into the space in front of the table; Imam Gamaliel managed to find a few feet of floor space in front of the door.

Halvar stacked two small books on top of three large ones on the larger table to make room for Selim to put her notebook. She appropriated the stool and sat down, her pen case with its vials of ink and her split-reed pens ready.

Imam Gamaliel followed her movements with narrowed eyes. Then he turned to Halvar.

"How long is this going to take?" he demanded. "There are lectures, classes…"

"Really? From what I've seen, most of the students at this madrassa spend their days either chasing balls and bladders or sitting in mokka-shops arguing," Halvar retorted. "I passed them on their way to Green Village yesterday. To be sure, it's Nativity, and Rest Day, but what about Yehudit? Is it a rest day for them?"

"Are you questioning the purpose of the madrassa? May I remind you, Capitán, that it is the Manatas Madrassa that attracts so many people to the city? We provide employment for servants, for sellers of books and paper. Those who attend the lectures must be fed and housed, which also provides employment, as well as a market for food vendors. The Manatas Madrassa is the most important institution on this island." Imam Gamaliel ended his tirade with a lofty sniff.

"I thought it was the feria brought trade here," Halvar observed.

Imam Gamaliel glared at this boor who dared to question the worthiness of his school.

"So say the merchants, but the ferias are only twice a year, whereas the madrassa is in session almost all the year around. The Manatas Madrassa is known as a haven for scholars of all sorts," he declared. "We may have begun as an adjunct to the Grand Muskat, as every muskat must have a madrassa to teach children their letters so they may read the Holy Book, and to educate the Faithful in the correct interpretation of the Prophet's teachings, but under the direction of Calif Don Carlos, of blessed memory, this madrassa was expanded to include such disciplines as law and medicine and rhetoric. We attracted teachers from Oropa and Bretain as well as the best of Al-Andalus. Our students come from all over Nova Mundum to absorb knowledge."

"You didn't mention natural philosophy, and alchemy, and mathematics. Which brings us to Master Kupernik. How did he come to be here? What do you know of his family, his background? Did he have any particular friends, lovers, enemies?"

"Master Kupernik arrived here some years ago, shortly after I did," Imam Gamaliel said. "At that time, he presented me with several letters from masters at the Collegium in Parigi attesting to his ability to instruct students in mathematics. It was brought to my attention that we did not have such a person on our faculty, and that this lack should be addressed. It was decided—"

"By who?" Halvar snapped.

"By the senior members of the madrassa," Imam Gamaliel retorted. "Myself, Rav Nahum, Master Rufford, and Mullah Abadul, who inserts himself into matters that do not concern him, but who insists that, since the Madrassa is a dependency of the Grand Muskat, he should have a voice in its affairs." He stopped for breath.

"Mullah Abadul doesn't care for Yehudit or Kristos," Halvar observed. "Did he make any objection to taking on Master Kupernik?"

"He did, but he was overruled," Imam Gamaliel said, with smug satisfaction.

"And how did that work out? From what I heard yesterday, Master Kupernik was not universally loved. And he had a few other quirks. How did you feel about his stargazing, for instance?"

Imam Gamaliel stroked his beard.

"I do not concern myself with the personalities of those who instruct our students. I ask only that they be proficient in their fields. In that, Master Kupernik was perfectly suitable to our mission.

"Mathematics is not a popular subject, but we insist that all students entering the madrassa must pass a written examination to prove they have a grasp of its basic principles. Master Kupernik instructed his students well enough. We were willing to allow him to pursue his other studies, so long as he taught the mathematics classes."

Halvar frowned. "Entering the madrassa...How does that work? For instance, young Selim, here...if he wished to join the madrassa as a student, how would he go about it?"

Imam Gamaliel eyed Selim.

"He is the sultan's son, is he not? There would be no difficulty in his entering. I believe he was tutored by one Leon di Vicenza, who has taken the name of Frater Leonidas and is now at the Green Village Fratery. How old are you, boy?"

"I will be sixteen on my next birthday," Selim quavered.

"Hmmm." Imama Gamaliel pondered this. "One more year, young man. Perhaps after the Fall Feria you may apply."

Selim's face fairly glowed as she bent over her notebook.

Halvar nodded. "What about someone who isn't so well-connected? I've been hearing a lot about a youngster called Snake, a messenger lad from the waterfront, who had aspirations of attending classes at the madrassa. Don Felipe, may he live long, made it clear when he became calif he would continue his grandfather's policy—anyone who could pay the lecture fees could attend the madrassa classes. Now I hear this fellow, Snake, was 'not madrassa material.' Why not? How does a Bretain from West Caster whose whole life's ambition seems to be to chase a little ball around field get in, and a clever lad born here in Manatas can't?"

Imama Gamaliel huffed. "It's not all that simple, Capitán. It's true anyone can apply to attend classes and lectures, but to become a member of the madrassa, to attain the honor of becoming a master, that is something quite different. The prospective student must show his worth by passing the examination not only in mathematics but in rhetoric, with a written statement—"

"In Arabi," Selim put in, from her place at the table.

"What if they can't speak or write Arabi?" Halvar asked. "The Bretains and Franchen Kristos, they don't usually study Arabi. In fact, the young man who was killed at the feria, young Owen, he could barely speak Arabi at all."

"In that case, they must take remedial classes," Imam Gamaliel said.

"Like the one Benyamin gives," Selim added.

Imam Gamaliel ignored the interruption.

"And if the student can find a sponsor, someone already connected with the Manatas Madrassa, so much the better."

"A sponsor?" Halvar thought that over. "So, if this fellow, Snake, who doesn't have a high-born father and isn't well-schooled, had the fee, and could find someone to vouch for him, and could pass your tests, he could become an official student? And then what? What's in it for him? What's the point of all this learning?"

"Knowledge is a goal in itself," the imam pronounced. "But, if you mean, what material gain is there to be had, may I remind you that most of our students are planning to become leaders of congregations of their own, either in some of the settled towns in Nova Mundum or carrying the Prophet's words to the far reaches of the hinterland.

159

The Locals still worship their forest demons, and there are far too many Afrikans who continue to believe in their false orishas."

"Besides, it's a mark of respectability to have been to the Madrassa, even for one or two seasons," Selim added. "And once he had the certificate, he could make a place for himself as an advocate, or maybe be a tally-man at the Rabat."

"And there's the purely practical stuff, like law and medicine," Halvar admitted. "A doctor or lawyer has to know what he's doing, and you don't want someone messing about with alchemy unless he knows exactly what he's about. I don't see Snake as a preacher—he was a devout Roumi Rite Kristo and the presters have their own schools, but he might have had his eye on a position at the Rabat, maybe as a tally-man, or even in the Town Guard."

"Like Tenente Ruiz," Selim suggested. She didn't bother adding that Ruiz had met a sorry end.

"Precisely so," Imam Gamaliel. "However, I'm not sure how much any of this will help you in finding out who killed our beloved Master Kupernik."

"Beloved?" Halvar scoffed. "He seemed to be intent on arguing with everyone and anyone he met. The only reason he didn't take me on was because I didn't speak to him. He insulted several of the masters in my presence, including Frater Leonidas, and this fellow LaPierre."

"I was not aware of such animosity," Imam Gamaliel said. "You must ask Rav Nahum about Master Kupernik's personality, since it is he who insisted he be added o our company."

"In that case, I'll have a word with Rav Nahum next," Halvar decided. "Thank you for your time, revered imam. Send in Rav Nahum."

The tubby Yehudit edged into the room behind Imam Gamaliel, squeezed past him through the open door.

"I don't know what to say!" Rav Nahum, who must have overheard the others' discussion, stuttered. "Master

Kupernik was respected by all, even those who disagreed with his theories of celestial bodies and their movements."

"And his disdain for alchemy," Halvar pointed out. "More to the point, what do you know of his personal life? Did he have any particular friends? What were his vices? Did he visit brothels? Gamble at cards, or tables?

"Brothels! No!" Rav Nahum exclaimed. "Certainly not! As for gambling, no one would play cards with him. He was far too knowledgeable about numbers. I have never seen him play at tables, although he was not averse to a game of chess now and again."

"If he didn't have a sweetheart, or go to brothels, did he have any friendships with young men?" Halvar suggested.

Rav Nahum's face reddened.

"Of course not! Such a thing is forbidden! If you are implying…"

"I'm trying to understand why someone would want to kill him," Halvar reminded him.

"If we hadn't been there, no one would have suspected it was murder," Selim pointed out.

"True," Halvar observed. "So, Rav Nahum, how many people knew of Master Kupernik's, um, possible peculiarity regarding nuts?"

Rav Nahum shrugged. "I cannot say. We noticed that he did not eat nuts, but we assumed it was only a peculiarity, as you say. We keep a kosher kitchen here, not merely halal. You would have to speak with our cook, the estimable Fru Zelda, for information about Master Kupernik's dietary habits. She knows all our little ways—that Master Vanderplatt prefers herring above all other fish, and that Master Uri Geller is not fond of sour cabbage soup. I myself have a difficulty with onions." He patted his rotund stomach.

"So, she'd know not to set anything with nuts before Master Kupernik," Halvar said. "And he wouldn't eat something if he didn't know what was in it. What about *nguba*?"

"Those Afrikan ground-beans?" Rav Nahum looked blank. "I have no idea. My field is rhetoric, that is, the proper use of language and oratory. I teach literature, the works of the Old Greco and Old Roumi. One of the Bretain masters also lectures on the Scanian and Bretain epics. I know nothing of natural philosophy or the properties of plants, nor do I attend the lectures on such matters."

"Stick to your own field, eh?" Halvar thought this over. "Never bother with alchemy, or mathematics, or astronomy?"

"I leave such things to those more knowledgeable than I. Although, I did attend that debate on the waterfront during the heat of the summer, when Master Kupernik was invited to present his theories of the motions of the stars to the public. A disputation at the Mermaid Taberna, that place on the waterfront. It was the idea of the fellow who calls himself Frater Leonidas. Then, he was—"

"Leon di Vicenza."

"Indeed." Rav Nauhm's voice sharpened. "A most unpleasant person, a scoffer. He offered to set up a public disputation of the sort popular in Corduva to break the monotony of the hot days between the Spring and Fall Ferias."

Halvar tugged at his mustache as he considered this.

"At the Mermaid Taberna. Gomez told me those debates used to get very heated, to the point where students drew knives on each other. Was this one of those occasions?"

"That one was something special," Selim enthused. "It was just after the Longest Day, what some call Midsummer. The Spring Feria was long over, it was really hot, and Leon thought it might be fun to have a debate in the plaza in front of the Mermaid Taberna. Everyone came, even my father, to hear the disputation between Master Kupernik and a frater from Green Village and one of the imams on the subject of the movements of the planets. Even the women from Maiden Lane and the Waterfront Rats came. It was very exciting!"

162

"A debate?" Halvar shook his head. "Manatas must have been very short of entertainment that day."

"Not at all," Rav Nahum huffed. "Intellectual stimulation is as important as physical stimulation. And there was much discussion afterward."

"Who won?" Halvar asked.

"Sultan Petrus was the judge, and he decided that since no one had ever actually been to the stars or the moon, all discussion on the subject was pure speculation," Rav Nahum said. "He awarded the honor of the disputation to Master Kupernik for his ingenious argument. Leon, who is now Frater Leonidas, was not pleased."

"I see where I'm going to have to have a very long talk with Frater Leonidas," Halvar mused. "So, what happened with regard to the *nguba*?"

Selim shrugged. "I wasn't paying much attention to Master Kupernik."

"I was sitting next to him when one of the Afrikan women came along with baskets of roasted *nguba* beans," Rav Nahum said. "I took one. I happen to enjoy them, and they are, after all, *pareve*—acceptable food at any time. I offered one to Master Kupernik, who had apparently never seen them. He put one into his mouth, then started choking and spat it out immediately. One of the men selling cider gave him a cup, he rinsed his mouth out, and said that he must never again eat those things."

Halvar nodded. "And who saw this, besides you?"

"I suppose anyone who was present could have." Rav Nahum sighed. "I couldn't tell you who was or was not there. It was quite a crowd, with Mullah Abadul preaching that Master Kupernik's theories were blasphemy, and our own Rav Shimon Layzar saying that the Holy Book is open to interpretation, and several of the seamen offering their opinions, based on their observations of the stars as they navigated the oceans."

"And then things got really interesting," Selim added. "Leon and the Seekers of Truth got into a fistfight with some of the Waterfront Rats, and someone yelled that the

Scavengers were picking pockets. And Tenente Gomez and his men had to break things up, before anyone really got hurt."

Eli popped his head in at the door.

"Rav Nahum, the messenger is at the kitchen door. Are there any packages, any messages to go to the other schools?"

"Messenger?" Halvar's head went up. "What messenger? This is Nativity Day, Kristos aren't supposed to be working."

"He's here anyway," Eli said. "Shall I have him take the message about Master Kupernik's untimely demise to the rest of the schools?"

"I'm sure Imam Gamaliel will see to that," Rav Nahum said.

"I want to see this messenger," Halvar decided.

He followed Eli to the back of the house, through the kitchen, to the pantry and the door leading to the alley. Three teenaged Scavengers in ragged kaftans, wool hats pulled down over their ears, were wrestling a basket of food refuse into a dogcart. Another youngster, taller and broader, in a faded jacket and baggy trousers stood next to them.

"That's Bull!" Selim called out from behind Halvar, pointing at the taller boy.

The three in kaftans turned to stare at the fourth boy, who backed away from the door.

"Hey, boy, I want to talk to you!" Halvar called out.

The Waterfront Rat turned and ran.

"Get him!" Halvar yelled.

And the chase was on!

Chapter 23

IN THE BRIEF MOMENT BEFORE THE YOUNG
Scavengers could understand what was being asked of them,
Bull ran through the alley, splashing through the muck. He
was clearly headed for the gap between the houses that led
to the tangle of streets and alleys comprising the souk, the central marketplace of Manatas.

Halvar paused on the threshold of the kitchen door to
orient himself in the geography of Manatas. If he was correct, he was facing west, towards the Great River. Therefore, the souk was on his left, to the south. Dark shadows
pressed in on him as the sun slipped behind the houses
facing west. The short day was coming to a close. Already,
the muezzins were calling for evening prayers at the Grand
Muscat behind him.

Selim didn't hesitate. She shoved Halvar out of the way
and ran into the street to rally the Scavengers behind her.

"Follow me!" she called out.

Two of them took off after her, while the third held on to the dog's harness, trying to restrain its eagerness to do likewise. It was no use—the animal sensed a hunt, and his ancient instincts took over. With an eager bark, he, too, joined the chase, forgetting there was a frail cart tied behind him.

The cart tipped over, spilling its contents across the ground. Slimy leaves, bones with a bit of flesh still clinging to them, stems and twigs covered the alley, mixing with the muddy residue left by the recent snow melt and refreeze. Little patches of ice were already forming as the evening chill set in, making the footing even more treacherous.

Halvar slipped and slid over the muck, caroming off the walls on both sides of the narrow passageway between the houses, wincing as each contact jarred his wounded shoulder. This was the part of Manatas no visitor ever saw, the back alleys where the Scavengers plied their trade, picking up the detritus left by householders for them to cart away to the pits at the end of the town wall.

He grabbed onto whatever rough edges he could, cursing under his breath as he felt the muck sinking into his boots, the cold creeping into his toes, as he tried to keep up with the younger pursuers.

The alley ended abruptly at an open junction with a side street, lined on both sides with sheds, shacks, and a few more substantial shops and houses, some shuttered, some open for business. Late-afternoon shoppers were making purchases from carts pulled by donkeys or dogs, while Afrikan and Local women were still hawking their roasted yams or ears of maiz from braziers set up in any available corner that was out of the wind. Nativity Day or not, Islim Rest Day or not, someone was sure to be selling something in the souk.

Halvar staggered into the street, peering over the crowd to catch sight of his quarry.

"There he is!"

Selim was already halfway down the street, gathering more young Scavengers as she ran through the stalls.

"What's happening?" one of them shouted.

"It's a Rat!" the dog-handler yelled back. "Get 'im!"

Bull dodged from behind a shed covered with used coats and jackets that flapped in the growing wind. He skidded around the donkey carts, shoving passers-by out of the way. A woman in a burka shrieked and dropped her basket as he pinched her, and a man yelled a Danic curse when Bull tried to push him into the middle of the street.

Behind Bull, the Scavengers and Selim left a trail of outraged shoppers in their path, while Halvar forged ahead, mentally regretting his lack of exercise over the past months. Sitting at a desk had left him weak. He should have been outside, running.

The chase wound around the sheds and shacks toward the posts that marked the entrance to the souk, the junction of the main path and the Broad Way marked by the arches of the facade of the Madrassa Assembly Hall. Bull stopped briefly and clung to one of the posts, his chest heaving.

Selim and her gang rushed to catch up to him.

"Where is he?" Selim tried to leap high enough to see over the crowd.

"He's at the Madrassa Assembly Hall," the dogcart Scavenger announced.

"If he can cross the Broad Way, he'll be out of our territory," another Scavenger reminded them. "The Rats own the East Side, we get the West Side. We've run him off!" There was a cheer from the Scavengers.

"I don't want him 'run off'!" Halvar panted as he caught up with them. "Don't let him get to the Waterfront."

"What do you want him for? He's just a Waterfront Rat," sneered a Scavenger who had slowed to stay next to Halvar.

"He knows something we want him to tell us," Halvar said. "Don't kill him!"

167

"We won't!" Selim yelled over her shoulder as she raced on. "Come on, let's get 'im!"

The young gang swarmed shrieking through the crowd, pursuing their quarry toward a tall guardsman standing on the Broad Way, halberd in hand, posed to present the most flattering picture of a man guarding the streets of Manatas from just the sort of rabble now heading towards him.

"Zoltan!" Halvar shouted. "Get that boy!"

The guardsman turned around as Bull barreled past him, followed by the rest of the screaming mob of teenagers. He waded into the crowd as they pounced on Bull, kicking, hitting, spitting their wrath and used the butt end of the halberd to shove the gang out of the way. Then, he grabbed Bull just as the boy scrambled to his feet and was poised to flee.

"Not so fast, youngster!"

"What is going on here?"

"What has this boy done?"

Shoppers gathered around Zoltan and his prisoner. Women in burkas, accompanied by their fierce-looking servants, were joined by men in kaftans and caps, while the dogs of the Local women added their voices to the growing din. A group of soberly clad Yehudit, led by Mendel the Bookseller, looked on in terrified fascination.

"Help me!" Bull pleaded. "I didn't do nothing, I swear it! Those Islim Scavengers, they chased me—"

"He's wanted by Capitán Don Alvaro!" Zoltan shouted. "Capitán! I've got him!"

"Tateh!" Benyamin puffed to the front of the line of Yehudit to stand next to his father. "I have to tell you…" He stared at Bull. "That's the messenger!"

Halvar had managed to shove through the crowd of holiday shoppers and worshipers to where Bull struggled in Zoltan's iron grip.

"Don't hurt him," he warned Zoltan. To the crowd, he said, "This boy is wanted for questioning, that's all. We're taking him to the Rabat."

"What has he done?" Mendel the Bookseller demand- ed "Where are you taking him?"

"He just told you." Benyamin gulped for air. "It's about Master Kupernik...he's dead."

The Yehudit muttered in great consternation.

"When? How?" Mendel exclaimed.

"Last night," Benyamin told him."We think, that is, Don Alvaro thinks..."

"Someone gave him something that made his throat close up," Halvar said, staring at Bull. "The doctors are open- ing his stomach right now to determine exactly what it was. All we want to know from this lad is whether he brought a package to the Yehudit House at the madrassa last night."

"And what if I did?" Bull blustered. "It's what I do! I deliver packages, messages..."

"Not in the souk, you don't!" one of the Scavengers retorted. "That's our territory! No Waterfront Rats allowed!"

Halvar intervened. "Whoever sent him to the Yehu- dit House knew what was in the package, and that's all we want to know—who sent that package. That's why we're questioning him. It's getting dark, it's getting cold, and we can't do it here. So, if you will allow us to do what you good folks pay us for, we'll just take this lad to the Rabat."

"Questioning?" Mendel said with a sneer. "We know about that kind of *questioning*."

A murmur was growing in the crowd. Things were beginning to get ugly.

"I didn't do anything! I'm just a messenger, one of the Waterfront Rats," Bull yelled. "They say I killed someone, but I didn't do anything! I just delivered a package, that's all I did!"

"If that's all you did, then you can tell us all about it in a place that's a lot warmer than this one," Halvar re- peated. "And then I will take you back to the Kristo chapel myself." He looked around at the crowd. "And if any of you wants to come to the Rabat and wait at the gate, you

169

are welcome to do so. But like I said, it's getting dark, and it's a cold night. And don't you Yehudit do something with lamps at this time of the year?"

Mendel consulted with his son, then turned to his friends.

"Benyamin says that this youngster may know who sent poisoned food to our well-known scholar Master Kupernik. If so, then we should let Capitán Don Alvaro find out what he knows. Master Kupernik was a respected member of our community. His loss is considerable."

"Who cares about another Yehudit dead? They killed the Redeemer!" Bull yelled.

Zoltan gave the boy a shake. "You mind your tongue, Rat," he warned. "If Don Alvaro don't get you, I will."

"Enough, Guardsman Zoltan," Halvar said. "I'll take care of this Rat...or should I say, Bull? That's what they call you?"

"Tauro, that's right. Although my name is Tomas." Bull squared his shoulders, standing tall, meeting Halvar's gaze. "And I won't tell you nothing."

"You've already told me something," Halvar said. "And you will tell me more." He turned to the Scavengers. "Thank you for your efforts, but I think you have to tend to your dog."

The animal had knocked down a stall where sausages were being sold and was eagerly consuming as many as it could find.

"Jolly! Stop that!" One of the Scavenger lads ran to haul the dog away from his treat, another held out a hand, the universal sign for alms.

Halvar sighed, took out his string of wumpum, and slid a purple bead off one end and four white ones off the other.

"The purple will pay for what the dog ate, and the whites are for you and your friends. And don't tell that emir where you got them."

The rest of the Scavengers took off after the dog.

170

Zoltan sneered. "You shouldn't have paid them, Capitán. Those Scavenger brats are all over the souk, picking up this and that. Half of them are cutpurses and pickpockets, and the rest are soliciting."

"That's why I put you here, Guardsman," Halvar said. "Good work, stopping the boy. Carry on until sundown, then you can go to the barracks for your meal."

Bull twisted out of Zoltan's grip, only to be grabbed by the collar by Halvar.

"No, you don't, laddie. You're coming with us!"

Halvar marched him along, with Selim hovering behind well out of Bull's line of sight. He wanted answers, and he would wring them out of this lad before the night was over.

Chapter 24

TORCHES WERE BEING LIT IN THE COURTYARD
as Halvar, Selim and Bull were let into the Rabat by one of
the guards on duty.

"Bring mokka and one of those hot yams to my office," Halvar ordered. "And bring a fire-pot, too." He looked
around the courtyard. "Has Tenente Flores come back from
the Street of the Afrikans yet?"

"No, Capitán," the guardsman said. "He only left a few
minutes ago."

Halvar made an exasperated noise. Flores had surely
had enough time to get to the Street of the Afrikans and
back by now. Granted, he'd had to persuade the sultan
to sign the firman that would allow him to enter Igbo's
residence, but it shouldn't have taken that long, even if
Sultan Petrus wasn't inclined to discomfort the Afrikan
traders on whose good will the prosperity of Manatas
depended. He'd have to have a talk with his tenentes about
obeying orders speedily.

Meanwhile, there was the matter of the messenger, the package he had delivered, and, possibly, the whereabouts of Snake over the last few days.

Bull glowered at Halvar as he was thrust into the small room Halvar used as a private office. It contained the Oropan-style table and chair that suited Halvar's long frame better than the low table and cushions preferred by his predecessor, a small table and low chair, and a three-legged stool. Selim took her place at the small table, where a lamp had been lit, and placed her notebook and pen-case at the ready. Bull was shoved onto the stool by the guardsman who'd led the procession to the office, while another guardsmen bustled in with a brass fire-pot. The Local woman who supplied the guardsmen with snacks and mokka delivered Halvar's late-afternoon treat, salaamed, and left, along with the first guardsman. The second stood in the doorway, waiting for orders.

"Stay by the door, outside," Halvar told him. "I don't think this lad will bolt, but he may be stupid enough to try it. And let me know as soon as Tenente Flores gets here with Heer Samuel Igbo."

Bull squawked, "Igbo!" and jumped off the stool. The guardsman blocked his way.

"Sit down, laddie," Halvar ordered.

Bull cringed back onto the stool.

Halvar sipped his mokka, eying the youngster, taking his measure. Bull was a good name for him; he was already broad in the shoulders, with a round face surmounted by a mop of reddish-brown hair that peeked out from under the wool cap covering his ears against the cold.

Halvar's eyes narrowed as he recalled another overgrown youngster, cringing before his superiors, knowing he'd made a grievous error in judgment and fearing the punishment he knew was coming. Twenty years ago, that lad was he, lured away from his post by a pretty Yehudit girl while her kinsmen rifled the storeroom he had been set to guard. Was Bull like him, easily taken in by false promises? Or was something else going on, something

173

deeper and more sinister? How much did this lad really know?

Bull shivered and pulled his jacket tighter across his chest as he glanced around the room. His eyes lit on Selim, who cowered back into the shadow.

"I know you!" he cried. "You're the one who follows the capitán around Manatas. I thought I knew you last night at the chapel, only you were dressed like a girl then."

"And what of it?" Halvar countered.

"That isn't a boy. That's a girl!"

"And just how do you know that?"

"Because...because..." Bull stuttered.

"Because you assaulted her," Halvar finished for him. "You tried to rape her."

"Rape?" Bull yelped. "I didn't! He...I mean, she...went to the dormitory while we were serving the Holy Meal. I followed her, to see what she...he...was up to. I found her bending over Snake's bed, and grabbed her..."

"You put your hands right under my shirt!" Selim interrupted his excuses.

"I sure did, to stop you from taking whatever you found from under Snake's mattress. I wasn't sure if you were a boy dressed as a girl or a girl dressed like a boy, but I knew I'd seen you at the Mermaid Taberna, and you were there when they found Capitán Girard behind the whore's crib on Maiden Lane. And when I felt tits, I knew you're a girl, not a boy. I know the difference, I've been to the cribs, I know what a girl feels like, and this Selim isn't a boy, she's a girl. So I tried to stop her by laying on top of her."

"You tried to kiss me!" Selim protested.

"I didn't want you yelling," Bull retorted. "And then... she...he...hit me!"

"I gave you a smack, that's all. And you let go, and I got away, and I ran back to the Broad Way, with Snake's papers," Selim finished with a satisfied smirk.

"I'll tell Prester Nicodemus, and he'll tell everyone else."

174

"And if you do, you will find yourself in great trouble, Bull, or Tomas, whatever you want to call yourself," Halvar broke into the squabble. "This is the child of our sultan, and if you announce that Selim is no boy, then you will have to explain how you know, and that means confessing to attempted rape. Do you really want to do that? When you know the sultan will be the one to pass sentence?"

"Then she shouldn't have gone up to the dormitory," Bull grumbled. "And she shouldn't wear boy's clothing."

"Selim wears boy's clothes so that louts like you won't do what you did. And she went to the chapel to find out more about Snake. And to find out exactly who was the messenger Captain Girard sent when he came into port, where the message went, and what the answer was, if any."

"It was like Prester Nicodemus told you," Bull said. "Snake went out when the Franchen captain came into port, and then he came back. And when we heard the captain's body was found, he was very disturbed, but he only did his usual rounds—the madrassa, the west side of the Broad Way, up to the Street of the Afrikans."

Bull stopped for breath.

"What about the next day? The day of the storm? Why did he go out then?"

Bull rubbed his nose. "I'm not sure. I think he said something about having to pick up a package at the Street of the Afrikans, and he went out. That was while we were all watching you fight that Bretain milord with the sword, and the ship was trying to get out of the harbor."

"Snake went out and didn't come back." Halvar considered his next question. "When the Franchen captain came to the chapel, did he ask for any particular messenger, or was it the luck of the draw? Why did Snake go, and not you, for instance?"

Bull glowered resentfully. "Prester Nicodemus told the Franchen that Snake was the cleverest and fastest, and that he could be relied on to deliver the message properly. I could have done it just as well."

175

"Think yourself lucky you didn't," Halvar told him. "Otherwise, it might be you lying in Dr. Moise's shed instead of him."

"No, it wouldn't," Bull retorted. "Because I wouldn't have been so greedy. Snake got a whole silver imperial for running that message to the Street of the Afrikans, and he didn't even share it with the rest of us."

"And how do you know that?"

"Because he showed the coin to Mouse, in secret. I followed him when he took Mouse up to the dormitory and showed him his private stash of coins. Oh, he gave his tips, all in wumpum, into the general store, but the coins—the silver imperial and the Bretain penny and the iron Afrikan token—those he kept for himself. And he was going to spend them on himself, too, and not share the way Prester Nicodemus told us was the way of the Redeemer and his Followers."

"Spend them how?"

Bull could not contain his anger any longer.

"He told Mouse now that he had the money, he could get into the madrassa. He wanted to improve himself, get learning, maybe join the tally-men at the Rabat, or be an assistant in a advocate's office. He was even practicing writing in Arabi, copying words out of the *Gazetta*. He said he a sponsor, one of the professors at the madrassa, who would speak up for him and see him through the examinations."

"Ambitious," Halvar said as Bull's rant grew more and more frenzied.

"And for what? To be a tally-man, entering numbers in a book? To be an advocate, writing contracts all day? No one would allow a Waterfront Rat to sit with the sons of merchants and planters of kutton and tabac, no matter how many examinations they passed." Bull sneered. "We're the Waterfront Rats! That's all we'll ever be!"

"You might consider joining the Town Guards," Halvar suggested.

Bull spat his contempt. "Town Guards? For what? To stand out in the cold and rain every day? To chase the Scavengers in the souk? And for a few wumpum and a meal at the barracks? Being a Waterfront Rat is better. At least no one comes after you with a knife.

"But Snake thought he could do better, and he was wrong. Me, I'll stay at the chapel as along as I can, and when that's done, I can take a place with one of the merchants. They're always sending runners into the backcountry, to the Local villages. I can talk Munsi. I don't need a madrassa."

"The calif Don Felipe made it clear he wants all the folk in his realm to learn their letters, at a madrassa or at a chapel school," Halvar said. "And he's all in favor of anyone, rich or poor, attending the lectures at the higher madrassa, whether in Corduva or Manatas."

"The calif? Much he cares about Manatas. The only reason he came here was because Imperator Lovis kicked him out of Hispania, together with the rest of the Islim and Yehudit." Bull retorted. "Snake thought himself so clever because he could write and read, and it got him killed!" The boy's face twisted in pain as he rocked back and forth on the stool, tears leaking out of his eyes. "He thought he could get more money from the one who got the message, the one from Green Village, and the Afrkian, the one who was the middleman. I told him not to do it, I said they were too big for him, but he thought he was so clever! And he paid for it!"

"You saw it, didn't you," Halvar said, realization dawning. "While I was chasing after the one who killed the captain, Snake took a message to the Afrikan Igbo that the Franchen was dead, and whatever meeting was supposed to take place, the deal was off. Then Snake went to Igbo to extort more money from him to keep quiet about the arrangement with the Bretains, and you followed him, because you are a jealous, greedy boy, and you wanted to grab some of that silver for yourself."

"No! I didn't…it wasn't that way…" Bull blubbered. "I just wanted to know where he got the coins. I didn't think… I didn't know…" He took a deep breath. "It was the way Snake acted, when they took the Franchen away that morning. He was worried, and he went off by himself to write a note in Arabi, looking at the *Gazetta* to copy the words."

"The note he sent to Kupernik," Selim whispered.

Bull went on. "He did his rounds, going to the madrassa, and the Street of the Afrikans, and when he came back for dinner, he looked right smug, like he'd done something very clever. And the next day, just after they found the dead whore, before the snow came, he went out after we'd had our break-the-fast. And I followed him because… because…" Bull stopped.

"The whole business smelled wrong," Halvar finished for him, with a knowing smile. "You wanted to find out why Snake was so upset and then so sure of himself. So you followed him."

Bull nodded. "I did. Snake went to the Street of the Afrikans, to the house of the merchant, Samuel Igbo, the one with the big red markings on it, like the ones from Afrika."

"I knew it!" Halvar smacked the table. "Igbo! He's at the bottom of this business! What did you do next, laddie?"

Bull spoke with more confidence. "I hid behind the baskets and jars where the waste was set for the Scavengers to pick up. I saw Snake go to the back door in the alley where we always get the packages and letters. He called out, but Igbo didn't come out. Instead, a Bretain came around the side of the house—"

"What Bretain? Did you see his face" Halvar interrupted.

"I didn't know him, but it had to be a Bretain. He had one of those big hats, with the wide brim, and he had some kind of cloak that covered his chin, and he wore dark trews instead of wool breeches or a long robe, like the Oropans and the Andalusians. He came up behind Snake, took a pistoia out from under his cloak…" Bull's voice cracked, and he choked on a sob.

"And shot Snake in the back, in broad daylight," Halvar finished the tale. "And you did nothing? Said nothing? Didn't send for the Town Guards, didn't rouse the neighbors?"

"What could I do?" Bull cried out. "I could see that Snake was dead! Samuel Igbo came out of his house, and I didn't want him to see me, so I went back to the chapel."

"And still you said and did nothing? Didn't you even wonder about whether Snake's body would be found?" Selim cried out from her corner. "You left him lying there, in the street!"

"Samuel Igbo was there, I thought he'd take care of it," Bull blustered.

"Oh, he took care of it, all right," Selim spat out. "He got one of the Scavengers to carry Snake's body around the gate and throw it behind the wall for the animals to eat! Only it got covered up with snow, so they didn't eat it, and the Mahak patrol found it instead, after two whole days had passed. You are disgusting!"

Bull wiped his nose on his sleeve.

"I prayed for his soul," he quavered. "I hoped someone would find him, and they did."

"But you didn't tell anyone who shot him," Halvar reminded him.

"I didn't see exactly who it was, only that it was a Bretain. And it could have been someone else, even an Afrikan, wearing a tall hat and a cloak." Bull looked from Halvar to Selim. "And I couldn't let the other Rats know I didn't trust Snake. And I was right not to trust him. He'd written something and left a message with someone at the madrassa. And he hadn't told me anything!"

Halvar sighed. "I've already got someone looking for the Bretain who got the message from Snake," he said. "Now you can tell me about last night. Who gave you the package to take to the madrassa?"

179

Bull shifted uneasily on the stool.

"I'm not sure. It was going on for dark, and all I could tell was that it was an Afrikan. At least, he sounded like an Afrikan, and he was wrapped up in one of those long capes the Afrikans wear, the ones that cover their heads with a hood, so I couldn't make out his face. But his voice was deep. He wore gloves, too, so I didn't see his hands." But I will swear to you by anything you like it was a man —a tall man—not a woman."

Halvar thought this over.

"Did this Afrikan come to the chapel? Did he ask for you, in particular, or would any of the messengers have done?"

Bull shrugged. "He didn't come to the chapel. I was doing my rounds, along the mokka-shops on the Broad Way, delivering the last messages for the day, and I was about to go back to the chapel to serve the Holy Meal for the Watch-Night, but then there was this man behind me. He stopped me and said he had one last task for me to do before dark. He gave me a package, told me it was to be delivered to the Yehudit House behind the madrassa, and gave me six white wumpum to do it. That's twice the usual fee."

"And you thought you could hand over the three whites and keep the other three for yourself," Selim sniffed.

"Why not? Snake did! I was going to give half to the general fund," Bull protested.

Halvar brought them back to the topic at hand.

"Exactly what time was this? Was it before or after mid-afternoon prayers?"

"It was after, nearly dark. I delivered the package, and when I came back to the chapel, you were there telling Prester Nicodemus about Snake. And I was glad, because now I didn't have to worry about Snake not being found and his spirit roaming, haunting us."

"If he haunts you, it's because you left him there, alone, in the alley, instead of doing what a good Kristo would do—finding a doctor to tend him in case he was still alive, and sending for the Town Guard to get the one who did it." Halvar dismissed the idea of spiritual revenge with a wave of his hand. "So, you delivered the package to the Yehudit House at the madrassa. What kind of a package was it? Hard or soft? Could you tell what was in it?"

"It was wrapped in paper, like the goods you buy at the souk," Bull said. "It wasn't a box, or a book—it wasn't hard. I supposed it was a festival gift, since it was going to the Yehudit House, and they're having their Festival of Lights, when they send gifts back and forth. Cakes and other sweets, sometimes boxes with little toys or books. Things like that."

"Cakes," Halvar muttered. "Cakes, baked by Afrikans, who use ground *nguba* like flour. And you delivered it to Master Kupernik yourself?"

"Who?" Bull asked with a puzzled frown.

"The package, these cakes–they were to go to Master Kupernik."

"Wasn't he the funny one, the one who says the moon goes around the Earth, and the Earth goes around the sun? The one who was at the big fight on the waterfront? No, that wasn't him. The package was to go to Master LaPierre, and that's exactly who I gave it to!" Bull exclaimed. "You can't say I didn't! I went to the kitchen, and I put the package right into his hands."

"Master LaPierre? The alchemist? Why would he be getting cakes from an Afrikan?" Selim asked.

"A good question, which I am going to pose as soon as I can find him." Halvar said. "Meanwhile, I think I will take this fine lad back to the Kristo Chapel, where he can pray for the soul of his poor friend."

"And that's all?" Selim cried out. "He's not going to be punished?"

"I think he's been punishing himself for the last three days," Halvar said. "And he's going to get a lot worse from Prester Nicodemus. Come along, laddie. As for you, Selim, I told you what you have to do. Stay here, go over those papers we took from Master Kupernik's desk, and see what you can make of them. Look for anything connected with alchemy, especially black powder. I'm starting to get an idea of what has been brewing at the madrassa, and why someone felt that Master Kupernik was dangerous."

He left her puzzling over the sheaf of papers she took out from under her jacket.

Bull allowed himself to be marched back to the Rabat gate, where Halvar stopped to let Flores and his squad pass by.

"Where's Igbo?" he demanded as he realized the Afrikan was not among them.

"He's gone." Flores confessed. "Capitán…it took some time to get that firman you wanted. Sultan Petrus was napping, and we couldn't wake him up, could we? It was nearly dark by the time we got to Igbo's villa, and he was not there. I went in, searched the place, even got Lady Tekla's cook to go into the harem to make sure he wasn't hiding among his women, but he's gone."

"Thor's Hammer!" Halvar swore.

"He can't have gone far," Flores soothed him. "It's full dark, and no one's going anywhere tonight. It's freezing cold, and this wind makes it worse. The East Channels' full of ice, he's not about to swim in it! We'll be after him tomorrow at first light."

"And make sure you get him alive," Halvar warned him. "I'm taking this lad to the Kristo Chapel on the waterfront, and then I'll be at the Mermaid Taberna for my dinner after that. And let's hope no one gets killed before tomorrow morning."

He headed towards the gate, only to be stopped by Dr. Moise.

"Where do you think you are going?" the Afrikan demanded.

"I am taking this lad to the Roumi Rite Chapel, and then I am going to the Mermaid Taberna, where I will have some of Fru Marta's excellent cooking and play a game or two of tables with Baltasar," Halvar said. "And I am

182

willing to lay any wager you like that you found the remains of some kind of cake in Master Kupernik's stomach when you opened him up."

"I didn't do the opening, that young sprout Efrem Russo insisted on doing it," Dr. Moise grumbled. "But we did
find something that looked like bread or cake, something
with grains and bits of nut-meats in it."

"And that's what killed him," Halvar said. He started
towards the gate.

"And you are going to come inside and get your bandage changed, if you don't want to join him in the next
world," Dr. Moise warned him. "Eva Hakim has given me
some kind of Local salve that she swears will draw the
infection from your shoulder."

Halvar sighed, and loosened his grip on Bull. The Waterfront Rat wrenched away from him, ran across the courtyard, and slid out the gate before anyone had the wit to
stop him.

"He's heading back to the chapel, where Prester Nicodemus will protect him," Dr. Moise assured Halvar. "You
won't be any good to anyone if you are raging with fever."

Reluctantly, Halvar followed his chosen physician to
the infirmary and allowed him to remove the bandage, smear
an odorous salve on his shoulder, and replace the bandage
with a clean one.

"You've been in a fight," Dr. Moise clucked, regarding the oozing wound.

"I banged up against some walls," Halvar explained.

"Take the advice of your doctor. Go back to your warm
taberna, have nourishing broth and fowl, and go to bed,"
Dr. Moise chided.

"And so I will," Halvar promised. "Just as soon as I
have a few words with Prester Nicodemus. Those Waterfront Rats could be a valuable source of information."

"If they'll give it to you," Dr. Moise muttered as Halvar proceeded back to the Waterfront.

Chapter 25

NATIVITY NIGHT WAS THE OCCASION FOR FES-
tivities in the Kristo homes just south of the Town Wall, even
as the Festival of Lights drew to a close in the Yehudit Quarter behind the souk. Many mokka-shops closed early; the
few that stayed open past nightfall hung lanterns in front of
the door to let those folk who had no place better to go know
here, at least, was food and company.

Halvar proceeded down the path behind the Mermaid
Taberna, noting how lights flickered in all three cottages
on Pearl Street.

"Milord is dining at home," he murmured. "So much
the better! I won't have to look at his fat face or listen to
his loud voice."

Hannes Zilberstam had set lanterns in front of the taberna to light the way for his customers. Halvar inhaled the
luscious aromas of roasting meat and baking bread. The
mokka and yam he'd had as an afternoon snack had merely whetted his appetite for more substantial fare.

The ringing of the chapel bell reminded him his day was not over. He still had one more interview to conduct, and it would not be a pleasant one.

First, there was the matter of the Holy Meal. It would never do for the Redeemer and Mother Mara to think that their devoted follower Halvar Danske had forgotten them in his pursuit of murderers. He crossed the plaza, passed the pawnbrokers shop (now being run by a group of Local women), and went north on Maiden Lane., following the last worshipers to crowd into the wooden shack where the Roumi Rite Kristos held their services.

The unheated shack drew an odd group to praise the Redeemer and his Mother— Franchen sailors in canvas breeches and jackets; the women who serviced the sailors, decked out in striped or checked skirts and matching jackets, or faded silk dresses that might have once belonged to wealthy Franchen merchants' wives; Local women in deerskin skirts and bead-trimmed cloth blouses, huddling under fur wraps. Baltasar and Lukas, the gamblers who frequented the Mermaid Taberna, squeezed in behind Halvar, shoving their protege, Little Jeannot, ahead of them. Halvar found himself wedged into the corner, where he could observe everything and everyone without being seen himself.

He checked the room again. In the corner opposite his he saw a wide-brimmed hat with a plume. Devallon must have decided to attend the Roumi Rite after all. There was no sign of Milord Summersby or his constant companion, Edgar Norris. Presumably, they felt they had done their religious duty at the Erse Rite service the night before.

Prester Nicodemus, his usual black robe covered with a red stole trimmed with gold, stood in front of the carved table that served as an altar, which had been covered with a white cloth. A large gold crux, a silver goblet, and a plate with the Holy Bread had been laid out for the ceremony. Foxy stood at one end of the table holding a round brass censer; Bull stood at the other end, his hair still ruffled but his face serious, evidence he knew the importance of his

185

part. Little Mouse and the rest of the boys stood to one side, prepared to sing the responses to the prayers in the sonorous Old Roumi few could understand but Episcopus Innocente had decreed was the only language holy enough to address the Redeemer, his Father, and Mother Mara.

The Roumi Rite Holy Meal was more elaborate than the Erse Rite, with incense waved about and bells rung after each prayer. Prester Nicodemus prepared the bread and wine, and the Waterfront Rats sang shrilly, drowning out the other responses. Prester Nicodemus served the bread and wine only to himself and the boys; everyone else had to make do with a blessing.

At last, Prester Nicodemus announced, in Old Roumi, "*Ita missa est.*"

The final bell rang, the crowd filed out, and the boys began to remove the ceremonial items from the table. Prester Nicodemus stood by the door, making the sign of the crux as each of his congregants passed by.

"I see you have decided to join us," he said to Halvar.

"I wanted to make sure your lad Bull got home safely," Halvar said. "He's been under a great burden. And I have a few more questions I think you can answer."

Prester Nicodemus sighed. "Bull has been unusually silent these last few days. I thought he might have something to tell me, but he is a headstrong young man, and prefers not to confide in me."

"Not even in the confessional?"

"If he had done that, I could not tell you," Prester Nicodemus reminded him. "You said you had more questions? I have already told you what I know of Snake. I don't see what I can add."

"I was wondering about how the lad came to be sent out out so late at night, alone, in the dark. Your lads don't deliver messages after dark, do they?"

"Not as a rule, no."

Foxy came up behind the prester to remove his festival mantle. Prester Nicodemus dismissed him with a wave.

"Go to your dinner, Foxy. Tell the others I will join them as soon as Capitán Don Alvaro has gone."

"You take good care of those lads," Halvar commented. "Which makes me think you know more than you are saying. Don't tell me you weren't worried about him, Prester. And don't try to lie. I already know a good deal about what went on that night.

"I know that when the Franchen, Captain Girard, came into port last week he wanted a message sent, even though it nearly night, and there was a storm on the way. I know Snake took that message. Was there any reason he was sent, and not, say, Bull? Or the redhead—Foxy? Or even little Mouse?"

"I really couldn't say why Snake went," Prester Nicodemus said. "Captain Girard may have asked for him, or Snake may have offered. I cannot say which."

"You didn't send him yourself?"

"What? Are you suggesting I deliberately sent the lad out at night? It was a message, that was all. He had a lantern with him, and I made sure he had on a warm jacket and wool hat when he left."

"What kind of message? Written or spoken?" Halvar persisted.

"I can't recall." Prester Nicodemus moved toward the door, obviously wanting to end the conversation.

"Try," Halvar pressed him. "Because whatever that message was, Snake was told to pass it on to someone in Green Village, which he did. The following day, we found the body of Captain Girard, which disturbed Snake greatly, according to young Bull. That same day, he went first to the madrassa, and then to the Street of the Afrikans, and when he came back, he seemed quite relieved, even smug. And the day after that, right after we discovered the dead woman on Maiden Lane, the day of the storm, Snake went out and didn't come back.

"I have to wonder, Prester Nicodemus, why you were not worried about him. I would be. If a lad in my care went

187

off and didn't return for two whole days, I'd be very worried. So, why weren't you, Prester Nicodemus?"

Prester Nicodemus paled and bit his lip.

"I *was* worried. But I got word he was in Green Village—"

"Got word? How? From whom? I thought your boys were the only ones carrying messages in Manatas."

Prester Nicodemus was growing more and more flustered.

"I cannot say how. That is, it might have been an Afrikan servant, or maybe one of the Scavengers, but I told the boys that Snake had been detained by the snow. As to whether Snake offered to go, or I sent him, or Captain Girard asked for him in particular, I only know that he went, that he returned, and that he went out again two days later. I was somewhat worried, yes, but I…that is, Snake was quite capable of talking his way out of any difficulty." He stopped, red-faced.

"And you never thought to call for the Town Guard to find him, when he'd been missing for three days?"

"There was the furore over the dead Franchen, and the business with the wreck in the harbor," Prester Nicodemus countered. "And I had been assured he was safe."

"Safely in the next world," Halvar said grimly. "You can get his body from the Rabat tomorrow, now that Dr. Moise is finished with it, and put it into the earth in the Kristo cemetery."

Prester Nicodemus made the sign of the crux.

"I will do so. You may not believe this, Capitán, but I am truly unhappy at how Snake met his end."

Halvar nodded, turned to go, then turned back.

"One more thing…your lad Bull—does he take Snake's place as head of the Waterfront Rats?"

"I suppose so," Prester Nicodemus said. "He is strong, speaks well…"

"And loudly," Halvar agreed. "He and Snake were rivals?"

"You might say that. In the way of lads, they were always trying to best each other. Bull is strong but sometimes slow, doesn't always understand what he sees, or what a joke means. Snake was not as strong but had a quicker wit, and a vicious tongue he sometimes used to make jokes at Bull's expense. I do believe he might have gone far, well beyond the waterfront, had he not been cut down." Prester Nicodemus sighed loudly. "I even considered sending him to the Roumi Rite school at Bella Mara for training as a prester."

"I saw some papers, copies of the *Gazetta*, where he had copied words from Old Roumi to Arabi letters. He was apparently trying to teach himself Arabi script so he could take the examination for the madrassa. I found a note on the desk of Master Kupernik asking for a meeting."

"Kupernik!" Prester Nicodemus's placid expression had turned to one of loathing. "A Yehudit scoffer, one of those who called for the Redeemer's death, who deny the Redeemer's grace, who dare to refute the Holy Book, who argue that the heavens were not perfect, and who said he would prove it when he got his spying-glass and could show there were things in the sky we could not see with our own eyes! He was shameless, even took his heresies to the people, speaking in the plaza during the summer—"

"So I heard." Halvar murmured.

The Kristo ranted on. "Snake was enthralled by the idea of a public disputation, free to anyone who cared to attend. I told him not to go, but he insisted, and listened to the man's theories."

"You said he attended the debates at the Mermaid Taberna."

"Snake attended those, yes. Against my better judgment, but I did not try to stop him. He had it in his head that if he could get someone to sponsor him, he could enter the madrassa. A vain hope!"

"I know he tried to get Leon...that is, Frater Leonidas... to do it."

"Leon di Vicenza!" Prester Nicodemus spat the name. "A lecher, a lover of men! He was seen at the forge all last summer, mooning over the Mahak apprentice. Disgusting man!"

"He's in the Green Village Fratery now and swears he's changed his ways," Halvar said. "More to the point, might Snake have tried to get one of the other masters to sponsor him? One of the ones who spoke at the Mermaid Taberna debates? Master Kupernik, perhaps"

"It is possible," Prester Nicodemus said thoughtfully. "Right after the disputation in the plaza he changed his route, from the east side of the Broad Way, where the mokka-shops are located, to the west side, where the madrassa schools are. He let Bull do the mokka-shops. It was odd, because until then he kept the mokka-shop route for himself, since the scholars at the madrassa are notorious for not giving gratuities, whereas the patrons of the mokka-shops are merchants, who are generous with their wumpum."

"Someone was generous," Halvar said. "Snake had a silver imperial and a Bretain penny sewn into his jacket, together with an iron Afrikan token."

"That was not right," Prester Nicodemus said. "All funds are to be held in common."

"Except that Snake didn't want to put those coins into the common fund," Halvar pointed out. "I think he was planning to use something he found out on that last run to persuade Master Kupernik to sponsor him for the madrassa examinations. Maybe even to coach him in the examination so he'd do well enough they would overlook his poverty and lack of family."

"Poor lad," Prester Nicodemus mourned. "Whatever he knew, it died with him."

"Maybe not," Halvar said. "Master Kupernik may have written it down in one of the papers we found when we searched his desk this afternoon."

"Searched? But...why?" Prester Nicodemus asked with a puzzled frown.

"I don't suppose Daoud the News-crier has gotten to the waterfront with this information yet. Master Kupernik was found dead in his rooms earlier today."

"What? How?" Prester Nicodemus sputtered.

"It seems someone sent him a festival gift, a cake with something in it he should not eat. Not poison to anyone but him. And it also seems that cake was delivered to the Yehudit House by none other than your prize pupil, Bull. I would suggest you take very good care of that lad, Prester, lest he suffer the same fate as Snake."

With that, Halvar bowed to the crux and left the chapel. The lights of the Mermaid Taberna beckoned. He could almost taste the long-overdue festive meal he had waited all day to consume. He only hoped he would be allowed to finish it.

Chapter 26

HANNES ZILBERSTAM HAD LEFT HIS YULE DECOR-
ations up to adorn the Mermaid Taberna until the Turning
Night. The scent of pine boughs nearly overtook the aromas wafting from the kitchen. Candles were placed on each
of the small tables set around the main floor, leaving space
for whatever entertainment would appear. Apparently, Willem of Cos had decided to remain at the Gardens of Paradise;
the space was empty.

Halvar scanned the room, mentally checking off familiar faces. The sailors from the *Belle Fleur* had discovered the Mermaid Taberna was more welcoming than the
Maison Rouge and sat at a table near the fireplace. He
spotted several Danic merchants, drawn by the hope of a
good, plain dinner without the exotic spices preferred by
Andalusians. And there, right next to his own table, was
a large hat with a plume, and under it…

Devallon sprawled on the bench beside Halvar's favorite spot, the table against the wall next to the stairs that
led to his quarters.

"Landsman!" Hannes greeted Halvar effusively. "We were worried about you. You didn't come home last night."

"It's a long tale, and I'm dry. Mulled ale, and something solid to go with it," Halvar ordered. He glared at Devallon, who edged over to allow him to sit on the bench.

"How's the shoulder?" the musketman asked.

"It hurts," Halvar replied, easing back against the wall. "What are you doing here? Why aren't you dancing attendance on Milord Summersby?"

"Milord has a new fancy," Devallon said. "He saw the animal in the field last night. What they call the mountain cat?"

"I think the Locals call it a cougar," Halvar informed him.

"Whatever it is, he's decided to go a-hunting. I'm here to see if anyone else wants to go with him. Edgar's gone to the house where the Bretain students live, the ones who know the ways of the beasts in Nova Mundum. He thinks they can show him where the animal can be found. It would be easier if we could enlist the Locals, but they're making themselves scarce. How do you find that fellow, the big one, the one you call Firebrand?"

"I don't find him; he just comes when he feels like it," Halvar groused. His bad mood dissipated as Hannes bustled forward with a large tankard of steaming liquid. He seized it and took a hearty swig. "My thanks, Hannes, I'm chilled to the bone. What's for dinner? I'm famished!"

Hannes recited the menu.

"Fru Marta has roasted an entire gobble-bird in the oven, with yams and carrots, and she's made the giblets into a good hearty soup, with wheaten noodles to make it heartier. There are pigeons, freshly taken, cooked on the spit then put into a pie. A sallet of greens, if you wish, and ears of maiz, roasted in the ashes, as the Locals do. And several sweets, for the end of the meal."

"Bring on the soup, then the bird, and whatever else you like. Just put the lot on my bill."

"If I may…" Hannes said, hesitantly. "This bill of yours, it's mounting up. When will you settle it, Capitán?"

"I said I'd pay, and I will." Halvar shot back. "Just fetch me something to eat."

"And me, also," Devallon added. He produced two purple wumpum. "I believe this will cover the cost?"

"Indeed it will!"

Hannes bowed to the Franchen, scowled at Halvar, and hurried back to the kitchen.

"Can't pay your bills, pikeman?" Devallon twitted his old enemy.

"I can, but not right now." Halvar took a long swig of the hot ale and let out a deep sigh. "I needed that. I've been chasing here and there all day, and nothing to show for it."

"Still looking for the Bretain who shot the messenger?" Devallon accepted a mug of ale, regarded it with a dubious grimace, and took a taste. "Faugh! How can you drink this stuff?"

"It's not wine and it's not cider, but it's got a bit of a bite to it," Halvar said. "How do you know it was a Bretain shot Snake?"

"Who else would have a pistoia in Manatas? Surely not the law-abiding Islim, or even the ones who don't abide by the law. And I suppose I have you to thank for stranding me at that smelly pit with the King of Thieves. I was lucky to get out of there with my life, let alone my purse, and in the end, he had nothing to offer. He said the Afrikans pay him to guard their houses during the time they are in the south, and he doesn't want to disrupt that profitable arrangement. Milord Summersby remains at the cottage with Edgar."

"So, you came here for companionship?" Halvar smiled wryly.

"It's better than sitting there watching Milord drink himself into a stupor, or Edgar writing in his notebook."

"Is that how Master Norris spends his time? Writing? To what end?"

Devallon shrugged and tried another sip of ale.

"Who knows? He was out all day, on what business I cannot tell you, because he certainly didn't tell me. I assume it was about this hunt of Milord's."

A server came to the table with a platter of small fish, covered in a sour-smelling white sauce.

"Herring!" Halvar speared one with his ever-present dagger and closed his eyes in ecstasy as he enjoyed this taste of home. "Care for one?"

Devallon's nose wrinkled at the pungent odor.

"I'll wait for the bird," he demurred. "It's the same as what I'd get at the cottage. The Yehudit woman Edgar found has been feeding us on nothing but fowl and fish. Can't you get a round of beef on this island?"

"Cows are for milking," Halvar told him. "And don't even think about pork! This is Islim territory, not a pig to be found on this island, not even in Green Village. The animals are far too clever to be penned in, and when they aren't, they go wild in a month or two and breed like mad. If one sow with piglets got loose on Manatas Island, it would be a disaster for anything else that moves. They eat what they can dig up, and that includes the filth in the latrines."

"You know a good deal about swine, for a pikeman."

"I was raised on a farm, musket-man."

"As was I," Devallon admitted. "Ah! Pigeons, in a pastry shell! At last, something I can eat!"

The serving-lad set down a bowl with a pastry crust and a large spoon. Devallon broke the crust of the pie with his knife and speared one of the bits of meat floating in the gravy.

"Not at all bad," he decided, spooning up some of the gravy.

"Fru Marta is an excellent cook, and Hannes is lucky to have her." Halvar dug into his own serving. "So, musket-man, tell me again how you left Franchenland and wound up here."

"I already told you," Devallon said between bites of pigeon pie. "I didn't want to join Lovis Younger's army and take orders from the Lad, I don't have an estate like the Toff, and I'm not one for religion like the Prig. I had an offer to sail with Girard, escorting the shipload of women to Kibbick, and I took it. No more to be said."

"Indeed? Who made the offer?"

"What difference does it make?" Devallon motioned to the boy for a refill of ale. "The offer was made. Why bother about who made it?"

"It doesn't sound likely," Halvar said. "There must have been other soldiers on the loose in Paris. Why choose you? Did you know Girard before you left Franchenland?"

Devallon finished the pie, sopping up the gravy with the remains of the crust.

"I can't say I knew him, but I'd seen him from time to time at a certain house," he hedged.

"Where certain women could be found?" Halvar hinted. "Run by one Dame Brigitte?"

"All right, if you must know, it was Charlotte's idea. She introduced me to Girard when he was in Paris. We got on well enough, he needed someone to look after those women, and he was willing to pay for my services. I had nothing better to do, and I took him up on it."

"So, you sailed from...where?"

"Nantes," Devallon said. "With twenty young women, most of whom were virgins. A few widows...and Charlotte."

"And Dame Brigitte," Halvar said with a knowing smirk. "And once you got to Kibbick...what then?"

"The girls went to their prospective husbands, and Charlotte married Summersby." The bowl with the dregs of the pie was replaced by a platter of sliced meat covered in gravy, with yellow root vegetables arranged around the edge of the plate.

"Yams and carrots!" Halvar grinned. "Eat up, musket-man!" He dug in, delighted with the fare. Devallon wasn't so eager to sample Manatas cuisine but admitted the gobble-bird was unusually tender.

196

The food was consumed while Halvar continued to question his reluctant guest.

"Whose idea was it for you to take service with Milord? Charlotte again?"

"Who else?" Devallon shrugged.

"A woman with many ideas, Charlotte Besson," Halvar commented between mouthfuls of bird, gravy, and vegetables.

"Always was," Devallon said. "We grew up together, near neighbors, until her father got in the way of Lovis's army, and she had to go to Paris, and I wound up in the Company of Musket-Men."

"But you never quite lost touch, eh?" Halvar leaned back with a contented sigh, then winced at the pain in his wounded shoulder.

"Oh, we saw each other, now and again, whenever I was in Paris. I knew where she was, she knew where I'd been sent."

"So, when this opportunity came along, she promoted you for it?"

"So it would seem."

"And you didn't question why?"

Devallon grew defensive. "Why should I? Did you ask questions when you got that plum position following a young prince around Corduva?""

"In fact, I did. I said I didn't know Arabi, didn't know the young man, and didn't know if I could do the job. The old man told me that was all to the good. I couldn't be bribed if I didn't speak the language, and I'd be able to deal with Don Felipe better if I hadn't grown up with him. So, yes, I'd have wondered why a seafarer would take on a fellow who's never been on a ship in his life. What did you have to offer, aside from a strong sword arm and a manly presence? Why should Girard cart you clear across the Storm Sea?"

"Why not? He had another army man with him, a stout young fellow who kept prating about how much he was looking forward to meeting the Locals, how he wanted to go inland, explore the country. He needed someone like me to keep the girls in line, especially when Dame Brigette was laid low with the *mal-de-mer*."

"And once you got to Kibbick?" Halvar persisted. "What then?"

"How many times must I tell you? The girls were auctioned off—"

"With the proceeds going to the governor," Halvar interrupted. "What about the rest of the cargo?"

"Eh?!" Devallon frowned in puzzlement.

"The muskets," Halvar said. "The real reason the *Belle Fleur* had been dispatched to Kibbick."

"Muskets? What muskets?" Devallon's frown deepened.

"You really didn't know?" Halvar leaned back again. "When the *Belle Fleur* was salvaged, a shipment of muskets was found in the ballast. You don't put a cargo into a load of rocks and bricks unless you don't want it found. That, musket-man, is called smuggling. You were being used, Devallon. Girard didn't want your military presence, he wanted your military expertise."

Devallon's face grew red. "If he did, he didn't tell me!"

"Not then, not in Kibbick," Halvar said slowly. "But you might have seen some crates being taken off the ship there."

"I didn't pay any attention to what was taken off the ship," Devallon said. "They took all sorts of boxes off. I thought they were the girls' dowries, their linens and finery. No one said anything about muskets."

"But muskets there were," Halvar said. "And Girard was taking them with him to Bella Mara, in Terra Mara, along with Milord Summersby…and Charlotte."

"And Edgar," Devallon reminded him. "Who hung over Girard's shoulder all during the voyage, claiming that he'd studied mathematics at Oxenbridge and wanted to learn the art of navigation at sea."

"And who has also claimed a friendship with one of the masters here at the Manatas Madrassa." Halvar tugged at his mustache as he tried to put the pieces of the puzzle together. "Girard knew about the muskets. He comes to Manatas...why?"

"To sell them?" Devallon tried to follow Halvar's reasoning.

"Not when they were still in the ballast," Halvar said. "There's something else, something he didn't have. You can't use a musket without the powder and shot. So said the sultan, and he's right. What Girard needed was someone to get him black powder and musket-balls."

"The Bretains make black powder," Devallon said. "But he didn't bring any on board when he stopped at Bos-Town. I watched them loading kegs, but they were marked *rhum*."

"And rhum there was, because when I boarded, the sailors Girard had left to guard the ship were roaring drunk on it." He'd had to kill one of them, but he didn't like to be reminded of it. "But according to my Local informants, there were no kegs of powder found on the ship. So, I will bet a silver imperial to a white wumpum that someone on this island is either making it, or knows how to. And that, musket-man, is why Girard wanted to have you along when he sailed, and why he told Milord to hire you. Girard wanted someone who knew how to use a musket, who could presumably show someone else how to use it. A lot of someones."

"Me? Train an army?" Devallon snorted scornfully. "You're seeing Franchen spies everywhere, pikeman. I'm just an old soldier who needed a berth, that's all."

"And I'm just a pikeman who chases down murderers," Halvar countered. "And one of them is connected to this musket business of Girard's. And I *will* get to the bottom of it."

The server removed the remains of the meat course.

"Do you wish a sweet? We have nut pastry with honey, cream cakes..."

"No nuts for me, laddie. They're bad for the digestion," Devallon demurred. "Cream cakes will do. And if you have a bit of cheese? Nothing like a good slice of cheese to finish a meal."

"You don't eat nuts?" Halvar asked,

"Not since I was a lad. I get a cough from them."

"Indeed. So did Master Kupernik."

"Who's he?" Devallon smiled happily at the wedge of white cheese set before him.

"The master mathematician at the madrassa, the loud Yehudit from the party yesterday. After I left you at the Scavenger's Pit, I was called to open his bedroom door at the Yehudit House, and there he was, stretched out on the floor. It seems someone fed him a cake with nuts in it. It closed his throat, and he died of it."

"Bad for him. Nothing to do with me." Devallon nodded in appreciation of the cheese. "This isn't a bad cheese at all, not at all. There may be something worth my time in Nova Mundum after all."

"Other than tabac?" Halvar said as Devallon took a pipe from his pocket and prepared for a post-dinner smoke.

"Tabac is the best thing I've seen here," Devallon stated. "I just hope Edgar can find some way to get us off this island and back to somewhere civilized."

"Like Bel' Mar?" Halvar asked wryly. "I hear Sultan Calvera has made his new town the envy of all Nova Mundum. He's got plenty of tabernas, he allows alcohol to be sold, he's even got a theater to present dramas and history plays. Why, you could have a whole new career there. You could set up as a rival to Willem of Cos. You tell clever tales, you sing, you dance. You could become a prime entertainer."

"I'm a soldier, not an actor," Devallon declared. He stretched out, replete. "Do you feel up to a game of tables? I guarantee you a good match."

"I've had enough excitement for one day, and I'm going to my bed," Halvar countered. "You may remain here, if you like. Balthasar plays a good game of tables, but watch his hands—he'll move the spots if you're not careful. Goodnight, Devallon. And a Blessed Nativity to you all."

He waved to the rest of the diners and mounted the stairs, wincing at each step. Hannes had left a jug of water for him to splash on his face and rinse out his mouth before falling into the huge bed Leon had installed in the windowless alcove that served as a sleeping-chamber.

Halvar eased himself out of his coat and boots. *One of these days, I'll get a servant,* he thought as he fell back onto the featherbed.

He considered everything he had learned that day. Of one thing he was certain—the death of the messenger Snake was somehow connected to that of the eminent Master Kupernik. He just wasn't sure how.

"Something I should have done…I didn't do…I missed something…" he mumbled.

Then darkness overtook him.

Chapter 27

HALVAR WOKE TO THE SOUND OF A HORN BLOWN
right under the stairs leading to the latrine in the alley below. Gleeful shouts, donkey brays, and the neighing of a
horse added to the din.

"Thor's Hammer!" he swore as he dragged himself to
the outside landing to see who or what was making the
racket, forgetting he was clad only in his shirt and braes.

Milord Summersby and his minion, Edgar Norris, were
just below in the alley. Milord was mounted on his sorry
nag, clad in a gorgeous coat of bright red trimmed with
black braid. Edgar Norris stood next to the horse, his usual dark suit covered with a short cape. Devallon made a
third, in a leather jacket that had seen much wear, a sword
at his side.

"Halloo!" Devallon waved up at Halvar. "Care to join
us?"

"What's all this?"

"Surely you know it's the custom for Bretains to go a-hunting on the day after Nativity. Milord has decided he is going to find himself something to shoot."

`What does he have in mind?"

"That cat-thing we saw on Watch-night, the one that chased the deer. It spooked his horse, so now he's got a grudge against it. We're going to get some of the Locals to lead us to it and get rid of it. And to tell you the truth, if we happen to kill a few deer, I wouldn't mind a bit of venison to add to our diet of fowl. Something to get our teeth into!"

"I've got other prey to catch," Halvar called down. "But I wish you good hunting. Take care, Musket-man, the thing's the size and shape of a lion. According to what I've heard, it may take more than a few arrows to put it down."

"We've got more than arrows." Milord called out. "Edgar, show this Dane what the Bretains can do."

Edgar lifted his cape to reveal what he had been carrying under his arm.

"A musket?"

"One of the newest," Milord said, proudly.

"And the powder and shot?"

Edgar smiled. "I have prevailed upon my friend LaPierre to accommodate us. He has been testing his latest concoctions in a cabin in those hills, and he is as eager as we to see how well his new powder works."

"Devallon! Edgar!" Milord commanded attention. "Don't bother with the Dane. You said some of the students at the madrassa were familiar with the ways of this beast. Let's see if they will join our hunt. Tally-ho!"

He kicked the horse, which let out a loud neigh in protest but moved briskly enough. The hunting-party proceeded towards the Broad Way.

Halvar considered stopping this endeavor, then decided it would keep Milord occupied for a day and couldn't do any harm. He very much doubted the cat would get hurt. Cats of all sizes were wily creatures, and this one must be clever indeed to have managed to get to Manatas Island at all.

He returned to his rooms and shrugged into his coat and breeches. He checked his chin and decided he didn't need a shave. He ran a hand through his hair by way of toilette and grimaced at the stab of pain in his wounded shoulder. He'd have to stop at Dr. Moise's shed before he set out for Green Village for another chat with Leon.

He thought over the events of the previous day as he descended to the main room, where where Hannes had set out his morning meal of mush and mokka.

"Are you well, Landsman?" Hannes hovered over him while he munched and sipped his break-the-fast.

"Well enough, Hannes. Just a small scratch, nothing to worry about. Tell Fru Marta I'll be here for dinner."

That done, Halvar made his way back to the Rabat, where Flores and Selim were already waiting for him in the courtyard, along with Zoltan, the tall guardsman from the souk, and his shorter companion, Fergus.

"Salaam aleikum, good morning, and what's to do to-day?" Halvar greeted them.

"T've got the firman," Flores announced, waving the fold-ed document. "I've pulled Zoltan and Fergus off the souk detail to come with us to get Igbo. If that Afrikan puts up a fight, they'll bring him down fast enough."

"I doubt he'll do that," Halvar said. "How did you you miss him when you went to his house yesterday?"

"The Shaitan-led bastard must have run out when he heard we were on the way." Zoltan spat in contempt. "But we'll find him."

"Where would he go?" Selim asked. "Not to Lady Tekla, surely! And all the other Afrikan merchants—any who would shelter him, at least—are in the south."

"We checked the other houses on the Street of the Af-rikans," Fergus put in. "Just to be sure he wasn't in any of them. Most of them are boarded up, empty. The ones with servants swore they weren't hiding Samuel, and we believe them."

"He'd go to his friends in Green Village," Halvar decided. "The Pure Sect."

"But why?" Selim asked. "He's Islim, they're Kristo. He hates them, they hate him."

"'Ilha or Redeemer, it don't matter if it's a business deal.' So said Old Sergeant Olaf, and he was right. Igbo is hand-in-glove with the Pure Sect Kristos from Green Village, according to Lady Tekla, and she'd have no reason to lie about it."

"Doing what?" Selim waved at Avaram, who was waiting with his donkey cart.

"Arranging something to do with those muskets we found in the ballast of the *Belle Fleur*. Igbo was the middleman, just as he said, in some deal involving them. Otherwise, why would Girard have sent him a message?

"According to Bull, Snake carried messages to Igbo. And according to my constable in Green Village, on the Longest Night, Snake came to Green Village, inquired after the Pure Sect, and went to their quarters. So, Snake was the link between the three—Girard, Igbo, and the Pure Sect."

"But there are at least five Purists in Green Village," Selim reminded him. "Which one would Igbo seek out?"

"Andrew MacAlan is their leader," Halvar stated. "I want another word or two with that Bretain."

"But what kind of arrangement was Girard making?" Selim asked as the four mounted the cart and traveled slowly northward. "Sending muskets to Nova Mundum? Why? Who was supposed to get them, and for what purpose?"

"I'm not sure. Could be some idea of Lovis Younger's to foment rebellion, or maybe arm the Locals against the Afrikans, and then come in and mop up, like Caesar of the Old Roumi" Halvar mused. "Could even have been some plan of Girard's, to sell the muskets privately to whoever would buy them, Afrikan or Local." *And throw in Devallon's expertise as a bonus*, he silently added.

"Whatever the plan was, it's not going to happen, now that Girard's dead." Flores said.

205

"We don't know that," Halvar corrected. "Girard might have been part of something else, something bigger, that we still don't know about."

Flores was not impressed.

"You're seeing plots and schemes where they don't exist. You sound like one of the Thousand Nights and a Night tales, with stories within stories." He stared at a growing crowd in front of the madrassa. "What's going on?"

"It would seem Milord Summersby has managed to recruit some of the madrassa students for his hunting party" Halvar observed. "Halloo, Stephane Mercier! Shouldn't you be at your lectures?"

The Franchen student loped across the Broad Way to the donkey cart.

"It's Yehudit Shabat—no lectures from Benyamin today, and it's a fine, clear day for a hunt. I've got my fowling-piece, and Master Norris has shot and powder, so why not?"

"Cold, but not windy," another student agreed.

"*Master* Norris, is it?" Flores grumbled. "He's no master, he's no better than a servant."

"He went to Oxenbridge," Halvar said. "That makes him something more than a mere servant, no matter what he does for Milord. I wonder where he got the black powder and shot for the firearms?"

"Oh, that's Master LaPierre's doing," Stephane said cheerfully. "He's given us some of his new powder, to test how it works with the different muskets. The stuff he's been making in his cabin up-the-hills, behind the charcoal-burners' camp. I can't wait to try it!"

"Interested in alchemy, are you?" Halvar asked.

"More than dry stuff like law," Stephane admitted. "At least, with alchemy, you've got some excitement when the stuff explodes or stinks. And it's something that everyone wants, so you can sell it for a goodly sum."

"Be careful," Selim warned him as Avaram urged the donkey forward. "Mountain cats are fierce."

"I've hunted them before," Stephane assured her. "That's why Milord Summersby asked for me to lead this hunt with him." He swaggered to the front of the pack of would-be hunters.

"Fools!" Flores spat over the side of the cart. "They'll wind up cat meat!"

"More likely, they'll spend the day climbing the hills, getting cold and finding nothing," Selim said scornfully. "No one can catch one of those mountain cats when it goes into its den. And the hills at the north end of this island are full of little caves where it can hide. "

Halvar said nothing, but thought over what little he knew about muskets and how they worked while the donkey cart jogged along the Broad Way.

"Street of the Afrikans," Avaram announced. "Do we stop here?"

"No," Halvar ordered. "Go on to Green Village. I want to have a word with Frater Leonidas while Flores, Zoltan, and Fergus take that firman and explain to our argumentative Pure Sect Bretains how the laws of Sharia and Al-Andalus work. And if you happen to find Samuel Igbo, take him into custody. I just hope we're not too late. If I'm right, someone is trying to eliminate anyone who can link him with Franz Girard."

"And you think that someone is MacAlan," Flores said. "We'll get him, Capitán!"

"Just don't kill him," Halvar warned. "I've got to find out how deep this rot goes before we send him to Sheol."

Chapter 28

THE FRATERY CHAPEL BELL WAS TOLLING FOR midday prayers when Avaram finally reached Green Village. The remains of the bone-fire, which had been hidden under snow, were now evident in the center of the common ground. Several Bretain men were removing the ashes and some of the half-burned logs. Women stood around them, gossiping. Apparently, Green Village folk were not quite ready to resume their everyday chores in the interim between Nativity and the Turn-of-the Year festivities.

Flores, Zoltan, and Fergus hopped off the cart easily. Selim slid down, while Halvar took his time clambering off.

"Where's Tenente Donal?" He looked across the common to the iron gates that led to the Gardens of Paradise.

"Probably sleeping off his Nativity drunk," Flores sniped. "It was a mistake putting him in charge, Capitán. One of our own would have been better."

"Donal was already keeping order here," Halvar pointed out. "Halloo! Tenente Donal!"

It took a few minutes for Donal to shamble through the gates, blinking in the winter sunlight.

"Capitán?"

"What's happening with those Pure Sect people? I sent word yesterday that you should keep watch over them."

Donal winced at Halvar's sharp tones.

"Yesterday? That was Nativity Day, Capitán. Surely, you wouldn't make me work on Nativity Day!"

"*I* did!" Halvar shot back. "As did Tenente Flores, young Selim, and even the Mahak, Firebrand."

"Flores and Selim are Islim, it don't matter to them," Donal whined. "And the Pure Sect folk weren't going anywhere, not in this cold. Where can they go, eh?"

"They might try the bridge," Flores suggested. "Or they might try to hide in the rocks up-the-hills."

"With the mountain cat on the loose?" Donal sniffed. "Who'd be that kind of fool?"

"Enough of this!" Halvar cut the quarrel short. "Tenente Donal, Tenente Flores. You will go to the house where the Pure Sect are lodged. You will arrest the man known as Andrew MacAlan on a charge of murder. I have a witness who saw him shoot the messenger Stephen, known as Snake, on the day of the snowstorm."

"What makes you think it was MacAlan, and not one of the others?" Donal asked. "And where's the warrant? This is Bretain territory, you don't take a man without a warrant. That's our law!" He glared pugnaciously at Halvar.

"MacAlan is the tallest, he has a pistoia," Halvar said. "Flores has the warrant, the firman, signed by the sultan. And remember, Tenente Donal, Green Village is now a part of Manatas Town, not Bretain or Local. No one can hide from the laws of Al-Andalus."

"What about this witness? Who is he?" Donal persisted. "Why didn't he come forward before this?"

"Because he couldn't, without opening himself to another charge," Halvar told him. "Now, Tenente Donal, summon your own men, if any are awake, and get yourself over to the house where the Pure Sect lodge, and bring them back here to the Gardens of Paradise for questioning."

"And while we are doing this, where will you be?" Donal glared at Flores, who returned the glare with a one of his own.

"I will be at the fratery—I have to consult Frater Leonidas on a few points. And if Fru Glick objects to our presence, tell her she has the warmest place in Green Village, and the only one large enough to hold everyone."

Donal led Flores across the common while Halvar and Selim took the path that led to the palisade surrounding Green Village Fratery. The gate was open. The surly porter was on guard, allowing a donkey cart loaded with baskets of maiz and other produce to enter.

"I'm here to speak with Frater Leonidas," Halvar announced.

"He's decorating the chapel," the porter grumbled. "More pictures, more images. The place will look like a Roumi Rite chapel by the time he's done."

Halvar and Selim headed for the small wooden building just outside the palisade where the Holy Meal had been offered two day before. Then, it had been heated only by the fervor of the congregation. Now a small brass firebox gave off a modicum of heat.

Leon stood near the firebox, notebook in hand, frowning at the back wall. He didn't look up from his work when he felt the draft from the open door.

"It's not time for more prayers," he said irritably, still scribbling in his notebook. .

"No, it's not," Halvar said. "More paintings? I thought the Pure Sect disapproves of them. Something about graven images, from the Holy Book."

"Abbas Mikhail is not of the Pure Sect," Leon said. "What brings you here, Halvar? Still chasing murderers?"

"I've got my men doing that. What are you planning to put here? The Redeemer on his crux? Mother Mara and the infant Chesu?"

"I'm not sure yet." Leon regarded the back wall with half-closed eyes. "Perhaps the Judgment of the Dead, to remind worshipers of the fate that comes to all of us. Is this about that lad who was killed in Manatas Town? I told you all I knew about him."

"Not quite." Halvar looked for a place to sit down and found none. Instead, he leaned against the table where the Holy Meal was prepared. Selim propped up her note-book and took out her pen-case. "I think you know more than you're telling me. You spent the better part of a year at the Mermaid Taberna, so you must have seen him around the waterfront with those messenger boys, the Waterfront Rats."

Leon watched these preparations warily.

"Perhaps I saw him once or twice on the waterfront, that's all. I told you, I didn't know him."

"He must have known you if he approached you about sponsoring him for the madrassa. What gave him the notion of applying for classes at all? Prester Nicodemus has a school that teaches Roumi Rite letters and basic numbers. Most of the other lads are content with that. What made Snake suddenly think he could do better?"

Leon smirked. "I suppose it was my little discussions at the Mermaid. They drew some of the madrassa students away from the Broad Way to the waterfront."

"I heard something about a big discussion. A disputation, Prester Nicodemus called it. Something about the stars and their movements?"

"Oh, that." Leon's smirk deepened into a malicious grin. "That was my idea, to draw a crowd to the Mermaid in return for the use of the upper rooms. It worked, too. We got quite a gathering. Even Sultan Petrus and Mullah Abadul came to hear Master Kupernik and Master LaPierre going at each other, with commentary by the mullah and a few choice words from myself."

211

"According to one of the lads at the Roumi Rite chapel, it disintegrated into a brawl and had to be stopped by Tenente Gomez and his men."

"It was a grand and glorious evening," Leon gloated.

"And afterward? Did this messenger Snake approach you then?"

Leon was jerked out of his contemplation of past victories.

"He might have. Wait…let me think…." He closed his eyes, presumably recalling everything about the event. "I do remember the lads from the chapel…there are five or six of them. A big, blonde brute, something like you, Halvar. A little boy, like a mouse. A redhead—they call him Fox, I think.

"And, yes, now you bring it back to me, Snake, the ugly one. Spots on his face, big nose, stringy hair, not quite ready to grow a beard but trying to. And a whiny, high voice. He asked questions about the validity of the Holy Books that had Mullah Abadul and Prester Nicodemus actually agreeing on one thing—that the Holy Books were true in every particular, and that questioning them was heresy."

"And then Snake came to you, to ask you to sponsor him?"

"Oh, he'd already done that. I turned him down, as I said. I don't know what he could have been thinking. It's all very well for a messenger boy to attend a discussion, but to take part in it himself? That's overreaching. And I could have told him not to ask Kupernik. That man is a total snob."

"I heard how he treated you, twitted you for being an apothecary's son," Halvar agreed. "You may not have heard, but he was found dead in his rooms about this time yesterday. I'm looking into that, too."

Leon's grin faded. "Found dead, you say? Of what cause?"

"That's the interesting part." Halvar shifted slightly. "Someone gave him a cake with *nguba* in it. Seems he had a sensitivity to the beans—they choked him, and he died."

"An accident, surely?" Leon said.

"Not quite. I found a little piece of wood jammed into the space under his door, and his water jug had been emptied. Someone didn't want Master Kupernik to get help if he was in difficulty."

"And you thought I...?" Leon gasped, affronted.

"It crossed my mind," Halvar admitted. "But then I found out the cakes had been brought into the kitchen by one of the Waterfront Rat messengers, directed to someone else. You were at the party before I got there, stayed until after I left, so it couldn't have been you who sent the messenger. Of course, you could have paid someone else to do it..."

"With what? I have no money here!" Leon snapped.

"Exactly so," Halvar agreed. "So, I decided you weren't the one responsible for Master Kupernik's death."

"Thank you for that," Leon said with an ironic twist of his lips. "So, Don Alvaro, who do you think murdered the mathematician?"

"I'm not sure," Halvar admitted. "But it would have to be someone who lived at the Yehudit House, because anyone else would be noticed by the house-master, Eli. It has to be someone Kupernik knew, because he was found in his nightclothes. My guess? Someone came to Kupernik's room with the cakes as a festival gift. This person emptied the water jug and jammed the door when he left."

"You're certain it was a man?" Leon sniped.

"The only woman in the house is the cook, and she's got no reason to kill Kupernik, no matter how much fuss he made over his food." Halvar tugged at his mustache in thought. "Someone who disliked Kupernik...What do you know of this Master Albrecht LaPierre?"

"Very little," Leon snapped. "He's an alchemist, the experimental type. He came to Manatas at about the time I was...removed...from my lectures, thanks to that meddling Mullah Abadul."

"He's not Islim," Halvar mused. "He lives in the Yehudit House—I saw him there—but he doesn't wear Yehudit garb. Albrecht is a Danic name, but LaPierre? That's Franchen. Where's he from?"

"I've no idea," Leon shrugged. "My best guess is the disputed territory between Franchenland and the Dane-March, very close to where you spent your youth, my dear Halvar. Is there anything else you want to know? Because I have just had a grand idea as to what to do with this bare wall."

"One more thing. What do you know about gunpowder?"

"Gunpowder?" Leon repeated. "I know enough not to meddle with the stuff. One of my best students in Corduba was badly burned trying to manufacture it."

"And how do you do that?"

"You mix certain ingredients. Sulfur—that's a sort of yellow rock. Charred coal, the half-burned logs of certain trees. Saltpeter—that's a substance distilled from urine, among other things. Grind them down, distill them, and you get gunpowder. Or so the alchemists claim."

Halvar tugged at his mustache thoughtfully.

"Mix this and that, as Master Kupernik said at the party at the madrassa. Is it really that simple?"

"No, it is not." Leon's voice took on a bitter edge. "More than one reckless student has met a very unpleasant end trying to emulate his masters. The ingredients have to be very, very pure, for one thing, and the portions have to be exact. And as I told you, I will not touch the stuff. Some of those ingredients are deadly if they are not properly prepared."

"So, if someone at the madrassa—say, this LaPierre—wanted to mix up batches, he'd have to do it far from the town? Where would he go?"

The fratery bell rang out.

"I have no idea," Leon said. "And now, my dear Halvar, I have to go to refectory. The bell calls me. And I hope you find out who killed Master Kupernik. I didn't like him, he didn't like me, but he had a most original mind. The world has lost a great thinker."

With that, Leon left Halvar and Selim in the chapel.

"Did you get all that down?" Halvar stood over the fire-box, warming his hands.

"I did, but what does it mean? Did you really think Leon had killed Master Kupernik?"

"For a while, I did. After all, they didn't like each other, and he could have given him the cakes with the nguba in them. But when I thought it over, I knew the timing was wrong. Leon was well away from the Yehudit House when Master Kupernik received his guest. Then Bull told me he'd been given the cakes to deliver to Master LaPierre, not Master Kupernik."

Selim's heavy eyebrows nearly met over her nose in a puzzled frown.

"Master LaPierre? Why would he kill Master Kupernik?"

"That is what I am going to ask him," Halvar said. "Just as soon as we finish this business of the Pure Sect. They're connected somehow, and Snake is the link between them."

As Selim and Halvar crossed the common together, Halvar's attention was drawn to the rowdy crowd gathering in front of the gates to the Gardens of Paradise. Milord Summersby had assembled as many idlers, students and Scavengers as he could find to join him in his quest. Whether anyone else wanted it or not, Milord would have his lion hunt!

Chapter 29

AS LONG AS THERE WAS A CROWD, DANI GLICK would be sure to take advantage of it. She stood at the gates of the Gardens of Paradise, every inch the Yehudit matron in her woolen skirt and jacket, wrapped in a fur stole, her hair tucked under a colorful silk scarf, while her servers passed out cups of steaming-hot liquid. Milord tried to control his restive steed, and Edgar Norris orated in Erse to whoever would stop and listen.

"We are searching for the mountain cat that has been seen near this place. Does anyone know where the beast may be found?"

Firebrand and his men came down the path from the woods at the north end of Green Village.

"Where have you been?" Halvar didn't bother with polite greetings. "These people want to chase that cat. I have other prey in mind...Aha! Flores! Donal!"

The two guardsmen thrust through the hunters. Halvar looked past them.

"Where's the Pure Sect? Where's MacAlan?"

Flores sneered at Donal. "Who knows? This drunken Kristo was celebrating his Redeemer's Nativity when he should have been keeping watch. He didn't even post a guard on their house! No one's seen them since yesterday."

Halvar took in Donal's state of undress, his obvious distress, and his reluctance to meet his eye.

"Tenente Donal? What have you to say for yourself?"

"Nativity?" Donal quavered. "No one goes anywhere on Nativity. It's a holy day."

"Which these Pure Sect don't accept," Halvar reminded him. "Take me to that house of theirs. Now!" he barked, jolting Donal out of his stupor.

Dani Glick was drawn to the sound of loud voices.

"What's going on here?"

"Your man Donal got drunk instead of keeping an eye on those Pure Sect troublemakers," Flores snarled before Halvar could speak.

"I gave orders to watch them." Halvar added.

"We have a warrant to search their house," Selim concluded.

Dani pulled her fur tighter around her neck.

"Cormack!" she called out.

The Bretain ironmonger, ostensibly the leader of the Bretains in Manatas, left the gang of hunters.

"Come with us. Capitán Halvar Danske wants to speak with the Pure Sect. You should be present, to make sure all is done according to the law."

It was quite a group that marched around the common—Halvar and his guardsmen, Donal and his constable, Firebrand and his watchmen, and Dani Glick and Cormack MacCormack. They arrayed themselves in front of the cottage at the northernmost end of Green Village, opposite the gates of the fratery palisade.

Halvar pounded on the door.

"Open, in the name of the Calif Don Felipe! You are wanted for questioning in the matter of the death of Stephen, called Snake, a messenger in Manatas!"

There was no answer.

"There's no smoke," Selim observed.

"Go around the back," Halvar ordered. "We have the warrant. If necessary, use the back door."

Flores led Zoltan and Fergus around the cottage. They returned with a shivering lad of Selim's age in worn trews and a knitted tunic.

"Who's this?" Halvar demanded.

"I'm Seth," the boy quavered.

"He was in the jakes," Zoltan explained.

"Hiding," Fergus sniggered.

"It was Andrew. I think he's gone mad!" Seth stammered. "He's gone up-the-hills, with the Afrikan."

"What Afrikan?" Donal asked.

"The one who came last night," Seth said. "Nearly dark, it was. He talked to Andrew—"

"In Erse or Arabi?" Halvar asked.

"Erse, of course. Andrew doesn't know Arabi. We don't speak Arabi in in Bos-Town, only Erse."

"What did this Afrikan have to say that was so important he couldn't send a messenger?" Halvar wanted to know.

Seth looked from one unfriendly face to another, and fixed on Donal as being the one most likely to understand him.

"He said that the Town Guards were after him, that the Dane was already suspicious, and that he would not have anything more to do with us. Then Andrew laid hands upon him and said he was already involved in our undertaking, and he would have to go with us, will he or nill he."

"Go where?" Selim piped up. "There are no boats running in the East Channel at this time of the year. Not even the ferries. Too much ice in the water, it's too dangerous."

"What about that bridge of Leon's? How is it faring in this winter cold?" Halvar tried to remember how far the building project had gone before it was shut down until the spring thaw.

218

"He's got boards laid across some of the pilings," Donal said. "And there's a jetty, with a small rowing boat, to get from one side of the channel to the other."

"No one has come there," Firebrand assured him. "My people watch that place carefully. If Huron try to get across, we are there to stop them."

"Never mind the Huron. They're miles away from here, up north. What about Bretains coming from this side?" Halvar fumed.

Firebrand consulted his men in Munsi, then turned back to Halvar.

"No one seen today. But Muskrat thought he saw smoke over the hills, where they burn bricks."

"Those are the Afrikans from Egypt," Selim recalled. "I suppose they're still at it."

Seulemon spoke up.

"Too far away for bricks. Too thin for tree-burners."

"The ones who make charred coals," Selim translated. "There is a camp for them, all the way up-the-hills, at the very north end of the island. There are stands of birch there —that makes for fine wood to burn."

Halvar tugged at his mustache as he put several small pieces of information together.

"Have you or your men heard odd noises coming from that direction?" He waved at the distant hills. "Thunder, when the sky is clear? Maybe smelled something odd that wasn't a sekonk?"

More Munsi chatter. Firebrand reported, "Sometimes, in the summer, when it is very hot, there is thunder but no rain. We do not go into the rocks up-the-hills. Why should we? There is nothing there. The Oropans who make bricks and the ones who make leather from deerskins are close to Manatas Town. We know them, we do not interfere with them, they do not bother us."

"Is this about the muskets?" Flores asked suddenly.

"Not exactly," Halvar said. "It's about what you need to make the muskets worth anything. Someone's making

219

gunpowder in those rocks, and if I'm right, that's where our missing Purists have gone."

"Gunpowder!" Donal blanched. "Is that why…?"

"That's right!" Seth exclaimed, awestruck at Halvar's acuity. "Andrew said he'd found a place where we could put our new manufactory, to make gunpowder, that it would be safe because there was a fellow-Bretain who would allow us to use some of the land to build on and not tell the Locals. How did you…? I mean, who told you…?" He stopped, conscious that he had said too much.

Firebrand was the first to recover from the shock of learning just how badly their trust in Donal had been betrayed.

"It seems your constable has been taking bribes to allow someone to build on Mahak land." Firebrand glared fiercely at Donal, who moaned, either from fear or hangover.

Dani Glick rounded on her bouncer.

"Donal, spit it out, right now! You are walking a very thin line! You got your position as constable because I vouched for you. If I find out you've been taking bribes behind my back.!"

"Not a bribe, just a consideration," Donal quavered. "Oh, my head! It was a master alchemist from the madrassa who approached me first. A most reputable young man. He just wanted a quiet place to do his experimenting, he said. I thought he was mixing paints or potions, maybe seeking Elixir of Life! No one told me he was making gunpowder!"

"I'm telling you now, Donal, and you'd better lead us to that cabin." Halvar looked over at the hunters. "I think this has turned from a cat-hunt into a man-hunt. Dani, don't feed those men any more alcohol. I want them clear-headed. Whoever or whatever has taken shelter in those rocks up there, it's not about to go quietly."

The rabble on the common grew louder under the influence of the hot cider and uskebaugh. Milord waved grandly from his place in the saddle.

"Forward, my hearties! We'll capture and kill this beast!"

He started out, only to be brought up short by a loud bang from the direction of the rocky hills ahead of him.

"That was no mountain cat!" Halvar shouted. "Milord, I think we're both going a-hunting, but my prey is a lot more dangerous than yours. Flores, Donal, you're with me. Firebrand, you go with Milord and his people. If you find the cat, kill it if you can, but don't kill Andrew MacAlan. I want him alive to tell me what he knows about muskets, gunpowder, and who wants to bring them to Manatas!"

Chapter 30

FLORES, DONAL AND FIREBRAND CROSSED THE
common with Halvar and Selim close behind them.

"With me!" Flores yelled in Arabi.

"To me!" Donal shouted in Erse.

Two groups sorted themselves out of the pack, one
that spoke Erse, one that understood Arabi.

"Wait just one minute!" Milord protested. "This is my
hunt!"

"Not anymore," Halvar told him. "Green Villagers!"
He called out in Erse. "There's a man who's already killed
once that I know of, maybe more. He's running up-the-
hills. I want him, and I want him alive!"

"Who?" someone called from the crowd.

"Andrew MacAlan," Donal told them, trying to regain
some of his lost authority.

"What proof have you?" another voice cried.

"Proof enough," Halvar declared. "There's a witness
saw him kill a lad in cold blood. We'll get more when we

catch him." He strode toward the tumble of rocks that marked the boundary of Green Village. "All of Manatas is now under one law, and that law is Al-Andalus. I have enough proof to satisfy any court, Andalusian or Bretain. The more we stand here chattering, the farther away he gets!"

"We'll get him." Donal gulped down whatever was rising in his throat. "There's a path...this way!" He indicated a faint track through the bare trees, towards the hills that rose on the north end of the island.

Halvar looked at the scarp in the distance and cringed inwardly. He did not enjoy climbing. He hated heights. He had grown up on the flat land of the Dane-March. Looking out from a tower was all very well, but a ledge with a drop below it was the stuff of nightmares.

Still, he reminded himself, he'd walked over the Alps, and he'd crossed an ocean. He could certainly climb a few rocks!

"Follow me!" He waved to Flores, Zoltan, and Fergus. Selim pattered after them, and the rest of the Green Village constabulary straggled along the trail, eagerly at first, losing some of their ardor as the day wore on and they grew cold and hungry.

They skirted the brickyard, where the ovens were already fired and spewing smoke into the frosty air. North of the brickyard, they could smell the rotting flesh and urine stink of the tannery, where deer hides and furs were turned into leather for everything from garments to tools.

Halvar could hear his men behind him, thrashing through the dead leaves that coated the ground. Icy patches and leftover snow made the footing treacherous, but there were signs of someone's passing—broken twigs, scattered leaves, even a scrap of cloth fluttering on a low branch.

After an hour's slog, Halvar called a halt.

"Seth!"

The Bretain lad was shoved along the line of march to face the leader.

"Have you been to this cabin?"

Seth looked for assurance and found none.

"Once. When Andrew wanted me to see what Master LaPierre had set up."

"Master LaPierre, was it?" Halvar nodded. "It would be. How much longer to find it, young man? If you've got us chasing a wild goose…"

"It's a little way more, up this track," Seth assured him.

"It better be!" Flores growled. "Or you'll find out just how we treat liars at the Rabat!"

Before Halvar could rebuke him, there was another loud bang, followed by an unearthly howl.

"Thor's Hammer! What was that?" He looked wildly about him.

"I think someone found the cat," Donal offered.

"Up ahead." Flores gestured with his halberd.

Halvar grabbed the halberd and used it as a walking-stick, marching grimly forward, following the path around a pile of rocks that marked the opening of a small clearing in the woods. A log cabin had been built against the rock face, with a woodpile next to it. A small campfire smoldered next to the woodpile.

"They've got to be around here somewhere." Halvar scanned the woods beyond the cabin for signs of something moving.

Donal looked up at the cliff face. A pebble rattled down the rock, bouncing into the fire.

"There's a cave up there," he announced.

Flores shaded his eyes with one hand as he examined the landscape.

"I just saw something move inside that cave."

Another spatter of pebbles confirmed his find.

"Hoy! Andrew MacAlan!" Halvar called up. "We know you're up there! Come down now, and no harm will come to you!"

"He's up here! He's mad!" The high-pitched squeal in Arabi ended abruptly with another loud bang.

"I have removed the Afrikan traitor from this earth and sent him to his reward in Hell!" Andrew MacAlan called down to his pursuers. "I am the Avenger of the Lord God, who has sent me to purify this world!"

"He must be mad!' Donal gasped. "His son's death must have driven him out of his wits!"

"He was insane before he ever got to Manatas," Halvar said. "If he thought he could build a gunpowder manufactory here and no one would notice it."

"Like the bridge," Selim said with a smug nod. "You'd find out all about it."

"What do we do now?" Flores asked with an anxious glance upward. "He's got a pistoia, he's got the powder."

"And he's had time to reload the thing," Donal added gloomily.

"I'll have to take him on," Halvar decided. "If he won't come down, I'll have to go up. Maybe I can talk him into surrendering."

"He's beyond reason," Donal said.

There was a neigh somewhere in the woods. Milord and his hunters were coming closer. Two Mahak carrying bows and arrows emerged from the woods, followed by Stephane and his fellow students with their fowling-pieces.

"Have you seen it?" Stephane asked.

"We've heard it," Selim told him.

"Never mind the beast." Halvar settled the araghoun hat firmly on his head and grabbed Flores's halberd. "This ends now! I'll get that Bretain Purist down, and we'll find out just what's going on here."

He started up the pebble-strewn path that led to the cave opening, ignoring the protests from below him. He used the pole of the halberd as a prop, pushing the rocks out of his way, hugging the face of the scarp, forcing himself not to look down.

There was a ledge at the opening of the cave. Halvar stood, his back against the rock, and called inside.

"You can't get away, MacAlan. Give yourself up, now!"

His answer was another shot.

"It's not good, you know that."

"I will kill the infidel!" MacAlan roared out. "They offend the Lord God with their presence!"

"The Redeemer didn't want his people to kill their enemies," Halvar pleaded. "What happened to your son was not the fault of the Islim, or of the Mahak. It was a greedy, selfish man and his schemes. Your son was in the way of his plot, that was all. You can't blame all Mahak or Afrikans—"

"He was a martyr to the Cause!" the man in the cave howled.

"He was a victim of greed! Come out, man, and we can discuss this." Halvar heard something scrabbling over his head. "Come out, MacAlan. See? I'm laying down my weapon…"

MacAlan emerged from the cave, pistoia in hand, ready to finish what he had started, as Halvar edged toward the opening, halberd at the ready. Something huge and furry hurtled down from the rocky slope above the cave. Halvar thrust the halberd forward as the cat swiped a paw and caught MacAlan across the face. The Bretain howled in pain. The cat yowled back.

Halvar thrust again, distracting the cat from its first victim in a desperate dance on the narrow ledge. MacAlan stepped back, missed his footing, and rolled down the scarp, bouncing from rock to rock until he lay still at the foot of the cliff.

On the ledge, Halvar thrust the point of the halberd at the cat, who batted it away with one paw. He tried to keep his back to the rock face, while the cat, more sure-footed than he, leaped from rock to rock, screeching its war-cry. From below, he heard cries of fear and advice, but he ignored them, focusing only on the cat.

Once more he thrust, this time with the flat of the blade, trying to get the creature across the throat. He used the edge to catch the cat across the chest, then thrust the point

226

of the halberd into it. With one last desperate howl, the animal died, leaving Halvar gasping for breath, braced against the rock.

He staggered down the scarp to the cheers of the crowd below.

"I wanted to shoot, but I didn't want to hit you," Stephane said.

"You were moving too fast for the Mahak to aim their arrows. And Milord was going to use his musket, but Tenente Flores wouldn't let him." Selim bounded forward to take his arm and lead him to the fire.

"You killed the cougar! A good fight!" Firebrand congratulated him. "We must take his skin. You will get a new name—Cat-Killer!"

"Never mind that. What about MacAlan? Is he alive?" Halvar wiped sweat out of his eyes.

The crowd parted to display the remains of Andrew MacAlan.

"Thor's Hammer! I wanted him alive!" Halvar handed the halberd to Flores, suddenly weak from his exertions. Flores and Donal caught him before he could fall and eased him down onto the woodpile.

He leaned forward, his head in his hands. His eye was caught by the chips of wood surrounding the pile of logs that had been neatly split, ready to be added to the fireplace inside the cabin he could see through the bare branches of the trees farther up the path.

"Who is it?" someone called out. "What was he doing up there?"

"He was the one who killed Snake, the messenger from the Waterfront Rats, the one whose body we found," Selim told the crowd. "And he would have killed as many of us as he could," she added, in case anyone regretted the man's death.

"I'm not sorry he's dead. I wanted to know who else was with him in this scheme," Halvar said.

"We know one," Flores said. "The alchemist, LaPierre. That lad, Seth, said he was the one MacAlan dealt with, to make the gunpowder. And that Afrikan, Samuel Igbo, he was another."

Halvar nodded. "You're right, Flores. Donal, you can take this body back to Green Village and give the man a decent burial. Tenente Firebrand, send one of your people up to that cave. If Samuel Igbo is still alive…"

Muskrat had already climbed the cliff.

"There's an Afrikan here!" he called down. "He's been shot."

"I suppose he's not alive, then," Halvar sighed. "Very well. Get him down. Make a litter, something to haul these bodies back to Green Village."

Firebrand's men fetched the lifeless Igbo down from the ledge.

"What will you do now?" Flores asked.

"Get back to Manatas. Finish the investigation."

"But…it's over," Donal said. "MacAlan killed the messenger—you said it yourself. He's dead, so it's over."

"No, it's not," Halvar said. "MacAlan was only half of the scheme. Tenente Donal, what did you find in the house the Pure Sect lived in?"

"The usual household goods. And some small kegs, about the size of a man's arm from hand to elbow."

"Did you open any of them? What was in them?"

"They were nailed shut. But there were some black grains under one of them…Is that gunpowder?" he asked in alarm.

"Probably. He must have sold some of his stock at the feria," Halvar decided. "That's what brought him to Manatas in the first place, not placing his son in a school he didn't approve of. I've got to get back to the madrassa…"

"Not now," Selim warned him. "You need to rest! Your shoulder's bleeding again, and the cat must have given you a swipe."

Halvar looked down at the woodpile as he heaved himself onto his feet. He kicked the chips of wood that had fallen from the split logs.

"I can't stop now. Get me to that Frater Iosip at the fratery. He'll put one of his moldy-bread poultices on the shoulder. Then get me back to the madrassa. I just remembered what I forgot to ask." He picked up one of the chips and handed it to Selim. "Keep this, laddie. It may be enough to hang a man."

"What do we do with the bodies?" Firebrand asked.

Halvar waved vaguely. "Make a litter, carry them back to Green Village."

Firebrand gave orders in Munsi. Somewhere in the woods, the Mahak broke branches, used vines to lash them together, and placed the bodies on the makeshift carriers.

Halvar heaved himself onto his feet, and prepared for the long slog back to Green Village. He only hoped he would not disgrace himself by fainting before he got there.

Chapter 31

THE PROCESSION HEADED BACK ALONG THE track to Green Village with a story that would further enhance the reputation of Capitán Halvar Danske, Cat-Killer. Firebrand's runners had reached Green Village well before the rest of the hunters and spread the tale of the encounter with the ferocious mountain cat. Padraig wrote feverishly, and Simon Singer set the type for a special edition of the *Gazetta*. The news-criers were dispatched to Manatas Town, in advance of the printed word.

"Dangerous beast slain by noble Capitán Don Alvaro Danico!"

Milord Summersby led the march through the woods on his steed, which had rediscovered his former glorious self and fairly pranced down the narrow path. Behind him, two Mahak dragged a roughly-built litter of branches lashed together with vines, with the body of the cat displayed on it. The less-conspicuous litter with the bodies of Andrew

MacAlan and Samuel Igbo was decently covered by a blanket found in the cabin.

Halvar brought up the rear, clutching the halberd for support, flanked by Tenentes Flores and Donal, with Selim hovering behind him. He slogged through the muck of mud and dead leaves, one step after the other. He could have cried with relief when he spotted Avaram and the donkey cart at the wide place on the path that marked where carts brought hides to the tannery and took finished leather back to Manatas.

"I thought you might need a lift," Avaram explained as he helped Halvar onto the cart.

"You were right. Thank you." Halvar leaned against the wall of the cart. He willed himself not to give in to the impulse to close his eyes and lose consciousness. "Selim! Did you do what I asked last night? Did you go over those papers we took from Kupernik's desk?"

"Yes, Don Alvaro. I even have them with me."

"And what about that little chip of wood? The one we found under the door?"

"I have that, too. Is it important?"

"It may be. I'm glad I have someone knows how to obey orders." He took a deep breath and let it out again. "Avaram, take me to the Gardens of Paradise. Then get Frater Iosip and Frater Leonidas and bring them to me there. When we get to the Gardens of Paradise, Flores, Donal, get something hot for yourselves. Not alcohol!" he added for Donal's benefit. "Then we go on, back to Manatas Town. There's more to do before we can rest."

"What more is there?" Donal protested. "We've got the cat, and we've got the killer."

"MacAlan killed Snake because he could identify him," Flores reasoned. "And he killed Igbo when Igbo tried to get away from him. He was mad. There's an end to it."

"Not so," Halvar gritted out between jolts, holding on to the side of the cart. "There's also the matter of the poisoned professor at the madrassa. What has he to do with this? What's the connection between him and MacAlan?"

"Suppose there isn't any," Selim said

"There has to be," Halvar said stubbornly. "Snake was involved with both of them." He peered over the edge of the cart. "What's all this?"

A cheering crowd surrounded the cart as it arrived at the edge of the Green Village common.

"You're a hero," Selim told him. "You killed the mountain cat!"

"*It* nearly killed <*me*," Halvar muttered. "Avaram…"

"We're at the Gardens of Paradise," the driver said. "What now?"

Dani Glick was waiting at the gate.

"So, Halvar, you're not dead yet." She stepped out of the way as Flores and Donal assisted their leader out of the cart.

"Apparently, the Redeemer and Mother Mara have other plans for me." Halvar grunted loudly as he tried to gain his footing. "I see Firebrand's watchmen have already spread the news. MacAlan's dead; so is the beast. I'm still alive."

"I've already sent for the physicians from the fratery. I thought you might need them. Come in out of the cold. And get that thing out of my sight!" Dani shuddered expressively at the gory carcass on the branches.

"Firebrand thinks its hide will make a good coat," Halvar commented as he allowed himself to be led into the warm building.

"I'm sure it will look stunning. It matches your hair, what there is of it." Dani took him into the back room, where one of Malik's stoves glowed in a corner, sending its smoke through the roof through a pipe. Flores, Donal and Selim followed them, only to be ousted some minutes later by Frater Iosip, the rotund physician from Green Village Fratery .

"Everybody out! I need room to work! Not you, Frater Leonidas. I need you to hold this Dane still while I look at what the incompetents in Manatas have done to him."

He tutted over Halvar's wounded shoulder and applied his trademark moldy-bread poultice while Frater Leonidas looked on. Halvar endured the treatment with only the occasional hiss of pain. He had other things on his mind.

"Leon!"

"I am Frater Leonidas!" the painter objected.

"You're Leon di Vicenza as far as I'm concerned. How much more have you learned about our noble Captain Girard?"

"If you mean have I translated any more of his private journal, I haven't learned much more than I already knew. The man was obsessed with two things—money and women." Leon sniffed scornfully.

"Did you get back to his stay in Bos-Town? How many women did he bed, and how much money did he make? Ow!"

Frater Iosip tightened the bandage and replaced Halvar's shirt.

"I advise you to rest. Of course, you won't."

"He's impossible." Dani Glick bustled in, followed by her servers carrying a tray on which were a large bowl, a spoon, and a steaming tankard.

"What's this?" Halvar regarded the offerings suspiciously.

"Soup made from the innards of a gobble-bird and some mulled cider. You drink far too much mokka," Dani informed him. "And you need nourishment. Eat!"

"And then, rest," Frater Iosip added, with an approving glance at Dani.

"I will rest, I promise you, as soon as I've finished what I started." Halvar continued his questioning between spoonfuls of soup. "What does our noble captain say about the women of Bos-Town?"

"Not much, because he didn't bed any of them." Leon smirked. "He wrote that they were all hideously plain, even the sailors' doxies, and they weren't worth his silver or his time. Instead, he wrote some vivid descriptions of what he calls 'heretical hypocrites'. Meaning, I suppose, the godly Purists who run Bos-Town."

"According to Devallon, they arrested Milady Summersby for displaying herself on the docks," Halvar said.

"That's true enough. Girard gives a straightforward account of it, with a few comments about the 'old lechers' ogling Milady's décolletage. Then he adds something about their 'goods,' which he'd thought to buy but that were gone elsewhere. And he adds, 'must put in at M. to get goods.' Which, I suppose, means that he expected to find something here in Manatas he'd thought he could get at Bos-Town but didn't."

Halvar sipped the mulled cider as he turned this information over in his mind.

"He had the muskets…he needed powder….he couldn't get it in Bos-Town because…"

"Because the one who made it and sold it had come here." Selim had been shooed out with the rest while the doctors were doing their work. Now, she stepped back into the room to take her usual place at Halvar's side.

"MacAlan," Halvar said.

"And that was why Girard had to come to Manatas," she agreed. "He thought he could rely on the Taverniers to house him and his men while he negotiated with whoever the Pure Sect had sent here. Only he found out when he got here that Jacques Tavernier wasn't at the Mermaid Taberna anymore, and Hannes Zilberstam didn't know him and didn't want to help him."

"He didn't know how much things had changed, because he must have left Bos-Town before the ships came in from the feria with the news of what had happened to the Taverniers and Tenente Gomez," Leon said. "I'm no mathematician, but I calculate it takes at least six to eight weeks to get from Manatas to Bos-Town, with the wind and current pushing a ship forward. Against the wind, with the current against you, add at least two weeks to that. I expect our Franchen had to do some fancy sailing to get here as fast as he did, especially in that tub of a round-ship. It's no sleek dhow."

"So, let us say, he leaves Bos-Town at about the time the Peace Game was being played at the end of the feria. No one in Bos-Town knew then that the Taverniers were gone, and that Green Village and Manatas Town were both under one law. So, when Girard sailed in last week, it must have come as a nasty surprise when he went to the Mermaid Taberna and found a Dane instead of a Franchen in charge." Halvar chuckled. "So, what can he do? He has to find a middleman, someone in Manatas Town who can get to the people from Bos-Town who are in Green Village. Most of them are Afrikans. Who does he think of?"

"Lady Tekla?" Selim asked.

"Not her!" Halvar said. "Someone who would deal with the Pure Sect. Let us say he was already informed that Samuel Igbo was the merchant who handled business with Bos-Town. So, he'd have to send the message to Samuel he was arrived, and was ready to buy gunpowder from the man from Bos-Town who would sell it to him. How does he contact this Igbo?"

Selim tried to work it out herself.

"He goes to the chapel, and asks for a messenger. And Snake puts himself forward to take it."

Leon was drawn into the discussion in spite of himself.

"That miserable, ugly boy? Whatever for?"

"Because he wanted money," Halvar said. "The Franchen was offering a whole silver imperial, just to take the message. Snake thought he could wangle more out of Igbo, and he was right. Igbo gave him the Afrikan iron token to take the message to the Pure Sect in Green Village. And MacAlan gave him a Bretain penny to keep quiet about the business."

"And then Girard was killed, and Snake thought he could get even more," Selim said. "So, he went back to Igbo."

235

"A bad mistake," Halvar said. "MacAlan is a hasty man. He realized that if it were known a Pure Sect Bretain was dealing with a Roumi Rite Franchen there would be embarrassing questions asked."

"Especially if my father found out they were dealing in muskets and gunpowder. At the very least, he'd want to know who sold them, and where they were going," Selim put in. "And when Snake came back to demand more money from Igbo, he was shot down instead. MacAlan must have been mad to think he could do it and not be seen or heard!"

"It was a risk, but remember, most of the houses in the Street of the Afrikans are empty at this time of the year. And there was the storm. The wind muffled the sound of the shot, the snow masked the shooter. Even Bull, who saw it all, couldn't say for certain who it was, only that it was a Bretain. And, as we have seen, clothing can be deceptive." He gave Leon a meaningful glance.

Somewhere across the common, a bell sounded.

"That is the call to late-afternoon prayers at the fratery," Leon said. "All this is fascinating but of little account, now that MacAlan is dead. There will be no gunpowder sale, no sale of muskets."

"Perhaps, but it's not over," Halvar said. "There's still this little matter of Kupernik, and where he fits into this scheme."

"Assuming he does," Leon said dismissively. "Kupernik was a contentious man. His death could have nothing to do with muskets and gunpowder. Think of that, my dear Halvar."

He strode jauntily from the room, leaving Selim and Halvar alone, one puzzled, the other infuriated.

"What about those papers from Kupernik's rooms?" Halvar demanded. "What were they?"

Selim blinked rapidly, as if to bring her thoughts back into focus.

"The ones on Master Kupernik's desk? They seemed to be arithmetical calculations, all in different hands, but the numbers were more or less the same. Some of the calculations had different answers. I assume they were examination papers from his students. Master Kupernik had marked some with red ink and added comments, not very polite or pleasant. He was a strict teacher."

"So I thought. What about Snake's papers?"

"Most of them were copies of the *Gazetta*, like I said, but one had the same calculations as the ones on Kupernik's desk. Was Snake one of Kupernik's pupils? That doesn't seem likely, considering his state in life, how poor he was…"

"Examinations!" Halvar stood up, straightened his coat, and adjusted his cap and the araghoun hat over it. "We've got to get to the madrassa. There are more questions to be asked before this business is finished."

Chapter 32

A DELEGATION AWAITED HALVAR OUTSIDE THE gates of the Gardens of Paradise. Cormack MacCormack looked worried as he fended off the protests of the two Pure Sect elders and Seth.

"Don Alvaro! Capitán!" Cormack called out as Halvar tried to get to his transportation. "What do you want done with…this?" He gestured at the bodies of MacAlan and Igbo, stiffening on the rough litters.

"Igbo was Islim. His wives and children will want to mourn him. He didn't deserve his death; he was caught in a situation he couldn't control," Halvar decreed. "I'll take him back to Manatas Town so his family can make the proper arrangements with his imam for his burial. As for Andrew MacAlan, he killed a lad in cold blood, before a witness. He would have faced the gallows. Bury him where you will."

"If you don't mind, I'd like to come with you." Devallon strode up to the iron gate.

"Devallon, what do you want now?" Halvar snarled. "And where were you while I was fighting mountain cats?"

"He was trying to persuade me to lease my entire establishment to him and his Bretain master." Dani Glick had joined the protest party. "To which I replied that the Gardens of Paradise are open to all. If Milord Summersby wants to stay, he can pay the same as anyone else, have one room to himself like anyone else, and take his meals with everyone else. If that doesn't suit him, he can stay right where he is." She folded her arms and glared defiantly up at Milord, who was struggling to control his restive mount.

"I thought that, with the death of the breadwinner, it is possible the Afrikan's widow would consider allowing Milord to use some of the empty rooms..." Devallon began.

"That is the most outrageous thing I've heard you say yet!" Halvar exploded. "The man's scarcely cold! Islim or Kristo, common decency would have you wait before you started picking his bones!"

"Igbo's got two wives and several small children," Selim reminded them. "You wouldn't turn a widow and orphans out into the cold!"

"I wouldn't do that," Devallon protested. "Of course they would be allowed to remain in the house. Milord, Edgar and I would only use some of the front rooms..." He trailed off again, backing away from the now-hostile crowd. Even the most rabid of Kristos would not intrude on a house of mourning.

"Tenente Flores." Halvar heaved himself into Avaram's cart. "Put the the remains of Samuel Igbo on another donkey cart. The driver can follow us into town. We'll take Samuel back to his family, and they can do what has to be done there. Then we will find one more murderer, and then, maybe, I can go back to the Mermaid Taberna, have a decent dinner, and obey my physicians. All of them!"

"But what of Milord?" Devallon protested.

239

"He can stay in the cottage," Halvar ruled. "Flores, come with me."

"You know who killed the professor?" Flores asked as he took his place in the cart.

"I think I do, but I have to be sure before I take him before the sultan." Halvar adjusted his arm in its sling. "Tenente Donal."

The Bretain stepped forward. "Can you stay sober long enough to go back to that cabin in the woods and make a thorough search? Take this lad, Seth, with you. I want to know exactly what is in that cabin, whether any of it can be used to make gunpowder, and if so, how much and of what sort. Can you do that, Tenente Donal?"

Donal looked as if he had bitten on something sour.

"I can do it, but, by what right do you come in here and give orders? No one asked us if we wanted to be put under Sharia law. No one offered us a choice. We were just told we were part of Manatas Town. That's not how we do things in Green Village. We make our own choices, we make our own decisions." He looked around for confirmation and got muttered agreement.

Cormack MacCormack answered him. "You weren't consulted, Tenente, but I was. I spoke for all of us when the young calif came to me and suggested it would be a good idea to put all of Manatas Island under one law. If you don't like it, Donal, you can go back to the woods and trap furs for a living."

Donal's face grew redder. If he meant to reply, however, it was drowned out by a frantic neigh as Milord's steed objected to the proximity of the carcass of the mountain cat. All animosity vanished in general mirth at the unwanted stranger's predicament as he struggled to control his bucking horse.

Halvar took advantage of the distraction to make his escape.

"Let's go, Avaram. Flores, you're with me. Zoltan, Fergus, you take the cart with the body."

Firebrand's Mahak runners were already crossing the feria grounds when the two carts made their way along the path that led around the field. As they approached the Street of the Afrikans, Selim said, "I think I'd better be the one to tell Igbo's wives what happened to Samuel."

"Why you? You're a child!" Flores protested.

"Because Selim is the *sultan's* child," Halvar reminded him. "That counts for something here in Manatas. And because…because Selim can get into the harem, and a grown man can't."

"To tell the women they are widows," Selim added. "and maybe, to find out what they know of Samuel's business dealings. Although I don't think Samuel was one to let them know what he was doing. He was a very strict Islim, never let his women out of the harem unless it was to go to the muskat or the souk, and even then, they had to have a servant with them."

She led the party to Samuel Igbo's door.

"*Salaam*, those within. I have sad news," she called out.

The servant who opened the door took one look at the burden on the cart and let out a howl of anguish.

"Please to let us enter," Selim pleaded, "to tell the wives of Samuel Igbo that he is no more."

The steward showed Halvar and Flores into the anteroom, where they waited nervously for several minutes while Selim was escorted to the rear of the house. A shriek and a chorus of wails signaled that the sad news had been delivered.

Selim reappeared, leading a diminutive figure wrapped in a shapeless black garment. The woman's head was draped in a black shawl she held over the lower part of her face, so that only her nose and eyes were visible.

"This is Tahira," Selim announced. "She is Samuel Igbo's eldest daughter. She speaks Arabi. The other women don't."

"My mother and aunties speak our own language," Tahira said, with the musical accent common to Afrikans. "I am familiar with Manatas Arabi. What happened to my father? Why do you send guards to our house?"

241

Halvar willed himself to lower his voice to a tone suitable to a house in mourning.

"*Salaam aleikum*, Tahira. I regret to tell you that your father was killed by someone he was doing business with. A Bretain—"

"The madman! I knew he was evil!" Tahira burst out.

"You know this man?" Selim asked.

Tahira seemed to shrink.

"I...I was curious to see...."

Selim patted the girl's hand.

"Of course you were. Stuck in the harem all day, no one but your mother and the children. I know all about that kind of life. You were curious, you peeked through the grille when your father had visitors."

"He did most of his business at the mokka-shop, but these men came to the house," Tahira admitted. "Mother said I must not see or hear them. I was shameless, but I wanted to know. So, I peeked when they came."

"When was this?" Halvar asked. "How long ago?"

Tahira thought for a moment.

"At the time of the Fall Feria," she said. "The first time I saw the Bretain was when Father allowed me to take the children to the feria to see the Peace Game. There was a man there, a Bretain, and he greeted my father as if he knew him. My father told me to take the children away, and told the Bretain and the man with the hair that they should come to him later. Not at the mokka-shop, but to the house, after the game was over."

"Which I suppose they did, " Halvar said. Tahira nodded in agreement.

"MacAlan was the Bretain, that's for sure," Flores said. "But who is the other one? What was wrong with his hair?"

Tahira gestured, nearly losing her grip on her shawl.

"It was all over. He had no hat, no cap. Only much hair."

"Sounds like Master LaPierre," Selim said. "But where does he fit into this scheme?"

242

"He's an alchemist," Halvar reminded her. "MacAlan needed an alchemist to make his gunpowder." He turned back to Tahira. "So, these two men came here instead of the mokka-shop where Samuel conducted his usual business. Did that happen often?"

"Father did not do business at his home," Tahira said. "My mother said it was not right, that the home was the home. She did not want to have Kristos and Yehudit here."

"But your father had them here anyway," Selim said. "At least once, maybe twice?"

"But not where we could see them," Tahira said. "They only came to the front of the house, where Father has his study. Then I saw the man with the hair when he came to the market at the end of the street, near the Broad Way, where we buy our vegetables. He bought roasted *nguba*—he liked them. He asked about how they were grown, where they came from. He was very odd, but I did not think him dangerous. Not like the other one, the loud one. *He* shouted in Erse when my father used Arabi."

Halvar tugged at his mustache, thinking furiously.

"Girl, think back two days, maybe three, the day of the snow. Did you hear or see anything odd in the back alley? A loud sound, maybe a bang or a boom?"

Tahira nodded wildly. "Yes, yes! Mother and Auntie Shana said it was only the wind, but I know I heard something, a loud noise. And Father went outside, into the snow, to see what it was, but he said it was only the wind, that it had blown over one of the jars for waste, and the Scavenger woman would put it right, we did not have to worry ourselves about it."

"And that settles that," Flores said with an emphatic nod. "Igbo knew all about the murdered messenger. He should have told us as soon as he saw the body. He deserved to be killed."

"No one deserves that kind of death," Halvar chided him. "And be kinder to this girl. She's lost her father. Tahira, this man with the hair...you say he came to the market. Did he ever come to this house?"

"My father does not eat with infidels," Tahira said. "But the man with the hair, he came to the kitchen two days ago," Tahira said. "I remember, because it was after the End-of-Fast feast, and we always give the scraps to the Scavengers. I was giving the alms, and the man with the hair came to the back door, like one of the beggars. He said he liked the cakes that Afrikans make with *nguba*, and that he would like some to be sent to him, but the cook at the Yehudit House where he lived was very strict, would not let any but Yehudit kosher food into the house, so the cakes should be sent to him at the Blue Parrot mokka-shop. He said that if he was not there, the cakes could be sent directly to him at the Yehudit House by way of one of the Waterfront Rats, the messenger boys who carried packages. He even had a paper they could be wrapped in, with his name on it in Arabi and Erse letters."

"And were they sent?" Halvar asked.

"I suppose so. Our cook had some of the cakes left from the feast. She sent Bakka, our own messenger, to the mokka-shop, and Bakka came back without them, so I have to think they were delivered." Her eyes filled with tears. "What is to become of us? My brother is in Salaam-abad. He doesn't know that Father..." She started to sob loudly.

"I will send Eva Hakim, the Nizam of the Sisters of Fatima to you. She can help you through this sad time," Halvar told her. "I will also speak of your situation to Sultan Petrus and the Lady Ayesha, his wife. They are very charitable; they will see that you and your mother get the widow's inheritance."

"I'll tell Ayesha myself," Selim promised. "And I'll come back and visit as soon as I can."

"Thank you," Tahira whispered. She stepped back as the porter ushered in a fussy little man in the long striped gown and green turban of an Islim cleric.

"Imam Talib," the servant announced.

Halvar edged away, eager to be out of the house of mourning. There was nothing more he could do here, but he'd gotten what he'd come for. There was a link between Master LaPierre and Samuel Igbo, one that would lead to the solution of another murder.

Flores, Zoltan, and Fergus were waiting outside the house beside Avaram and the official donkey cart.

"Where to next, Capitán? The Rabat?" Flores asked.

"The madrassa. I want to have another word or two with Master Albrecht LaPierre regarding his experiments with gunpowder in that cabin in the woods. Let's hope he hasn't heard the news-criers."

Halvar mounted his vehicle. Selim hopped on beside him. Flores, Zoltan and Fergus formed an honor guard.

"To the madrassa!" Halvar ordered, Once more, he was on the track of a murderer. This time, he swore he would take him alive.

Chapter 33

BY THE TIME HALVAR WAS READY TO LEAVE THE Street of the Afrikans, word had reached the general population about the stirring events in the woods north of Green Village. Firebrand's Mahak runners had reached Daoud the News-crier, who now strode up and down the Broad Way hailing Capitán Don Alvaro Danico as the savior of Manatas, who had rid the population of a vicious beast and captured an equally vicious murderer into the bargain. Halvar found his progress impeded by well-wishers of all sects. Like it or not, he was a hero.

He smiled weakly as Stephane Mercier led a gang of students down the avenue, waving their fowling-pieces and regaling anyone who would listen with the tale of the fight on the ledge. He waved at Milord Summersby, still trying to control the horse, which had decided it was once again the mighty steed it had been in its youth and was behaving accordingly.

Avaram's cart traveled slowly southward with Flores, Zoltan and Fergus marching alongside, trying to fend off the enthusiastic people wanting to congratulate their hero on his feat of daring.

"Thor's Hammer!" Halvar cursed under his breath as the cart jolted over the brick-paved avenue. "By the time we reach the madrassa, LaPierre will know we're after him. He'll be gone, and we'll never find him."

"Where will he go?" Flores asked as he pushed the crowd away from the cart with his halberd.

"The Yehudit study-house," Zoltan suggested. "They all stick together, those Yehudit."

"Should I go there, then?" Avaram called over his shoulder.

"Not yet," Halvar told him. "First, Yehudit House behind the madrassa. I never really got started on the Kupernik investigation. I want to be very sure before I start accusing the eminent professors of killing one another."

The muezzin was calling from the minaret of the Grand Muskat as they turned into the street behind the madrassa. Eli, the house-master, was not pleased to see Halvar and his men at his door.

"What do you want now?" he complained. "It's nearly dark. We're saying evening prayers." A loud muttering from within made this obvious.

"We'll wait," Halvar told him as Selim, Zoltan, and Flores performed their prostrations, and Fergus went on one knee to recite his Patri Nostri. Halvar clutched his amulet and thanked the Redeemer, Mother Mara and Thor for rescuing him from not one, but two deadly dangers.

The sounds of prayer from within ended with a loud cry of "Mazel tov" and the clinking of glasses. Rav Nahum bustled into the hall, as Oleg and the other servants arrived to light the lanterns.

"What is the matter now, Capitán Danske? I heard you had caught the murderer, that it was some Bretain of the Pure Sect."

"He was a murderer, indeed he was," Halvar said. "But he did not kill your Master Kupernik."

"Then, who...?"

"Is there a place where we can sit and be alone? Perhaps that library room?"

"If you must." Rav Nahum led Halvar and Selim back to the book-filled cubbyhole. "It is the last night of our Festival of Lights. I want to get back to my family. We celebrate together with a feast and distribute gifts."

"I won't keep you long," Halvar promised. He turned to the guardsmen. "Zoltan, Fergus, go into the back alley. Keep watch for anyone trying to leave. If you see someone, especially a gangly fellow with wild hair and a mustache like mine, stop him. Don't kill him, just stop him! Tenente Flores, you watch the door. If LaPierre comes in—"

"I know, Capitán, stop him. I won't kill him unless he tries to kill me," Flores promised.

Zoltan and Fergus shoved several black-clad men out of their way as they tromped down the hall to the kitchen. Loud female noises announced the cook's displeasure at having her kitchen invaded by armed men.

Halvar paid no notice.

"I am sorry we have to disturb your celebration, Rav Nahum, but we must take Master LaPierre to the Rabat."

"Master LaPierre?" Rav Nahum stopped in mid-stride. "Is that what this is about? You suspect him of...No, he could not! It would be..."

"If you mean, do I accuse Master Albrecht LaPierre of killing Master Nikola Kupernik, I do indeed," Halvar said. "If you know where he is, you must tell me. Now!"

"He did not come to evening prayers," Rav Nahum said. "But that is not surprising. Master LaPierre is known to be a free-thinker. He seldom comes to prayers, not even on the Holy Days. He can be somewhat...abrasive...on the subject."

"So I have heard," Halvar said. "If he's not here, then where do you think he is?

"I believe he has built a cabin somewhere up-the-hills…" Rav Nahum began.

"I can guarantee you he's not there," Halvar said. "We've just come from that cabin."

Rav Nahum sat down in the one chair in the library that did not have some kind of reading material on it.

"I cannot think…Murder Master Kupernik? Why would Master LaPierre do such a thing? How?"

"As to why, I will have to ask him. As to how? He gave Kupernik some cakes that had been baked with *nguba* beans. He knew Kupernik had a sensitivity to such food, that it would choke him. He took steps to make sure Kupernik could not get help and left the room, certain that Kupernik would eat the cakes, choke, and die."

"Horrible!" Rav Nahum breathed.

"I should have asked yesterday, but I was distracted…Who lives in this house? Who has rooms next to Kupernik's? Did anyone hear anything, see anything that night?"

Rav Nahum stroked his beard as he thought.

"Not all our Yehudit masters live here. I do not—my house is in the cross-street, where I live with my wife and children. There are also two students who board with us and tutor my sons. Of those masters who reside here, Master Kupernik, as you know, had the big room at the head of the stairs. Master LaPierre has the room next to his, which he shares with Efrem Russo, the medical student."

"Who is also an alchemist," Selim reminded them. "He could have given Kupernik those cakes."

"True," Halvar commented. "But he was the one who pointed out exactly how Kupernik died. He'd hardly do that if he'd killed him himself. Much better to have us think he'd died of some seizure of the heart, being a choleric man to begin with."

"It was a festival night, but we still kept early hours," Rav Nahum said. "Except for Master Kupernik, who would stay up all night observing the motions of the stars."

"When did you last see Master Kupernik?"

"Let me think…we had the party, we had prayers. I left to have my festival dinner at home with my family. I sometimes dine here, sometimes there…" Rav Nahum muttered to himself.

There was a blast of cold air as someone opened the front door.

"Master LaPierre!" one of the men in the hall hailed a newcomer. "Where have you been? We had to send to the souk to get our tenth man for minyan!"

LaPierre looked wildly about him. Flores stepped behind him, halberd ready, blocking his way.

"Master Albrecht LaPierre, you are wanted for questioning in the matter of the death of Master Nikola—"

Before he could finish, LaPierre took off down the hall, heading for the back door.

"Stop him!" Halvar yelled as he and Flores shoved through the assembled Yehudit.

He stumbled over the threshold to the kitchen. The cook shouted angrily in a dialect of Danic he did not understand, but whose meaning was clear. Flores hustled through the overheated room, ignoring the protests of the cook and her assistants.

"Thor's Hammer, not another dark alley," Halvar muttered as he staggered after Flores into the same alley along which he had chased Bull the previous day.

In the gathering darkness, the passage was lit with a only few stray gleams of light from the back doors of the other houses in the row. Halvar reeled along, once again bouncing from wall to wall, his shoulder stabbing with pain every time he made contact with another brick or wooden surface. The ground was already slick with the refuse from the madrassa houses, and was now freezing as the cold took hold.

He could just make out Zoltan's tall figure and Flores's squat one at the end of the alley, framed by the walls, their silhouettes visible against the lanterns that marked the entrance to the souk. gasped for breath as he reached them to find they were holding a squirming captive.

"Got him!" Zoltan's triumphant yell marked the end of one more chase.

Albrecht LaPierre looked shabbier and wilder than ever in his shaggy woolen tunic and breeches. He glared at his captors.

"What is the meaning of this! Why am I being assaulted? Do you know who I am?"

"You are Master Albrecht LaPierre, and you are accused of murder," Flores told him as Fergus tied the prisoner's hands behind his back with the leather thong carried by all the guards for just that purpose.

"You can't do this! You have no warrant, no proof!" LaPierre shouted. "Help me, good masters! I am being taken prisoner with no warrant!"

The back doors of the Kristo and Islim houses opened. Heads popped out as the inhabitants tried to see what was going on.

Rav Nahum slipped and slid down the alley with Master Eli behind him holding a lantern.

"*Have* you a warrant, Capitán?"

"I've got a warrant, and I've got proof," Halvar assured him. "And if you want to advise him, Rav Nahum, you are welcome to come to the Rabat and do so. But this man killed his colleague in cold blood, maliciously, with careful planning. And I do not think any of your Yehudit advocates will be able to justify that.Take Master LaPierre to the Rabat," he ordered his men. "He's allowed food and water, and if he needs the jakes, he can use it. Then bring him to my office. He's got a few questions to answer."

He trudged back to the Yehudit House, where his donkey cart awaited him. Night had fallen, but the day was far from over.

Chapter 34

IT WAS FULLY DARK BY THE TIME HALVAR GOT
to the Rabat. The torches in the courtyard had been lit, and
a guard with a lantern escorted him to his tiny office in the
barracks.

"Send in a firebox," Halvar ordered. "Selim, light the
lamp. Flores, stand at the door. Master LaPierre, there's a
stool for you. Sit down, be comfortable. This may take some
time."

La Pierre ignored the stool. He stood defiantly, his arms
tied behind his back, and glared at Halvar, who had
squeezed into the chair behind his desk.

"Who are you to give me orders?" LaPierre demanded. "I am a master of the madrassa. I do not have to answer to anyone, let alone an ignorant Dane who was
jumped into office by a corrupt and idle prince."

"Dane I am," Halvar admitted. "And I can't read or
write anything but Danic, and that not well, so I suppose

one could say I was ignorant of a great deal of what's called learning, even though I sat through lectures at the Corduva Madrassa. But Don Felipe is far from idle, and to my knowledge is not corrupt. On the other hand, Master LaPierre, I have every reason to believe you are a murderer. It's up to you to convince me you're not."

LaPierre looked around the room for a friendly face and found none. Selim was carefully tending to her pen, sharpening the point of the quill. Flores glowered at the door, halberd ready to prevent another escape.

Halvar leaned forward, resting his arms on the desk.

"Sit down, laddie…"

"I am not a lad. I am Master Albrecht LaPierre."

"I know who you say you are," Halvar told him. "And there's no one to say you're not. You teach alchemy at the madrassa. That much is already known. As is the fact that you built a cabin in the part of Manatas Island where only beasts and charcoal-burners go. Very private place, that cabin. No one can see or hear what you're doing there. And if the Mahak do hear odd noises, you can always play on their superstitions, tell them it's ghosts, or forest spirits making the booms and bangs. That's where you're trying out the different methods for making gunpowder, aren't you?"

Flores stepped into the room to shove LaPierre down onto the stool, then took up his post at the door.

LaPierre struggled to maintain some dignity.

"What if I am?" he blustered. "Is that not the way of empirical science? To try different methods to see which one is best? No matter what Master Kupernik thinks!"

"No matter to me," Halvar said. "But Sultan Petrus will be very interested. He's no friend of alchemists who meddle with gunpowder. A cannon took away his leg, and he takes firearms very personally."

LaPierre lost some of his pugnacity under Halvar's bland gaze.

"I suppose I should have asked permission before building the cabin. At the time, the land was in the hands of the

Locals. They had no objection, so long as I did not bring in any livestock or plant crops."

"Too rocky for a farm," Halvar agreed. "And you don't keep animals. And it's not as if you were living there permanently—you have your room at the Yehudit House. But you have a fireplace. You chop wood. I have one of the chips right here. Very like the one I found on the floor of Kupernik's room when we pushed the door open. Selim?"

Selim looked up from her writing.

"I have inspected the two chips, one from the Yehudit House and one from the cabin in the woods. They look the same."

"A chip of wood? What does that have to do with Master Kupernik's death?"

"It has everything to do with it. It proves, Master LaPierre, that you deliberately jammed that chip under Kupernik's door, edging it in with your foot as you left him the night of the party. I wondered when I saw it how it got there. It wasn't a part of the woodwork of the house. That's dark wood. This is pine—light wood. That's what made me suspect there was more to Kupernik's death than a natural seizure."

"And the water jug was emptied into the chamberpot," Selim added. "Kupernik didn't do that."

"What did he do to deserve such malice, Master LaPierre? I heard him scoff at your alchemy. He referred to your testing materials, something about going 'boom'? Did he find out what you were up to? And perhaps, who was going to buy the product once you had perfected it?" Halvar's voice darkened.

"I...I don't know what you mean," LaPierre quavered.

"I mean your little deal with Samuel Igbo and Andrew MacAlan," Halvar snapped. "You make the gunpowder that Andrew MacAlan planned to sell to Captain Girard. Girard needed the gunpowder to arm the muskets he carried in his ballast."

LaPierre's face paled, then reddened.

"I do not know those names."

"You certainly know Samuel," Flores accused him. "You went to his house for *nguba* cakes, and had some sent to you at the Blue Parrot mokka-shop."

"But you weren't there," Selim said, "because we saw you at the party. So, the Afrikan gave them to the Water-front Rat who carries the messages from the mokka-shops, and he carried the package to the Yehudit House."

"And he told us all about it, because he had no idea that what he was carrying was anything but a festival gift," Halvar finished the tale. "So, Master LaPierre, we can con-nect you with the cakes Master Kupernik ate, which con-tained the *nguba* that killed him. And we know that you knew of his sensitivity to *nguba* because you were at the disputation on the waterfront the night he ate one and nearly choked to death on it. You had the cakes, you had the chip. You took the cakes to Kupernik, you emptied the water jug, you left the cakes with him, and you jammed the door as you left. All you had to do was wait until he ate them. A malicious murder, quite bloodless. If it weren't for Efrem Russo, we might have been fooled into thinking that Kupernik died naturally, of his own choler, or a seizure of the heart."

"Efrem!" LaPierre spat out. "A medical student who dabbles in alchemy. He *would* have to put his long nose into what doesn't concern him."

"And a good thing he did," Selim said.

"What I don't understand," Halvar said, leaning back again, "is what Kupernik said or did that drove you to this dreadful act? I understand he was something of a crank, a curmudgeon, who was rude to everyone. He scoffed at your alchemical studies, true, but he was just as dismis-sive of Leon di Vicenza's natural philosophy."

"He was a hypocrite," LaPierre grumbled. "Oh, he could speak about the motions of the stars, and how the Holy Book was wrong, but he still put on the tallis and t'fill-in, he prayed with the rest of them. He kept the commandments, he said, he claimed he ate only kosher food, but I saw him in the souk eating yams from one of the Local women. He never questioned where I got the cakes, just grabbed them, greedy man! Hypocrite!"

"Which is why you knew he wouldn't make a fuss about what was in the cakes," Halvar said. "I wondered about that. A man so finicky about his food, why would he eat something that came from outside the house? He had to believe the person who gave them knew about his sensitivity and would not give him something that was bad for him."

"I told him they were *pareve*," LaPierre admitted. "Yes, I went to his room after dinner. I told him I had a festival gift for him, something unusual, by way of an apology for my harsh words at the party. I didn't know whether he'd even eat them…"

"But you had a good idea he would," Selim said. "I saw how he gobbled down the cakes at the party."

"Greedy man," LaPierre repeated. "Full of himself. He never suspected how much I hated him."

"But greed and hypocrisy are common enough," Halvar observed. "What did Kupernik do to *you*, Master LaPierre, that you felt he had to die? It wasn't just that he scoffed at you. Was it that he had found out about your cozy deal with the Bretains, to supply them with gunpowder for the new muskets? The ones that use flint instead of a match? Was that it?"

"Kupernik knew nothing about those muskets," LaPierre scoffed. "He only cared about his mathematical and astronomical studies, and furthering the interests of those students he deemed worthy of his attention. He would reject applicants for no better reason than that he disliked them. They were not sufficiently noble, or they had not had enough education, or they were of low birth. Or they were Roumi Rite or Greco Rite Kristo, not Erse Rite. Or they were Sepharat Yehudit, not Askenat. Or because they were poor and might not be able to pay his fees."

"Poor boys like Snake." Halvar leaned forward again. "That Waterfront Rat, the lad who wanted to better himself. Is that what set you off, Master LaPierre? What was Snake to you? Perhaps, like Leon…"

"Don't be disgusting!" LaPierre retorted. "Leon di Vicenza is a disgrace to scholarship. He only wanted to attract personable young men to his so-called 'Seekers of Truth' to pervert them. Stephen wasn't like those hangers-on. He could have been something quite extraordinary. He asked pertinent questions at that disputation.

"He came to us afterward, me and Master Kupernik, while the guards were dispersing the crowd, to find out more. Kupernik wanted to shoo him away, but I saw something in him, something that could be molded and refined. He could have become my apprentice, and even, in good time, a master himself."

"You encouraged him," Halvar said. "You gave him instruction, even helped him with the mathematical examination for the madrassa."

"The papers on Kupernik's desk!" Selim scrabbled in her notebook and produced the one written on coarse brown paper. "This one…Kupernik has written, 'Illiterate boor! Booby! Do not attempt what is too difficult for a clod like you to ever understand'"

"You saw that paper on Kupernik's desk and made your decision," Halvar said. "You didn't have to give him the cakes. You didn't have to jam the door, or empty the jug."

"He was going to ruin that lad!" La Pierre cried out, in real agony. "I had to stop him!"

Halvar sighed. "What you didn't know, Master La-Pierre, is that when you gave Kupernik those cakes, Snake had been dead for two days. You told him that, if he could come up with the money for the madrassa fee, you would see that he got admitted as a full student. He could advance into the ranks of scholars, even become a teacher himself."

LaPierre's face crumpled. Tears ran down his face.

"He could have…What a waste…"

"When did you last hear from Snake?" Halvar asked.

"I got a note…it was the first day of the Festival of Lights. Master Eli gave me the note the lad had left for me."

"The one we found in Kupernik's room?" Halvar asked.

"It wasn't on the desk," Selim put in. "I found it on the floor, near the desk."

"It wasn't meant for Kupernik at all," Halvar said. "He'd got the money from Igbo and Girard and MacAlan. He left the examination paper with you…"

"And went back to Samuel Igbo while everyone was watching the fight on the docks; and the snow was falling, so no one would see him leaving, and no one would know where he was going."

"Except for Bull," Halvar said, sadly. "But MacAlan was waiting for him, and that was that. Flores, take this man to a cell. Give him some food, water, a piss-pot, and an extra blanket against the cold. I'll put the matter before the sultan, but I don't think he'll be very sympathetic. Gunpowder, muskets, secrecy—it all smells of intrigue. There's more to this than we've found, Tenente Flores. Selim, come with me. I have to make my report before I can finish this business."

Chapter 35

SULTAN PETRUS LISTENED TO HALVAR'S EXPLA-
nation in his overheated quarters, wrapped in several woolen
shawls, with Selim in her usual seat at the small table next
to his chair.

"And so, Excellent Sultan, it all revolved around Snake,"
Halvar explained. "Snake carried the messages from LaPierre
at the madrassa to Igbo at his mokka-shop. He knew about
the Pure Sect when they came from Bos-Town. When Girard sent him to Igbo with the message that he'd arrived,
and was willing to negotiate with the Bos-Town Purists
for gunpowder, Igbo sent him to Green Village. He was
the only one who could put Girard, Igbo, and MacAlan
together, and he tried to extort money to keep that link a
secret."

"To pay for a madrassa education?" Sultan Petrus
snorted indignantly.

"Why not? It's a noble aspiration," Halvar said. "You
could say it all began with Leon di Vicenza. If he had not

259

been cast out of the Rabat, he would not have gone to the Mermaid Taberna. If he had not been at the Mermaid, he would not have set up his debates and disputations. If those debates were not public, Snake would not even have known what he was lacking. And then, when he found out, the lad was eager to advance himself any way he could."

"But where does this fellow LaPierre come in?" Sultan Petrus sipped his mokka.

"I think LaPierre recognized something in Snake no one else saw," Halvar said, stroking his mustache. "Something like what I felt when I questioned that Waterfront Rat Bull, When I saw him in my office, I thought, *That was me twenty years ago.* I made a mistake then, and it nearly cost me my life. Instead, I got a second chance, and I found a good soul who was willing to teach me how to get on."

"Your Old Sergeant Olaf," Selim said.

"Old Sergeant Olaf it was," Halvar agreed. "He kept the rest of the recruits from taking their anger out on me just because I was the big fellow. He kept me straight, he showed me how to fight and when not to. He was the wisest man I ever met, always excepting the Old One, Calif Carlus, may his memory be for a blessing."

"And you think that Master LaPierre felt the same about Snake?" Sultan Petrus asked.

"I think he saw something in Snake that reminded him of himself. Snake wasn't a handsome young fellow who could attract the likes of Leon. He had bad skin, a whining voice, stringy hair. Not a charmer like Foxy, or a strong-arm bully like Bull. But a sharp mind, and a determination to use it. I only wish I'd known him better. He'd have made a good replacement for Tenente Ruiz."

"Not, I hope, with Ruiz's, um, personal habits!" Sultan Petrus harrumphed.

"I don't think so," Halvar agreed. "Not a devout Roumi Rite Kristo."

Selim sighed.

"All those ifs! *If* Leon had not been thrown out of the Rabat...*If* Snake had not got it into his head to apply to the madrassa...*If* Girard had not been murdered..."

"Too *many* ifs," Halvar told her. "Like Old Sergeant Olaf always said, 'If Grandma had balls, she'd be Grandpa; if Grandpa had tits, he'd be Grandma.' You can't think about ifs. What is...is. You can go mad wondering about ifs. If the Italian episcopus in Rouma had spent less time fighting each other and more praying, would we all be speaking Old Roumi when we pray instead of Erse? If the Franchen had got south of the mountains, would they have taken over Al-Andalus before now? We will never know, because it happened the way it happened."

Sultan Petrus sighed deeply.

"I will visit the house of Samuel Igbo myself," he decided. "I must show the people that their sultan has their well-being at heart. The murderer of Samuel Igbo has been punished by Ilha, may His name be blessed, in His great wisdom, by means of this beast. Is it true that you killed it with a thrust of the halberd?"

Halvar shrugged. "I wanted to get inside the cave to help Igbo, if he was still alive. I think the animal had made the cave its den, and it was only defending its home. Animals will do that."

"As will people," the sultan said. "Now, Capitán, I want to know more about these muskets. Where they came from, where they were supposed to go to. How this scheme was planned, and who planned it. And most of all, whether there are any more people involved, and if so, how many?"

"Questions which I agree must be answered. But not tonight, Excellent Sultan. With your permission, I have been advised by three different physicians to rest, and I should obey their orders. Salaam aleikum, Sultan Petrus. I wish you a good rest."

"Mmph!" Sultan Petrus grunted. "I have too many physicians. Eva Hakim, Dr. Moise, even my wife Ayesha. They all seem to think I'm an old man on the brink of death. I'm well enough to ride out tomorrow."

"And I look forward to seeing you out of the Rabat," Halvar said.

261

With a low bow, he took his leave.

Flores was waiting for him at the base of the stairs in the courtyard.

"What do we do with LaPierre?"

"For now, hold him in the cells. Give him food, water, fire, but make sure he doesn't harm himself. When the sultan decides to hold another Grand Divan, his fate will be decided."

"Waste of time and food," Flores grumbled. "Chop his head off now, get it over with."

"Not without a trial," Halvar warned him. "I'm off to the Mermaid Taberna. If anyone gets murdered during the night, don't tell me until morning."

The lanterns were lit on the Broad Way, and in front of the mokka-shops on the side street that led down the hill past the latrines to the waterfront plaza and the Mermaid Taberna. Halvar glanced down Pearl Street. The chickens were roosted, the goat was penned. He did not have to fight his way down the hill.

A hearty voice greeted him as he passed Pearl Street.

"*Salaam aleikum*, Capitán! Isn't that how they say it here in Manatas?"

"Devallon? Why aren't you at the cottage, celebrating the end of a glorious hunt with Milord?" Halvar had had more than enough of this boisterous Franchen.

"Milord has just broached another bottle of that disgusting wine," Devallon explained. "Edgar is writing an account of the hunt in his journal. What he intends to do with it, I have no idea. I thought I'd seek out some more congenial company at the Mermaid."

"Meaning mine? I'm not feeling very congenial tonight. I want my food, some hot ale, maybe a game or two of tables, and bed, in that order. What's this?"

Hannes Zilberstam stood in front of the door to the taberna.

"Capitán, Sieur Devallon, I think I should warn you—"

"Andres!" a plaintive voice called from behind the tavernkeeper.

Halvar and Devallon moved inside out of the rising wind from the bay. Before them was a diminutive figure—a pale, thin woman wrapped in a bedraggled red cloak, her wispy fair hair straggling out from under a plain linen cap. Her eyes were reddened, and the tip of her sharp nose was even redder than her chapped cheeks.

"Charlotte?" Devallon regarded the woman with horror. "What have they done to you?"

Halvar closed his eyes and sent up a hasty prayer to the Redeemer and Mother Mara. He didn't think Thor would be of much use. Milady Summersby had returned to Manatas.

END

GLOSSARY

AL-ANDALUS	Spain
AL-LARGATO	Alligator
ALGONKIN	Algonquin/Lenape Indians
ARABI	Arabic
ARAGHOUN	Raccoon
BATATAS	Potatoes
BRETAINS	British
CHESU	Jesus
CRUX	Cross
CORDUVA	Cordova
DANE-MARCH	Germany
DANES	The Germanic people (includes Denmark)
DANIC	Germanic language (written in Rune characters)
EAST CHANNEL	East River

END-OF-FAST	Eid Al-Fitr; Festival marking the end of Ramadan
ERSE	Gaelic language (written in Ogham characters)
ERSE RITE	Celtic Christianity as practiced in Northern Europe
ESCOUASH	Squash
FERIA	Commercial gathering/fair
FESTIVAL OF LIGHTS	Hanukkah
FRANCHEN	Language of Franchenland (written in Roman characters); a native of Franchenland
FRANCHENLAND	France
FRATER	General term for a Kristo cleric
FRATERY	Monastery
GREAT RIVER	Hudson River
HAMMAM	Communal bath
HEMP	Cannabis, Marijuana

HOLY BOOK	The Bible or the Q'ran, depending on who is speaking
HOLY MEAL	Mass
ILHA	Allah
ISLIM	Islam
IVRIT	Hebrew
KICK-THE-BLADDER	Football
KRISTO	Christian
KUTTON	Cotton
KIBBICK	Quebec
LOCALS	Native Americans
MACASSIN	Moccasin
MADRASSA	School/university
MAHAK	Mohawk/Iroquois
MAIZ	Corn
MANATAS	Manhattan Island
MOKKA	Coffee
MOTHER MARA	Virgin Mary
MUNSI	Native trade language (unwritten)

MUSKAT	Mosque
NATIVITY	Christmas
NGUBA	"Goobers," peanuts
NOVA MUNDUM	"New World," North America
OLD GRECO	Ancient Greece
OLD ROUMI	Ancient Rome, Ancient Romans
OPASSOM	Opossum
OROPA	Europe, excluding Al-Andalus
PARIGI	Paris
PATRI NOSTRI	"Our Father"/Lord's Prayer
PISTOIA	Pistol
POWHATAN	Native Name For Terra Mara – Maryland
RABAT	Fortress
RHUM	Rum
ROUMI RITE	Christianity as practiced south of the Alps, centered in Rome
ROUND ISLAND	Staten Island
SALAAMABAD	Philadelphia

SAVANA PORT	Savannah, Ga.
SEKONK	Skunk
SEQUANOK	Pennsylvania
SOUK	Marketplace
STUDY HOUSE	Synagogue
TABAC	Tobacco
"TAKE THE WATER"	Be Baptized
THE PIZZLE	Florida
THE PROPHET	Mohammad
THE REDEEMER	Jesus
THREE OLD WOMEN	Norns, Fates
WAMUS	A deerskin shirt with a fringed yoke and sleeves
WEST CASTER	Westchester / New England
WUMPUM	Wampum; Colored shells used as medium of exchange for small purchases
YEHUDIT	Jews / Jewish

About The Author

ROBERTA ROGOW writes historical fiction, although she sometimes twists the history. Her most recent stories take place in a Manhattan Island that was settled by Spanish Moors instead of by Dutch traders: *Last of the Mohegans* meets *Arabian Nights*, with a Spanish accent. Roberta retired from a 37-year career as a children's librarian in 2008. She now lives in New Jersey, and spends her time going to science fiction and mystery conventions when she is not writing mysteries or singing filk (science fiction folk music).

Malice in Manatas is the fifth book in the Saga of Halvar the Hireling.

About The Artist

Born in Chicago, WILLIAM NEAGLE graduated from the University of Tennessee with a BFA. Having done work for the US Department of Energy and other companies, his work has been distributed worldwide. He has done book covers for the writing team of Joreid McFate and for his own novel, *Catching the Ghost*. He resides in North Carolina with his wife and two children.

www.ingramcontent.com/pod-product-compliance
Lightning Source LLC
Chambersburg PA
CBHW031003260626
47169CB00002B/676